the
UKRAINIAN
WEDDING

the UKRAINIAN WEDDING

LARRY WARWARUK

COTEAU BOOKS

Edited by Geoffrey Ursell.

Cover painting, "Autumn Dance", by Anastasia Chemikos.
Cover and book design by Duncan Campbell.
Interior map illustration by Linda Hendry.
Author photo by Shalene Norrish.
Printed and bound in Canada.

The publisher gratefully acknowledges the financial assistance of the Saskatchewan Arts Board, the Canada Council for the Arts, the Department of Canadian Heritage, and the City of Regina Arts Commission, for its publishing program.

Canadian Cataloguing in Publication Data

Warwaruk, Larry, 1943-
The Ukrainian wedding
ISBN 1-55050-138-0

1. Title.

PS8589.A8765 U48 1998   C813'.54   C98-920122-8
PR9199.3.W386 U48 1998

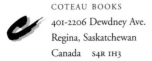

COTEAU BOOKS
401-2206 Dewdney Ave.
Regina, Saskatchewan
Canada   S4R 1H3

AVAILABLE IN THE US FROM
General Distribution Services
85 River Rock Drive, Suite 202
Buffalo, New York, USA 14207

For my mother,
Jean Slobodzian Warwaruk

In memory of my father,
Steve Warwaruk

LIST of CHARACTERS

THE MELNYKS

Mike Melnyk: *father – arrived in Canada 1903*
Anna Melnyk: *mother*
Lena Melnyk: *daughter*
Danylo Melnyk: *son – the groom*
Rose: *daughter – married to Yuri*
Dounia Zazelenchuk: *grandmother*
Metro Zazelenchuk: *grandfather*

THE SEMCHUKS

Panko Semchuk: *father*
Paraska Semchuk: *mother*
Nellie Semchuk: *daughter – the bride*
Nick Semchuk: *son – in the army*

OTHER CHARACTERS

Yuri Belinski: *a teacher*
Marusia Budka: *a young woman*
Hryhori Budka: *her husband*
Vasylko Gregorovitch: *a hermit*
Bohdan Kobzey: *a Ukrainian Catholic priest*
Ivan Stupych: *a storekeeper*
Isaac Gruber: *a Jewish merchant*

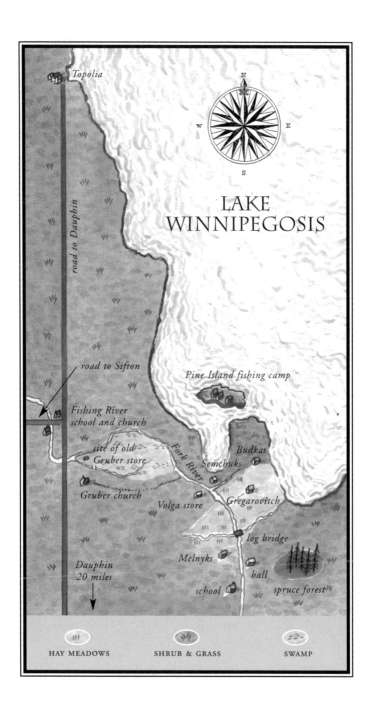

Topolia

road to Dauphin

LAKE
WINNIPEGOSIS

road to Sifton

Pine Island fishing camp

Fishing River
school and church

site of old
Gruber store

Fork River

Budkas

Semchuks

Gruber church

Volga store

Gregarovitch

Melnyks

log bridge

Dauphin
20 miles

hall

school

spruce forest

HAY MEADOWS

SHRUB & GRASS

SWAMP

ONE

Lena's father had said that if she passed her Grade Ten correspondence courses, she could go to Dauphin to buy an outfit for Danylo's wedding. She wants Naturalizer shoes, a red high heel with an open toe. *The Stardust.* Her older sister Rose had seen a pair on display for $6.95 in the showroom window at Hendersons. The store is having a summer sale the end of the week: July 3rd and 4th. Lena has saved more than $20.00 cleaning fish at Pine Island. She wants a blue suit in the military style, and a Kayser brand slip along with Kayser rayon stockings, like the jingle in the movie magazines, *Be wiser, buy Kayser.* And Rose said that Hendersons had Bestform bras at less than a dollar.

"Why let her go, Mike?" Lena's mother had said. "You spoil her. Don't you know the wedding is in two weeks? Who is going to clean the house if she runs off to Dauphin?"

Mike Melnyk had opened the pages of his *Ukrainian Voice,* holding the paper wide between himself and his wife. "Anna, don't worry so much. Besides, Rose can help with the cleaning."

Lena's mother all along had thought how stupid it was for Nellie Semchuk to insist on having her wedding in the middle of July when everybody's working. And how do you keep cabbage rolls from spoiling in July? She didn't even want Lena to continue with school this coming fall. What sense would it be for a girl? Who would do the cooking and house cleaning? What other training does a girl need? Her mother believed that if Lena went to the town school this fall they might take her to some office for the war. Like Prime Minister Mackenzie King said on the radio: "Everybody should do something to help in the war."

Her mother had lit candles at the church to pray that the army wouldn't take Danylo. Now they had even the Japanese to fight, she said, and there's no end to them. Father had been trying to tell her not to worry. Danylo has a farm exemption. She said then why did they take Nick Semchuk? Why do they always take the Ukrainian boys? Why don't they take the English? But Nick wanted to go. He said that the farm was a joke that didn't need his help to look after.

But Mother worried all the same. She was against Lena going to Topolia to live with Baba and Dido, just to study Grade Eleven at a high school. And if Lena wasn't bridesmaid for the wedding there'd be no going to Dauphin for her today either.

But how is she supposed to get there? With all the rain in June the twelve miles of road from the farm to Topolia are a mess. By the swamp the men have to lay down new logs where the bottom has sunk out of sight. The countryside needs the sun. Not only to dry the road, but it's time to cut hay. Rose had her husband Yuri bring her twenty miles from Fishing River to help prepare for the wedding. Yuri's a school teacher at Fishing River. Plowed mud all the way. Three times they had to get horses to pull their car out.

Yuri said he'd take Lena with the rowboat across the bay to the fishing station on Pine Island. The freighter from Topolia will be there with supplies this afternoon. She can catch a ride on it.

The north pasture runs narrowly to the bay with thick black poplar forest on each side. At the shore dried pieces of bulrush stems mat over the sand. In the early afternoon heat Lena's senses are sharpened by the tang of shoreline smells: the grass, snails, reeds, and alkali. A pelican swims far out on the bay's horizon. A frog croaks somewhere close in the reeds. Dragonflies buzz over the water, and two small gulls hover high above in the sky. The calm green water ripples gently to the east.

The water cools Lena's hot feet as she and Yuri pull the boat to deeper water. Lake Winnipegosis spreads forever to the north like an ocean, their only landmark the fishing camp on the island at the mouth of the bay. They wouldn't want to be rowing far. If the wind came up the waves would swamp them, even in the bay.

The sight reminds her of the stories. When Lena was a little girl her Baba told how the immigrants crossed the ocean years ago to come to Manitoba. She told of mornings on the ship's deck just before daybreak. The long-haired maidens rose between the waves, water maidens singing, Rusalkas beckoning for sailors to join them in the deep green waters. Baba sang those songs to Lena. Could there be Rusalkas in the muddy waters of Lake Winnipegosis?

Yuri's face is red like a beet. Strands of his black hair hang limp and wet on his forehead, and his moustache twitches with each grimace as he pulls on the oars. He sings in deep but quiet tones. When she asks he tells her it is the *Song of the Dnieper*. Yuri studied at the academy in Lviv. He is a scholar on things Ukrainian and he tries to interest the young people in the old culture. Funny that her sister Rose married him. Maybe better to marry an educated young Ukrainian than a bush Ukrainian like her brother Danylo. Lena's not interested in either choice. She's not much interested in the old culture.

Yuri asks her, "How's it feel to be sixteen?"

"How did you know it's my birthday?"

"Rose told me."

Odd that Rose even knows, Lena thinks. Nobody ever says anything. Lena's birthday is just another day. She trails her hand in the water, wondering how it feels to be sixteen.

"You want to know how it feels to be sixteen? No different than yesterday. Maybe a little different to be going to Dauphin." Yesterday she had to weed the garden. This morning too.

"At sixteen you should be looking for boyfriends already."

Lena splashes water at Yuri. "How do you know I haven't?"

"Nick Semchuk is coming home for the wedding."

"Nellie told me. She wants him to play the *tsymbali*."

"It is an instrument of Ukraine," Yuri says. Lena wishes she hadn't said it. He'll start up on Independence and how the people are suffering from the war. How Nick is in the army and how nice it would be if he was sent to Europe to free the Ukrainian people from Stalin and from Hitler. She can't imagine Nick Semchuk freeing the Ukrainian people. She wonders why Yuri hasn't been called up.

Along the bay's shoreline, back in the trees a half mile or so, are several farmyards, all of them hidden by the growth, including the Semchuk place to the west on the way to Topolia. Danylo's bride-to-be, Nellie Semchuk, lives there with her parents. Smoke curls up from the trees. Nellie's mother must be baking bread, or else Panko is cooking home-brew mash, getting ready for the wedding.

Panko's father Onufrey lost his feet on this lake. He was with an Indian in the winter time going for work to a fish camp further up the lake from here. In the afternoon a blizzard had mixed them up on their directions. For three days in the cold they walked on the ice. The Indian's feet stayed warm with moccasins, but Onufrey's feet froze and had to be amputated. Nellie tells how the sight and smell of the burlap wrappings on his leg stumps made her sick to the stomach. She tells how her mother Paraska had to wash these bags in wood ashes to get them clean. How her father Panko grunted to lift him up on the wagon to go to church. The rest of his life Onufrey walked on his stumps wrapped with potato bags. He was no longer able to farm. He spent his days making cabinets and sleeping benches, or picking bugs off potatoes with his wife in the garden.

"Would you like me to row for a while?"

Yuri doesn't answer. He smiles, and rows with extra energy as if to suggest he's teaching in a high school, engaging in a workout such as he'd demonstrate to a class on physical fitness.

"We want to get there today," he says.

Lena's thankful that finally they have a day without rain. The road has to be good for the wedding. Everybody will want to come, and who wants mud when you're wearing good clothes? Who will want mud when Lena's wearing her new blue suit with the padded shoulders and her red shoes? She picked an outfit from the Eaton's catalogue, but she's not going to order. The parcel wouldn't get here on time for the wedding, and she wants to try things on. Rose said to go to Hendersons in Dauphin. She'll have to pay more, but so what? She's not giving any of her money away. Not to Danylo to help pay for the mower, not to her mother for her Eaton's kitchen table. It was her own money. She had earned it. As soon as Lena had finished writing her correspondence school exams at the farm school, she went to clean fish for two weeks at the fish camp. Enough money for her outfit. She thinks she has enough even for the train ticket from Topolia to Dauphin. If she runs short Baba will always give her something. When she gets back from Dauphin she's going to stay at Baba's and help with the garden.

Lena wonders if she could ever move away. It's not the first time she wishes she was a grown-up living in some city, some place away from here. There's always Winnipeg. Other girls have gone there to work as housemaids and they send money home. Lena doesn't know if she'd do that: send money home. Now with the war some have taken the train to Toronto to work in the factories. That would really be getting away from here. Would she ever be brave enough to venture that far? Where would she find the money to travel, and how do you find one of those jobs? Could she be a "Rosie the Riveter" like Mr. Stupych showed her at the store in a *Life* magazine his brother sent from Chicago? Would Lena want to do man's work in the city? It's hard enough for a Ukrainian girl to be accepted, so how could she ever be a "Rosie the Riveter" and a Canadian woman all at the same time? She'd rather be like the women in Nellie's movie magazines. But you are what you are, and you only dream about what you want to be. Nellie will marry Danylo and she will live here on the farm. She will work in the house and the barn, in the field and in the bush. And she will have kids. But maybe Lena will be lucky. She will dream, and she will study hard at her school work. She's lucky even now to get to Dauphin for a day.

The sun shines on the water making it glisten, the sparkles striking her eyes when she looks in the direction of Panko's shore. South of his place are two more farm sites, both securely hidden, hardly farms, but at least places to live. On one of them lives the bachelor hermit Vasylko Gregorovitch. Lena has seen him now and then peddling his bicycle on his way to the Volga country store, or on some days all the way to Topolia.

The other farm belongs to Hryhori and Marusia Budka. They work for other farmers when they can, when people need them to hay, or stook, to pick rocks and roots, to cut bush. Hryhori married her in the Old Country just before they came to Canada. She was very young, just a girl, both of them very poor, like orphans paired together. At least they have strong backs to work, and Marusia is very pretty.

The rowboat approaches the fish camp.

"It looks like the freighter is nearly unloaded," Yuri says. "We're right on time." He steadies the boat alongside the pier as Lena steps out. Standing on the wooden platform holding on to a bag with her change of clothes, she watches as Yuri rows off the way they came. She yells to him. "Tell Rose I'll make the cabbage rolls when I get back." Lena doesn't know why she should feel guilty.

TWO

One week later, Panko Semchuk lumbers out of bed before the sun rises. This is unusual, for he likes his sleep. However, yesterday at the Volga store Marusia Budka had asked if anyone was going to town in the morning. She wanted to meet the train. "I like to meet the train," she had said. "And what can I do at home? Weed the potatoes. What fun is that?"

Of course Panko will take her to town. His son is coming on the train from the army. Danylo Melnyk is driving a car to pick him up, but Panko can be there too. After all, he's the father. It's no bother to hitch the horse to the buggy, and the road is starting to dry enough to get through. It's no trouble at all to take Marusia's can of cream to the station. His wife hasn't got a can ready to go yet, maybe after tomorrow's milking, but he knows that a Massey-Harris salesman from Winnipeg is arriving on the train, and Panko has an order to sell him two gallons of home-brew. He thinks that he can get the whiskey to Topolia and be back home by noon if Paraska wants him to help her with anything.

"Humph." Paraska glared at him. "Anything. Don't

you know the wedding comes in one week?"

"Of course I know," he told her. "I'll be back before noon. You don't believe me, but you'll see."

Marusia sways beside him on the seat as the buggy wheels jostle in the ruts from the rains. Panko smells sweet basil coming from her clothing, and he's curious to know if she carries a pouch of herbs around her waist. "Nice morning, Mrs. Budka." He reaches over, tempted to pat her on the knee, but instead points to a meadowlark singing on a fence-post. "Beautiful melody, don't you think?" Panko can't imagine a more pleasant situation, driving his horse slowly to town with this young woman on a warm summer day.

Marusia Budka is less than half his age. She is twenty-four, fair, and beautifully formed. Panko is short and fat with the moustache of a Cossack, thinning hair, and a red nose. But his eyes twinkle, especially around young women. Not that he would take advantage, if that were even possible, but they twinkle all the same.

At least they haven't sent his son Nick to England. The army pays him for sitting around, with free room and board on top. He makes more money than he can earn here. Panko turns again to Marusia.

"Are you coming to my daughter's wedding, Mrs. Budka?"

"You silly man. Why do you say 'Mrs. Budka?' Don't you know I'm not an old baba? I'm Marusia." She unties the knot on her yellow *babushka,* takes it off and combs her fingers through her hair. "My name is Marusia and that's what you can call me when we are by ourselves. We are not strangers." Her blouse gathers at the neck but can't hide the bold outline of her breasts. She tugs a little at the material, lifting where it clings to her flesh. Panko squints, then slaps the leather lines gently on the horse's rump.

"You know Nick is coming on the train?"

"Oh?" Marusia says. "Does he still play the *tsymbali?*"

"Nellie wants him to play at the wedding."

"The army lets him go to play the *tsymbali?*"

"Harvest leave," Panko says.

THREE

It's Lena's last day in Topolia. She's done her shopping in Dauphin, and she's helped with Baba's garden. Her mother didn't mind her going to help with the gardening. It's too hard for Baba to be always bending. It's so much more fun here than having to work at home. Baba Dounia said the garden came so early this year. Never before had she seen peas ready by the second week in July. She said the gardens were early like it used to be in the Old Country.

Baba gave Lena fifty cents just for picking peas. Money from her cream cheque. She said her granddaughter should have something to buy for herself at the café. Lena leaves the house and walks along the road to the concrete bridge, crossing over to the downtown, past the Roman Catholic Church and the big white statue of the Virgin Mary, past the grain elevator and across the tracks. A few people are already milling about on the station platform. Train time is ten o'clock. She came to watch the train yesterday morning, and the morning before that. She sits on the bench at the front of the station. From here she'll get a good look at Nick Semchuk in his uniform, but then she thinks she'll be noticed so she doesn't stay. She has to ride back to the farm with them anyway. She'll see the uniform then. Her brother Danylo is supposed to get Lena from Baba and Dido's.

Not a soul is in the café except Mr. Wong standing behind a glass counter, the rows of cigarette packages clearly visible to Lena's gaze. She notices that his eyes follow hers. The two quarters are wet in her hand.

"Something for you?" Lena looks up, startled, attempting to smile, exposing the palm of her hand with her money. Why should she be so nervous? After all, she's sixteen. "Can I have Black Cat?" she says.

She takes her cigarettes to the river bank underneath the concrete bridge. Baba says the Gypsies come here with their wagons every year around the time of the Green Holidays. Lena has never seen a Gypsy, but the way Baba talks, they have the power to read into the future. Lena's learned at school not to be superstitious.

She has tried cigarettes before. When she irons Danylo's suit, sometimes she finds a package of cigarettes and she'll take one cigarette. He probably knows, but he never says.

When she leaves the riverbank and gets back up on the road, she can see Baba's cow tethered by the barn. Between the cow and the house Dido Zazelenchuk stands leaning on his pitchfork, between two stacks of hay, wiping sweat from his brow with a crumpled hat. Baba sits in the sun on a bench against the house, shelling peas into a basin. Only then does Lena sense that someone's been watching her. She glances back towards the bridge.

Sure enough, the old hermit neighbour from the farm, Vasylko Gregorovitch, has been following her. Was he there when she was under the bridge? He's about a hundred yards away, halfway across the concrete bridge, walking with his bicycle. She had seen him earlier at the station, snooping around the freight shed examining the names on cream cans as if looking for something he doesn't even have.

She has to go home this afternoon to help with the wedding. At least she'll be back here next month when school starts. She loves the town. Last year she took Grade Ten by correspondence at the country school. But her father says she can stay at Baba and Dido's to go to high school in Topolia, if it's okay with Baba and Dido. And it is okay, Baba said. She said Lena could help clean house, and she could milk the cow. It will take a lot for her father to convince her mother. Who would do the housework at home? Who would milk? But Danylo's getting married. Nellie can do those things.

"Go to the cellar," Baba Dounia says. "I'm thirsty. Get me a bottle of Cream Soda, and for yourself."

The stairs to the cellar are under a trap door in the centre of the kitchen floor, and they're steep; another good reason for Lena to stay in town this winter. It must be getting harder and harder for Baba to get down here. A case of pop sits on the packed dirt floor beside a crock of sauerkraut, another of dill pickles, a keg of herring, a gallon jug of wine, and a two-quart sealer of Dido's home-brew. Shelves are filled with jars of canned fish, wild strawberries, raspberries, and high-bush cranberry preserves. A bag of dried mushrooms hangs from a peg on the wall. The smell of the pickle crock is the same strong garlic as the cellar at the farm.

As she climbs back up the cellar stairs she notices the brown trouser legs of an army uniform. It's Nick. Her eyes follow up to the top of his head. The rim of his tam runs in a line across his smooth forehead, slanting to the right, a gold-coloured badge pinned to the high side of the floppy fabric. His face is round, slightly oval. Light blue eyes glint under fair-coloured brows; thick lips shut tight. Nick has a pinched look, the collar of his tunic buttoned tight at his neck.

Dido Metro Zazelenchuk reaches out, touching the fabric of Nick's sleeve, and then he pats him on the shoulder.

"Men need a drink," Metro says. "Soldiers drink." He motions to Baba Dounia to go to the cellar.

"I'll go," Lena says, retreating a step downward.

"No," Dounia says, "I know where. I have to get jars for peas. I go. You get out." Lena does what she is told and the old woman in halting motions disappears into the cellar.

"Do you think she has grown in one year?" Danylo says, pointing to his sister. Nick's face turns red. Lena knows herself that she has grown. She's sixteen. Nick's sister Nellie is sixteen and she's getting married. Has she made her mind up about staying in Manitoba or will she try to talk Danylo into moving out East to work in a war factory or something? Danylo wouldn't go. She wonders if her face is red from Danylo's teasing. She never knows what to expect from him. Sometimes he can be the most generous brother a girl could have. She's almost certain that if she hadn't had enough money to buy her shoes, he would have found it for her somewhere. Yet he can say the meanest things and do the meanest tricks as if it didn't matter because she was a girl. He can get a laugh throwing a cat at her in the barn, or putting a lump of coal in a stocking she set out at Christmas because she wanted a different Christmas, like in the school readers.

"Yes," Nick says, "I guess she has grown." He takes off his army tam, then puts it back on, adusting it back and forth across his head. He's not so bad looking, if his head wasn't so round like a ball, and if his lips weren't so big. He's taller than she is, and slender, not husky like Danylo. He has gentle blue eyes, not penetrating like Danylo's.

Nick stutters, about to say something else, when Baba Dounia emerges from the cellar with the two-quart sealer of home-brew, some empty pint jars and a bottle of pop. She sets these on the table and gets two glasses and a small pitcher. Metro pours the whiskey from the jar into the pitcher, and then roughly measures an ounce of clear brew into one of the glasses. The pop he pours in the other.

"To God," he says to Nick and hands him the glass of whiskey.

"To God." Nick swallows it in one gulp then reaches for the strawberry chaser. Metro refills the whiskey glass and hands it to Danylo.

"To your wedding," Metro says.

"The wedding." Danylo drinks then shakes the glass. He doesn't need a chaser.

"How about you, Sister?"

Of course Danylo isn't serious. He knows she could never drink whiskey in front of Baba and Dido. Even if she was twenty-five years old, and not sixteen. She holds up her bottle of Cream Soda. There's wine in the cellar. She had hoped that maybe Baba would have thought to offer her wine.

"Let's go," Danylo says. He lifts the curtain on the kitchen window and looks out.

"Wait, wait," Baba says, "not before I send something with you. I baked *shyshka.*" From her cupboard she takes a wicker basket covered with a linen cloth. Lena knows what it is...*shyshka* loaves, Nellie told her about it...some kind of fertility charm. They used to hand them out at weddings, but it hasn't been done since before Lena's sister Rose got married.

Baba Dounia shuffles through the door into the east room, to the Holy pictures. She places the basket on a small table below the icon of the Virgin Mary. Three times she makes the sign of the cross.

"Take for Nellie," Dounia says. Lena lifts a corner of the cloth. In the basket are half a dozen glazed loaves in the shape of pine cones. Does Baba really believe these will help Nellie have sons? And what's so great about sons?

Nellie could believe in *shyshka*, for all that it matters. The Semchuks are Hutzuls. Baba Dounia says the Hutzuls come from the mountains in Carpathia, a land of shadows and demons. Panko when he is drunk says that life is for love, music, and whiskey. Panko is a Hutzul, and Nellie takes after him. Danylo will have his hands full with Nellie. She won't follow him around like a dog.

But why should Lena worry about Nellie and Danylo living in the bush? She should worry about herself living in the bush. Maybe when she's finished school she can get a job in Winnipeg. She'll have to earn some more money at the fish camp if she ever intends to leave home. Mother won't want her to go, and Lena's not too sure about it herself, one way or the other.

"Before I get my sister to the farm, I take Nick home, and maybe visit with Panko," Danylo says, downing one last drink. Danylo doesn't say a thing about seeing Nellie, his soon-to-be bride, the daughter of Panko.

Metro's moustache trembles, and he slaps his knee. "Panko! *Oi, oi.*"

Everybody knows Panko. Lena can hear her mother yelling at her in the morning, "Take that pail and get to the barn, you *Panko*. Can't you hear the cow bellowing?" Her mother would spit out the *ko* with emphasis, *Pan-ko. Pan-ko, Pan-ko.* Upstairs Lena should be dusting, but she'd lay on her bed reading stories from the school reader, now and then thumping the mop on the floor. All at once Mother was in the room staring down at her, "What is this? *Panko?* Get off the bed." Then, *thump,* with the mop across the legs. So often she heard the word used this way that it was hard to imagine Panko as an actual person. But he is for real all right. They will stop at his place on the way to the farm. Lena will see Nellie about the wedding. There is so much involved with being a bridesmaid.

FOUR

Panko leans against the station wall, rubbing a banknote between his thumb and forefinger. He struggles to think of an English saying. What do they say? *Ten dollars is nothing to blow your nose at?*

Home-brew is a good sideline, but he has to be careful. John Zwarichka wasn't, and he's sitting in Dauphin jail. You should learn to keep ahead of the police. The last two years, the week before St. Patrick's day, Panko delivered a twenty-six-ounce bottle to the town clerk in Topolia. He told him both times that it was for Corporal O'Hara in Dauphin, and to let him know that Panko found it in a ditch near Meadowlands. He told the clerk to say that somebody must be brewing it there. But now Panko has heard that O'Hara has been transferred to Brandon. Now he will have to find out what the new policeman is like. Isn't it always like this, Panko figures. Just when you are about to get ahead of things, misfortune falls.

Now he will have to be more careful.

Beside a rain barrel at the corner of the freight shed Panko is talking in a low voice to the salesman from

Massey-Harris. "The two gallons are buried in straw at the livery barn. On the left side when you're walking in. The last stall. You'll see it. The stall is filled with empty pails, a pile of harness, and two car tires."

Both men are watching Marusia Budka. She is talking to the drayman.

"Ice cream for Wong's Café," the drayman says, carrying the insulated canvas bag from the CNR wagon to the dray.

"I would like ice cream," Marusia says.

Panko leaves the horse tied to a post in the station yard. What should he buy with his money? Tobacco? Apples? A pocket watch? Of course he will buy an ice-cream cone.

While riding to town on the buggy, he had been contemplating that he should buy something for Marusia. Candy? Fruit? Would it have to be something to eat? Perhaps a ribbon she could put in her hair. Then he began thinking he'd be too embarrassed to give her a gift. What would he say to her? Wouldn't she wonder why is he giving her something? He is twice Marusia's age. Imagine, Panko being embarrassed. Who would ever think that?

He is half-way on his return trip home, his new watch showing the time to be five minutes to eleven. It will surprise Paraska that he's arriving at the farm before noon, but just the same she will ask "Where's Nick?" as if it is Panko's responsibility to get her son home.

The roads are still rutted and muddy from Sunday's rain, but in town everything was dry. It had looked like Topolia hadn't had as much rain. He notices that clouds are building from over the lake. It's going to be another shower. The air feels damp and the yellow-headed blackbirds are chirping as if there's no stopping them. He wishes that Marusia was returning from Topolia with him. She had said she wasn't ready to go home.

In his mind he can see her licking the strawberry cone, her tongue a darker pink than the ice cream, her lips sucking. People are lining up at the counter and Wong is scooping from two tubs: one vanilla and the other strawberry. "Five cents!" he says, selling as fast as he can.

Panko recalls Marusia licking the ice cream. Finally he thinks, forget it. "Come on, horse." He flicks the reins along its back. "Let's go to the farm."

Not only Panko had been watching Marusia lick, and not only were Ukrainian farmers watching. An Icelandic fisherman from Lake Manitoba visiting relatives was watching her lick, and the Massey-Harris man. The banker McCloud wearing a neatly pressed blue suit had come striding from across the street to watch. Even the barber was there, not to mention the café full of men, women, and children.

Everyone had been crowding to the counter to get the summertime treat that had arrived frozen on the train. They parted, leaving a space when they saw Marusia peeking in from the doorway. She gently closed the screen door, then approached the counter all the while smiling at the men on each side.

"Five cents?" she said to Mr. Wong, placing her

hand on his wrist. The ice-cream scoop rattled in the jar of milky water stained pink.

"Strawberry?" he said, the "r"s sounding like "l"s, and the sounds reversing when he said "vanilla."

"Strawberry," Marusia said.

Mr. Wong topped the cone with an extra dab of ice cream. "Free this time," he said. "Just for you."

FIVE

A few months earlier, during the Easter season, Panko and Danylo had engaged in the yearly rite of pouring the water. Normally the games were for the unmarried, but never would Panko miss out on such an event as this, never since he was thirteen years old. They had already been to several farms, and they not only poured water into the cupped hands of the maidens, but Panko had also collected a lard pail full of elaborately painted Easter eggs.

Water lay everywhere. The water nymph Rusalka had risen from the lake and combed the water droplets from her hair, flooding the meadow. Ducks quacked, muskrats swam, blackbirds chirped, perched on the brittle leaves of last summer's bulrushes, and in the sky the clouds billowed like plowed fields on the steppe, as they used to say in the Old Country. Panko gazed skyward to the sun, then looked around to every side. The tree leaves were still in bud, but promising soon to open, and here and there could be seen the beginnings of green grass. Everything was coming to life, including Panko and Danylo astride their horses plopping through the water.

"The bottle," Panko said. Danylo passed him the home-brew. Strong drink was as much of this spring water-pouring tradition as anything. At every house they were offered drink, but Panko had brought his own so they would have something between places.

"To spring," Panko said. They were on their way to Budka's. Men went out of their way for Marusia Budka, as if in rut, like it is in the spring when dogs trail a female. He thought of a saying from the Old Country; Marusia is *strong and fresh as a lusty turnip.* Does each man think she wants him because she is too much for Hryhori, her simpleton husband? If somebody asked Panko he would say that every man has a dream to breed her, even if it's not polite to say such a word. Maybe to say "service" wouldn't be as bad, but that's not the right word either. It sounds too much like working with cows and bulls. But with men, who can say? How can you tell what a man has on his mind, if he still has a head to think when it comes to a woman like Marusia Budka.

Panko wanted to perform the Easter ritual, to pour water into Marusia's cupped hands.

"She's not a maiden," Danylo said. "She's a married woman."

"What's the difference?" Panko said. He swayed on his horse imagining what he would do. He would pour the water. He would say "Christ has risen."

"He has risen indeed," Marusia would say on her knees. Then he would pour again. Three times he would pour into cupped hands.

He passed the bottle back to Danylo. "Look out!" Danylo said. Panko's horse had lowered his head to the water. Panko was sliding down its neck. Splash! Panko sat in the water with his pail of eggs. Danylo was laughing.

"What the hell," Panko said. He didn't even try to get up. He remained sitting in the water. "Lunch time," he said, and started peeling an egg. His horse nuzzled him in the back. A yellow-headed blackbird chirped, bobbing up and down on a bulrush as if mocking him.

"A beautiful day to you, too," Panko said. "What can be better than sunshine in the spring?"

In a few minutes Panko was back on his horse. The heat from the sun would dry him, he thought. They still had to go to Budka's. It wasn't long until they came to the big meadow, and in the distance they saw a man walking.

"Who can that be?" Panko said. "He is on his way to Budka's yard." They hurried with the horses to see who it was.

"It's my grandfather Zazelenchuk," Danylo said.

"Metro!" Panko said. "Have you walked all the way from town? And what are you carrying?" Metro had a shoebox under his arm. "What do you have in the box?"

Metro took off his cap and wiped his brow. "Do you have to know?" he said. He put his cap back on and took out his tobacco pouch. "Hold this," he said to Danylo and handed him the box. "Do you want a smoke?" he said to Panko. "And you, Danylo. How about you?"

Panko dismounted from his horse and took the offer of the tobacco pouch.

"But what do you have in the box?" Danylo shook it.

"Nothing much," the old man said.

"Nothing much?" Panko asked.

"What do you think I would have in a shoebox? Sausages?" He grabbed it from his grandson and took off the lid.

"Why they are shoes," Panko said, "Women's shoes!"

"Of course they are shoes!" Metro said.

"But what are you doing with women's shoes? What are you walking out here all the way with a box of women's shoes? Where did you get them?"

"I bought them in town."

"You bought them? Doesn't Dounia buy her own shoes? How do you know what to buy?"

"They are not for Dounia."

"Not for Dounia?" Panko said. "You bought shoes for Marusia Budka!"

"What's wrong with that?" Metro asked. "I saw at Easter church yesterday that she needs shoes. So this morning before breakfast I went to the Jew and bought shoes."

"Why not?" Danylo said, laughing, and nodding his head to the side towards Budka's yard.

"Of course 'why not?'" Metro said. "Who else would do it? What good is that husband of hers? Where can he get money to buy shoes?"

"You're going to buy shoes for Hryhori?" Panko said.

"You buy for Hryhori," Metro said.

BABA DOUNIA SOON HEARD ABOUT IT. The very next night in Topolia she had a visit from Panko's wife, Paraska.

The two women drank tea at the kitchen table. Paraska talked. "Such an early spring, isn't it? Do you still have cucumber pickles? I have a crock half full yet. Are your potatoes sprouting? Do you think there will be lots of wild berries this year with the spring coming so fast?" And then Paraska complained about her daughter Nellie's upcoming wedding to Danylo. Paraska didn't want to have it in July. Food was hard to keep from spoiling in July, and she was convinced that the young people didn't listen anymore like they used to. On top of this Panko was no help to tell her to wait for November, after the harvest. "Let her do what she wants," Panko had said. "Sure," Paraska told Dounia, "what does Panko have to cook? His home-brew. The more it spoils in the heat, the better he thinks it is."

"And how is Mr. Semchuk?" Dounia said.

"Ahhh," Paraska said. "Panko is Panko. I'm talking about Holy pictures, and he's talking about pumpkins."

They talked for an hour like this, but Dounia knew somehow that Paraska Semchuk had not walked all this way because she wanted potatoes, or that she wanted Dounia to do something about the wedding. But it was more than an hour before the real purpose of her visit began to unfold.

"Mrs. Zazelenchuk," Paraska said, "I have something to tell you."

"Oh?" Dounia said.

"About Metro."

"Metro?"

"Your husband, Metro. Is he in the house?"

"Sleeping in bed," Dounia said. "Since after supper. What did you hear about Metro?" She wondered what he could have done, an old man. From Paraska's eyes, Dounia knew as only an old woman could know that he had done something.

"You know, Mrs. Zazelenchuk, I don't like to tell you..."

"Tell me. Tell me. Why should there be secrets?"

"Well it isn't a nice thing. How you say...?"

"Come on. Come on, Mrs. You can tell me."

Paraska leaned forward, and in a hushed voice she said "Did you know your husband bought shoes for another woman?"

"Metro?" Dounia swallowed then tried to laugh, but when she discovered she couldn't, she reached for the teapot and poured herself more tea. What business was this of Paraska's? Why was she coming here with this gossip? She should instead have been doing something to get some work out of Panko. "More tea, Mrs. Semchuk?"

"Just a little," Paraska said, "and then I should go." She lifted the curtain and looked out the kitchen window. "You know, it's getting dark."

"Metro bought women's shoes?" Dounia glanced at the bedroom door all the while sipping her tea.

"He bought them for that Budka woman. Yesterday he took them to her."

"He took her shoes?" Dounia said. She thought about yesterday morning when he left the house. Took extra time to wash and shave. Asked her to find him a clean shirt when she has to force him to change his clothes to go to church. He said he wanted to go to the farm and talk to son-in-law Mike about the spring seeding. Dounia didn't look Paraska in the eye. "I don't know, Mrs. Semchuk," she said. "The Budkas are so poor they have nothing." Paraska said nothing, and instead she simply stared at Dounia, a forlorn look. Dounia brushed the air with her hand as if swatting a fly. "Baah!" she said, and brushed again. She didn't show anger, or surprise. If anything, she was angry with Paraska for telling her this nonsense but didn't want to let her know that. As far as Metro went, maybe being married to someone like him was what fate brought for a woman. She came here to Canada with Metro. He was young then, and so was she. Now they were old and he was a goat. "Ah," Dounia said, "Crazy men."

"Lazy, and crazy," Paraska said.

"Imagine," Dounia said, "those men chasing after that witch like a bunch of fools. Bah! That witch!" She felt better after making it sound as if Panko was chasing too. More than likely he wouldn't find the energy to run after a young woman, but it didn't hurt to make Paraska think about it.

"A witch?" Paraska said. "I don't think so. A man cries 'witch' if he's caught with his pants off."

"Mrs. Semchuk!" Dounia said, setting down her teacup and putting her hand to her mouth, then laughing.

"Let them play," Paraska said. "Maybe they will leave us alone."

Sure, Dounia thought. What woman would want

an old man like Metro? All these years in Manitoba. All these years with Metro, and he bought shoes for Marusia Budka. So what? She was Dounia, and she could look after herself, even if her life with him had been as rough as the moon bobbing on the clouds. There were good times too. If he wanted to make a fool of himself with women's shoes, he could go ahead.

"You have a ride to get home?" she asked Paraska.

"I don't worry," Paraska said. "Somebody comes along in a wagon. If not, it's full moon, and I enjoy to walk when everything is so fresh."

THE MOON WAS ALONE IN THE SKY and Dounia was alone in her backyard, as alone as she had been her first year in Canada, when she had left her daughter Anna with the baby and had to walk through the bush to the Gruber store and ask the Jew for salt and flour. This was before there had even been a road to walk on, and before there was a town of Topolia. What did old age bring? At least when she was young she looked forward to so much. Now what did she look forward to? Feeding Metro his prunes? Was it her fate to put up with him and do nothing? All her life without even giving it much of a thought she accepted that the woman listens to the man. Why change now? At least all these years he never beat her. What was the old saying she used to hear when the men were laughing and joking over a bottle of whiskey? *An unbeaten wife is like an unsharpened scythe.* Big joke. Had it always been this way? In her lifetime this was all she knew, but her grandmother once told her that a long time ago in Ukraine it had been different. A young woman did as she pleased.

Paraska said that Nellie doesn't listen. Maybe Nellie does as she pleases like grandmother said it was in the Old Country, long before Dounia's time, that's for sure. Nellie does whatever silly thing she can think of for her wedding, and she shuts her ears to her mother. But a girl is a girl and a marriage is a long time.

What had Dounia's grandmother said about weddings in ancient times? Many, many years ago, the single girls played a game, *Burning the Hair,* grandmother said. No boys could come. Each girl lifted her skirts above her waist and leaped over a bonfire. Why did Dounia have such a thought? Imagine, an old woman. But still she was a woman. Wedding tricks were for men only. What would they think if the women started jumping over fires?

Did Dounia want it like it used to be in those times? Not now that she was an old woman. She was content to sing at weddings. She kept the traditions as she learned them in her time, not her grandmother's fairy tales. Dounia was old and frail. Paraska still was strong. She had to be to look after Panko.

Maybe it *was* witches the men chased. The Evil One set traps. Why the Devil wanted to catch Metro, only the Devil knew. Certainly if Metro was so stupid, Dounia wouldn't go out of her way to protect him. If he wanted to buy shoes, let him spend his money.

Oi, oi, oi, she thought. What was there to enjoy

when you were old? Only to think of being young, and when she was young, there wasn't really much to enjoy. Only now when those times were in the past could she look back and enjoy the memory. Was it worth it to struggle? She didn't know any better. Oh, but why not have struggles? How many years ago was it when she and Metro came to Manitoba? How did she stay alive? Living in a hole in the ground. Eating rabbits. Chopping trees to make space for a garden. Alone in the middle of the bush, herself and two children, while Metro was gone most of the year working for an English farmer at Sifton. How old had she been? Twenty-four? Almost forty years ago. She had been old enough.

As she stood beside the well in the backyard, gazing up to the night sky, she followed the journey of the moon through the passing clouds, watching, as if her life was passing.

SIX

Danylo drives into Panko's yard blowing the car horn, Nick beside him in the front, Lena in the back seat. He honks again and chickens scatter and squawk. Lena can see that nothing changes here. The bush grows around old sheds with gaps between the logs where the mud has fallen away, nettles surround and grow through a rusty mower, and an outhouse squats, tilted back and to the side.

Paraska's garden is fenced off to keep out the chickens. Her house roof is newly thatched and the walls plastered. She's done it all herself. Panko is the kind of man who doesn't worry about such things. If he ignores them, these matters usually take care of themselves. Panko enjoys living in a fashion where he doesn't have to worry about anything, and he gets away with it because Paraska worries for him. He sits on his bench, hands on his knees, Paraska beside him, shelling peas. Panko beams at the arrival of his guests, proud that he's made it back from town in time to greet them.

"Praise be to Jesus," he says.

Danylo responds in the traditional manner. "Praise forever."

Both men use this religious greeting depending where they are and who they're talking to, depending how Ukrainian they want to be at the given moment. Panko, being older and closer to his origins, uses the greeting more often.

"Praise the weather," Panko says, laughing and pointing to the sky, to sunlight breaking through the clouds.

"Praise, praise, praise," Paraska says, ignoring, yet not ignoring the company. "Who else but my husband is an expert on sunshine? Look at him. Does he do anything else but sit gazing to the sky?" She takes a deep breath and sighs, then turns to her son. "Nick! *Oi, oi, oi.*" She rises to her feet, ignoring everyone but her son, letting him embrace her. She clasps her hands to her own cheeks and then to his, then brushes his shoulder. "How nice you look, everything pressed and polished. Look at me, shelling peas," she wipes her hands on her apron. "How long are you home?"

"October. Extended leave for the harvest."

"Ah," she says, "Good. Good. Stay for the harvest. Stay longer."

"I'm waiting for a call overseas."

"Stay all winter." Paraska sits back down on the bench beside Panko. She resumes shelling peas. "They can take Panko."

"A Cossack on my horse," Panko says. From Paraska's basin he scoops a handful of peas into his mouth, then reaches to the ground for an empty pod which he throws to the chickens. They run forward from around both sides of Danylo's car. Almost before the pod lands a chicken has it, scratching, pecking, then running with it. The rest of the chickens follow. They tug and pull the pod about the yard until nothing is left.

Panko winks, motions with his hands, inviting the visitors to join in watching this game with the chickens. Only when his eyes are full of tears from laughter does he resume conversation. "Ah, Danylo," Panko says, "You come for Nellie? Paraska, where is the Nellie?" He reaches down to the basin at Paraska's feet for more shelled peas and she slaps his hand.

"I shell just so you can eat?" she says. "Can't you at least wait until they are in a jar?"

"Hey," Panko says. "Wasylena. Do you think Nick is handsome in his uniform?"

Can't he just call her *Lena?* And does he think he's a match-maker? Lena wonders if she's red in the face. And there Nick is grinning, but is he blushing too?

Paraska takes another handful of unshelled peas from her pail.

"Shut up, you old fool," she tells Panko.

Lena's mother says that if Paraska had to depend on Panko to get anything done, she'd wait a long time. He has done nothing to modernize the farm. If anything, the place has gone back a little since Panko took over after his father Onufrey died.

Would Onufrey be disappointed? Is Panko altogether different from his father? There is a story about Onufrey that Panko likes to tell. In the Old Country years ago Onufrey laid bricks to build a smokestack for the landlord's factory. In the late afternoon he finished. Standing on the rim of this chimney fifty feet in the air, he lit his pipe, and danced the *Kolomeyka.* He dropped to his haunches, pipe in his mouth, arms folded across his chest, legs kicking out, and he danced around the circle. Suddenly he threw his cap, having it fall like a crippled bird to the ground, to the feet of his son Panko. This is what Panko likes to remember about his father, not frozen feet cut off after a blizzard. You can't dance without feet.

For Paraska the death of Panko's father had been a blessing. Panko's mother expected Paraska to do the dressings on the old man's leg stumps. Paraska did everything on the farm, just to get away from the old woman's bossing, to get out of the house and away from the in-laws altogether. She chopped out the bush and pulled roots by hand to make a bigger garden, worked in the fields, milked the cows, cut down willows to weave a fence. Besides this, she became a midwife. All of Lena's generation had Paraska there to help them into the world. She became everybody's Auntie: Tata Paraska.

How do they survive? They survive because of Tata Paraska. She and Panko will answer the call of other farmers to work in the hayfields. Baba Dounia says that Paraska can keep up to any man at building stacks. Panko usually quits after building one so he can sleep on its shady side.

As for Panko he does only four things: eating, making home-brew, sun-gazing on this bench beside the house, and playing his *sopilka.* On Saturdays up until the summer before Nick joined the army, two summers ago, Lena would sneak away from housework, walking to Panko's to hear the *sopilka*. She'd sit on a chair with just her toes touching the floor. She'd chew her nails and bounce her knees up and down. Panko would dig in his pocket and give her a nickel. Then he would show her how he made his *sopilka*, cutting a willow maybe two feet long, sliding off the bark, carefully, cutting the holes all in the right places, and then right away playing a tune as if he were an elf in the forest. He told her all kinds of things about the Devil and God that she would never in a million years hear from the priest.

What was more sacred to Panko than his *sopilka?* He would say that most things in this world were created by the Devil: wagons, knives and forks, houses, violins, anything you can name almost, things made with men's hands, steam engines, even the *tsymbali* that Nick plays. But God created the *sopilka.*

"The Devil created whiskey," Panko would say. "And the Devil created the fire that cooks the brew." He'd say that God didn't create much of anything; He didn't have to. Instead He stole from the Devil. He stole fire so the Devil got angry and threw water, "And what do you know," Panko would say. "That's how we got smoke."

Panko agrees with God to let the Devil do the work. "Farmers talk nothing but progress in this new country," he'd say. "And for what? Progress?" For this speech he'd get worked up. He'd nod his head up and down, and he'd shake his finger at the men he'd be talking to.

"Sure!" he'd say. "What is the proverb? *The wealth of one is the ruin of ten.* This progress business is nothing but the Devil's work and someday it will blow up in everybody's face."

But he knew that the Devil did not create the *sopilka.* The good Lord created the *sopilka,* and also Panko who plays it, and that's what Panko does. Some even say that he is not meant to farm. That he is more like an artist or a poet, not a farmer; that the world needs people like him to trill as do the birds, making music for everyone else.

But then Panko is too lazy to stand and play at a dance. He plays only while sitting on his bench. People wonder if it's some magic in the music from his willow pipe that keeps Tata Paraska from knocking him on the head with a post, and she could do it.

The screen door slams. Paraska turns her head to the doorway then clunks Panko on the knee with the pail. "If you don't get up, you will wear a hole in this bench," she tells him.

"Lena! Lena!" It is Nellie running out from the house. "I am so busy with these paper flowers I didn't know that anybody came." She looks just for a second at Danylo, and smiles, then quickly turns back to Lena.

"Come into the house," Nellie says. "I want to show you something." She pulls Lena by the hand, then closes the door. "Up here," she says. "I don't want anybody to see." They climb to the loft where Nellie has her bed. From under the bed she pulls out a small black suitcase, then takes a key from around her neck and opens the lock. She hands a pink box to Lena.

"Nellie!" Lena has never seen anything like this. This girl is a Hutzul for sure. How else can she get such crazy ideas?

"Pure silk," Nellie says.

"Sure, but Nellie! These are black! And this lace? Where did you get these? From the catalogue?"

Nellie lifts the fabric from the box and the silk flows through her fingers like water. "Do you expect Eatons to have such things? Of course not. I ordered from an ad in *True Romance* magazine. They come all the way from New York."

"What will your mother say?"

"She doesn't have to see. I don't sleep with Mother. Only Danylo will see."

Lena is embarrassed. Why should that be? The underwear is not hers, it is Nellie's. She holds up the box to Nellie's face. "Put them back."

"They won't bite you," Nellie says. "Here!" She tosses them on Lena's lap where the silk slithers across her thighs, falling to the floor.

"Are you crazy?" Lena says. Nellie laughs as her friend packs everything back into the suitcase and under the bed. Only once this is done can Lena relax. What a Nellie! Here she is having a stupid old-fashioned Ukrainian wedding, but she will be wearing black silk under her dress. She will wear the plaited myrtle leaves and coloured ribbons in her virgin head-piece, but her panties will be black, black silk that somehow frightens Lena. The *shyshka* loaves are in the car. Lena smiles. Nellie's black underwear will do more for fertility then a thousand loaves of *shyshka*.

SEVEN

Mud plugs under the fenders and Danylo has to stop and dig it out. The sun breaks through the clouds as Lena gets out of the car and walks in her bare feet, the mud squishing through her toes. She wades into the ditch, letting the water rinse away the dirt.

She hears Danylo cursing.

"How are you doing?" she asks.

Danylo wipes the sticky clay off the tire wrench he's using to probe under the fenders. "Goddamn! This shit is packed tight."

"We've got lots of time."

"Go to hell!"

Holding her skirt halfway up her thighs she wades further away along the ditch. She hears frogs croaking in the cat-tails ahead of her, and as she gets closer to them the noise stops. A yellow-headed blackbird flits ahead, bobs on a reed, then flies to another.

This spring they fished along this road. The ditches filled with water from the rising lake and the meadow flooded. Fish flipped about in the meadow grass. She ran after them, splashing, bending to grab a fish with her hands, and she fell face down in the cold water. They caught fish one after another with a wire snare on the end of a pole, so many fish that her father came to cart them home with the horse and wagon. "We'll have fish even for the pigs," he said.

Enough fish to feed the pigs. She scaled the fish, cut off the heads, gutted, packed the fish in jars. "Do this! Do that!" Always the same. "Mike, your daughter won't work!" Always, "Do this! Do that!" Last fall they were butchering. Her father stabbed and the blood spurted from the pig's neck. Mother caught blood in a basin. Stirring with a stick. Scalding hot water poured on the skin. Scraping off the hair. Entrails like sausages spilled on the ground. Mother put the liver in the basin of blood. After the killing, and gutting, and scraping, more women's work in the summer kitchen. Yuri and Rose were home for Thanksgiving. Some Thanksgiving for Rose, sweating at a hot stove, stirring fat rendering in a boiling pot.

"Wasylena," Mother said, "Go to the house for the sharpening stone."

"Why can't Rose go?"

"Go!"

Always it is me who has to run, Lena thought. And when she got back with the stone, Mother yelled at her again. "What took you so long? Do you think we have time to wait all day?" Mother concentrated on sharpening the knife; Lena started for the door.

"Where are you going? You have work."

Mother cut pork into thin strips, Lena was supposed to pack the strips into jars, and Rose ladled hot fat from a cast iron pot, filling the spaces in the jars. Lena was grease to the elbows.

"I can't wait till I'm finished high school and I can go find a job away from here."

"You'll find nothing. We need you here to work. Maybe someday a farmer will marry you. Who knows? God have mercy." Mother shoved Lena to the table.

"No!" Lena said. "This is stupid!"

"Do you want a slap?" Mother yelled, her hand raised in the air. Lena grabbed a piece of fat pork.

"Stupid! Stupid! Stupid!" and she flung it at her mother's face. Under her breath and in the Ukrainian language her mother swore. "Whore!" she said.

Why did she say that? Will she say it again? It's what her mother calls girls who smoke and wear lipstick. She had found Lena's tube of *Angelus* last year and had thrown it down the toilet hole. At least she won't be surprised when Lena wears her new lipstick to the wedding.

As THE CAR PULLS INTO THE YARD and up to the house, it starts to rain. Between the house and the road, surrounding the front garden, her father's wattled fence appears lush and plump. It's a weave of willow branches overgrown with ivy. The long dirt path leads from the centre gate to the veranda, also covered with vines. Plum and crabapple trees line each side of the path, and Mother's flower beds – pansies, clusters of sweet williams, poppies – fill the spaces between the fruit trees. The black poplars edge the garden, the grounds carefully groomed, every fallen twig swept away. Mother is particular about her flower garden, especially where people can see from the road.

She is particular about everything seen from the road. Lena has to wash clothes in the old house back up on the hill where the barn and chicken house are, the buildings out of the way. Mother makes her carry the wet clothes back down the hill to the clothes line beside the new house, close to the road. The neighbours will see how white the Melnyks wash their linens.

The flower garden is extra special to Mother. She used to say that if she could choose where to die, it would be in the flower garden. And sometimes when she was angry with Lena that's what she used to do, pretend that she was dying in the flower garden. She would go out and lie in the trench that bordered the raised beds. If Lena didn't behave, Mother would stay out there until she was dead. That's what she'd say, but Lena's older now.

Her sister Rose is standing on the back step, wiping her hands on her apron. "About time you got home." Rose wears a blue polka dot house dress and a little apron that has a picture of a kitten playing with a ball of wool. "Let's get in out of the rain. Let me take your parcels. Did you get the shoes?"

"Wait till you see them!"

Lena's father stands at the kitchen table. Mike Melnyk wears black lace-up boots, dark heavy denim trousers held up with braces, and a grey cotton shirt open at the neck. He is nearly bald, with the eyes of a Tartar, pinched at the corners, but they're blue. His moustache is not nearly as flamboyant as Panko's, nor his father-in-law Metro's for that matter. Her father doesn't hang on to the old ways. He was the first farmer in the district to farm with horses. He said that in Manitoba, heel flies and oxen don't mix. One summer's ploughing with them was enough. He would need ten men to hold a pig-headed ox from dragging the plough into a slough when the flies were biting.

He plucks the stub of a cigarette from its amber holder and drops it in a sardine can ashtray. He puts the cigarette holder in his shirt pocket. Mother keeps rocking, every once in a while looking over the top of her wire-rim glasses, at the same time twisting green paper-wrapped wire and pink crêpe paper, making a flower. She has an assortment of flower-making odds and ends and several rolls of crêpe paper in a basket on a kitchen chair beside her. She peers over her glasses again and stops rocking, sets her paper flower down in the basket, removes her glasses, and wipes her eyes. She does not get up from the rocking chair. Her mother is a big woman with a round face and a broad flat nose. Her salt-and-pepper hair is tightly wound into a bun at the back of her head. She wears a loose-fitting black-and-white-striped cotton dress, and a white full apron. Her brown stockings are rolled down to her ankles and her feet are covered in heavy wool socks.

All available counter space is covered with flour and dough. Rose has been working as only Rose can, and soon she will direct Lena to work, also as only Rose can. In the centre of the table, all by itself on the red and white check oilcloth, ready for the outdoor oven, sits the *kolach*. Lena looks at the intricate braids of dough. A hole is neatly made on the top for a candle. "You didn't make this, did you, Rose?"

"Of course not. Mother makes the *kolach*. "

Of course. Mother would not trust this chore to anyone but herself. Not even Rose. Tata Paraska and Baba Dounia made a *kolach* at Semchuks. Nellie herself made the little doves for decoration, but even with three women doing it, they could not match this one. Nothing is more sacred to the Ukrainian people than bread, and without a doubt no one shows this better than her mother, at Christmas, Easter, and now at Danylo's wedding.

EIGHT

Nellie insists that they drive around the country in the old tradition, inviting guests. Panko doesn't have a car, and it would take at least two days to make the rounds with a horse and buggy. Years ago they took the time, sometimes as long as three days, but this is 1942. Who would think to waste that much time these days?

"Inviting guests was easier in the Old Country," Baba Dounia says, talking to Paraska on Panko's bench outside the Semchuk house. "My mother said a match-maker was coming to our house. Metro wanted to marry me. After one week I was walking door to door inviting the guests, half the people in the village trailing me: children, old men, even the village dogs."

Lena wonders why they bother at all. Rose said it was old-fashioned nonsense for a bride to bow her head to the floor, then kiss the hand of an old farmer. Lena hasn't seen anybody make the wedding invitation rounds ever since Rose said she wouldn't when she and Yuri got married.

Dounia smiles, the look in her eyes far away, as if

the wedding makes her young again.

"What are you telling me?" Paraska says, standing up and grabbing a broom, sweeping dust off the step. "I was one of the children trailing behind you." She turns to Panko who has been washing his face in a basin of water on the bench, and is now combing his moustache. "What do you think you are? Some Cossack?"

"I'm going to invite guests," he says.

"You! Of course!" She shakes her broom at him. *"Oi, oi, oi,"* she says, affirming what everyone already knows, that there is nobody in the district old enough to remember a celebration taking place without Panko. "Foolishness!" Paraska says. "We are no longer living in the Old Country." She sweeps again. "Why didn't our people settle in a village, instead of in every bush? In the Old Country it was a simple thing to walk door to door. Here you have to drive from Volga to Meadowlands and back to Rice Lake."

"Ah, Paraska! How many times do I have to tell you? It is what Nellie wants. Maybe Lena can tell you. You tell her, Lena. My wife doesn't listen to me."

"Were the invitations your idea, Nellie?" Lena picks a purple sweet pea from the vines on the fence and weaves it into Nellie's hair, fixing ribbons on the headpiece that will get more work done to it tomorrow night at the wreath-plaiting. "I don't think you'd catch me on my knees kissing a farmer's hand."

"Danylo thought it might be fun going house to house. Hand me the mirror," Nellie says, "Over there where you left it on the bench. I want to see what you're doing to me."

Danylo, washing the car windows, throws a wet rag at Lena. "Catch this!" he says. "Why should you worry about kissing anything? Do you think anybody would marry you?"

"Come on! Come on!" Panko says. He climbs into the the car. "Let's go to Budka's."

Panko sits between Danylo and Nick in the front seat. Nellie, Lena, and Baba Dounia squeeze into the back.

"Hold this," Nick says, passing his *tsymbali* over the seat to Baba Dounia's lap.

"Watch out," Nellie says, tugging a pink ribbon from her headpiece caught in the instrument's strings. Lena opens the window, breathing fresh air and hoping she doesn't get carsick.

IF ANYONE IS COMFORTABLE VISITING HOMES, it is Panko. Christmas day, New Year's day, Easter Monday, Easter Tuesday, The Green Holidays, The Holiday of *Petra,* every wedding – Panko is on the road visiting. There isn't a household in the district he hasn't drunk in.

The Budkas live in the bush in a house not much better than a woodshed. Hryhori doesn't farm, and they have only a cow for milk and a few chickens for eggs. A garden plot is all the land that has been cleared. At least Marusia can grow beets to make borshch.

They have no children. Why, Panko wonders? Maybe Hryhori doesn't know what to do, or maybe she doesn't want him to do it. Maybe she wants somebody else. After all, Hryhori is twice her age. Dounia says his step-mother in the Old Country beat him when he was a child, and that's what makes him a little bit simple.

The farmers like to get the Budkas for bush work, especially if Marusia comes along. Hryhori will chop hour after hour. There is no stopping him. He doesn't work too fast, but he's always steady. It is the one thing he knows how to do. As for why he doesn't chop out his own bush to make a farm, who knows?

Panko has said, "What would please God more than to invite such people to a wedding? The Budkas need to enjoy life too." He has said this many times. But it's not just that he has a big heart. There is something about Marusia Budka that attracts all the men from the district. The story is that she was an orphan, and was married to Hryhori before her thirteenth birthday. They came to Manitoba not so many years ago. Panko has always wondered how they managed in bed on their wedding night?

Marusia greets them at the door. She is no longer a girl of thirteen, but a fresh and healthy twenty-four, and quite a woman at that. Her hair falls straight, a light brown with streaks of blond, beautiful hair that falls across her mouth and she blows away at the tips.

Panko likes to watch this: how her tongue licks her hair, and she makes little spitting sounds, like a cat. She shoots out her tongue over her full lower lip, and blows at the hair caressing her cheek.

Marusia has green eyes that light up when she is around the men. She smiles, her eyes flashing. She appears joyful at the arrival of her company. Her cotton house dress rides over her body, her breasts jutting and the curve of her hips showing as she sits on a bench in the middle of the room. Panko, Nick, and even the soon-to-be-married Danylo, do nothing but stare at her.

Hryhori comes directly from the barn and sits on the bench beside Marusia. He has milked, and the cows must have been eating green grass because his pantleg is smeared with runny manure, as is the back of his hand which he wipes on his knee. How can she tolerate spending her life with him? She doesn't need him. Panko doesn't understand how this union is possible. Marusia is not a woman to be tamed by any man, let alone this simple Hryhori. Even for anyone to try taming her would be a shame.

Nick is at the doorway playing a love tune on his *tsymbali*. The wooden hammers bounce only from their own weight, and move from string to string reluctant to leave, the hammers dropping slowly. Dounia leads Nellie to the couple on the bench. The old woman's singing is more of a lament, and she weeps.

Nellie bows low. Three times her forehead touches the hard-packed earthen floor. Her hands reach forward, palms flat on the floor.

"I invite you to my wedding," she sings. *"May I kiss your hand?"*

While Nellie is on the floor, Marusia is pulling up her dress to scratch her knee. Panko breathes in a bellyful of air. He wishes that he was down there on the floor closer to that knee.

Hryhori extends his hand. From the porch entry, craning her neck around the doorway, Lena watches until she's seen enough. She steps outside, her stomach queasy. Why does Nellie go through with this? Kissing his hand? There she is on her knees, and we are supposed to be living in Canada.

THE NEXT DAY ON THE EVE OF THE WEDDING, people are arriving at Semchuks for the plaiting of the wreaths. The men congregate outside, the women, carrying myrtle plants and cakes, go into the house. Panko stands by the edge of the bush, yelling at Danylo, instructing him to get the shovel from the garden. A year ago Panko buried a wooden keg in the floor of his home-brew shed and the time has come dig it up.

"Shliak trafyv," he says and laughs until tears fill his eyes. It is an old saying, swear words but not swear words. Panko is not even sure of the meaning; not all of it is Ukrainian, but something mixed with the German; *May you be struck by lightning.* The people say it when they are angry and it's a curse, or when they are not angry and it's not a curse but a joke. Panko's eyes twinkle and screw up at the corners, and he rubs his hands together saying *"Shliak trafyv."* He's not angry. He's thinking about the joy that will pour out of the keg. That it will be the best whiskey in the district, at least as good as Mike Melnyk's. "I would ask Nick to dig," Panko says, "but you know him. He's in the house with the women, plunking his

tsymbali." His still is a primitive contraption of his own design, a pail sitting on a fish camp stove in the corner of the shed. Mike quizzes him on how it works.

"Look," Panko says, "I show you. I have cut a hole in the side of the pail. Halfway up. Inside I have this pie plate and cut here too, in the rim. Then I solder this pipe to the hole in the plate. And you see that basin? On the bench? I put in ice and set it on top of the pail."

"Simple," Mike says and taps his cigarette holder against the side of the pail.

"Yeh, yeh. I hang the plate on a wire inside the pail. A bit of a slant, and the pipe comes out the hole in the side of the pail. When I cook the mash, the vapour cools on the bottom of the basin and drops on the plate. It runs down the pipe and you collect in the jar."

Panko has three two-quart sealers, all of them full, lined up on the floor against the shed wall. Mike points to the jars. "Let's try some of this fresh stuff before we dig. Just to compare."

"Why not?" Panko says, giving a twist to his moustache. "To compare."

THE WOMEN GATHER IN THE EAST ROOM. Lena sits with Nellie at the bride's table, the *skrynia*, the one fancy piece of furniture in the house, the chest which stores the household valuables – linens, Tata Paraska's coral beads, the land title, what money the family has. Tata Paraska has Holy pictures on the wall above their heads, each icon framed with crêpe paper flowers.

Lena unwinds Nellie's braid. She doesn't normally wear her hair in a braid, but for this part of the ceremony there has to be the *kosa*, the sign of the unmarried woman, the sign of a virgin. In the Old Country all young girls wore their hair this way. In Manitoba the girls have long ago given up the tradition of wearing this *kosa*.

The women sit on benches. Every woman has a few branches of the myrtle flower which they are braiding to add to the bride's headpiece. Even Marusia Budka plays with a branch of myrtle, but her fingers stumble. Every once in a while she cranes her neck to look out the window. Tata Paraska, Nellie's mother, has the headpiece to which she is sewing coloured ribbons. The women sing in chorus: *"Bless oh Lord the mother who is plaiting this wreath for her daughter...."* Lena's mother Anna sits with Tata Paraska, weaving the myrtle leaves and little white flowers into the crown. Everyone marvels at her skills. How is it in a district that always there is someone with the special talent for such things? Everybody knows that nobody can match Anna in making the bride's crown. Of course most of the women have made flowers before, but none with her touch.

Nick is at the doorway smiling mournfully as only Nick can, striking at the strings of his *tsymbali* with the little wooden hammers made by Panko. For that matter, it's not only the hammers Panko has made. Panko has made the *tsymbali*. He ordered piano strings from Eaton's. Nothing was in the catalogue so he got Mike Melnyk to write a letter. Mike knows how to write better than Panko in English. The wires came and Panko pieced everything together for the *tsymbali*, all from memory, even if he was just a boy when he came to Canada. Did his father tell him? He cannot remember. All he knows is that for him it is easy to make the *tsymbali*.

Each strike that Nick makes with either hammer is modest and delicate, and a sound rings on as if by itself. If Nick is an oaf, all is forgiven with his music, and the mud-walled dwelling of Panko is transformed into a palace when Nick plays.

Lena's mother brought her myrtle plant with her to Panko's. This plant was taken from a slip given to her by her mother. Baba Dounia brought it from Galicia.

They sing each time a woman comes to add something to the headpiece. Dounia has made two small myrtle wreaths which she sets beside the *kolach* on the bride's table. These the priest will place on the heads of the bride and groom at the church tomorrow.

When Lena finishes combing out Nellie's hair, Tata Paraska takes the comb, and Nellie sings: *"Comb my hair, Mother, with your white fingers, with tears...."*

Paraska gives the headpiece to Baba Dounia. At this moment the men enter the house.

"The priest!" A whisper runs through the room. "The priest is here." From the shed the men heard a car drive into the yard, saw the priest in the back seat. They ran out of the bush to greet him, and now Panko leads the procession of men into the east room.

Panko had asked him to come. Not often does the priest attend the party; it used to be he took part only at the church. In the Old Country a priest did not like to mix with the people.

Panko escorts Bohdan Kobzey around the room, the women bowing and crossing themselves. Hryhori Budka follows, lifting the priest's robe to keep it from touching the floor. Kobzey sprinkles Holy Water to every corner.

Dounia steps forward to the table in the same manner she did the other day when she approached Lena with the basket of *shyshka*. She is chanting. The song is for the crowning of the bride: "*The white blossom of the cranberry has flowered; the wreath glistens in beauty; let us put it on the head of the bride.*" Nellie kneels, touching her forehead to the floor three times. Dounia makes the sign of the cross three times and places the headpiece on the bride. Red, pink, yellow, and purple ribbons fall down Nellie's back. She looks up and her eyes sparkle like the tiny flowers on her crown. She rises and goes first to the knees of Tata Paraska and Panko, bows low, forehead touching the floor again, the ribbons of her headpiece falling along the length of her body to the floor. "*The bride deserves to wear the wreath,*" Dounia sings, "*Her virgin purity is intact.*"

Lena is standing beside Nellie, adjusting the bridal ribbons trailing from the headpiece. She hears the words of Dounia's song and wonders if all the people are looking at her or at Nellie. She follows Nellie, standing directly behind her as the bride stops before each woman in the room and bends to her knees, bowing three times and singing her thanks for the wreath.

"A drink," Panko says to the priest, "To good

health and God's blessing on tomorrow's wedding. Play the *tsymbali*, Nick – a fast one." He raises bottle and glass to Danylo's father. "What do you say, Mike? Tomorrow we are related. Let's have a drink for everyone."

Lena wonders if she is the only one embarrassed by all the ritual. Why does Nellie put up with all this? She must know better. Surely her parents wouldn't insist on traditions that the young people wished everybody would forget. But then Panko is Hutzul and those people live in the past. Nellie is Panko's daughter. Maybe that explains it. Who can say?

Lena looks around the room, at the women and the men. She wonders what Panko thinks. He would probably say it doesn't pay to think, and then he would laugh. If someone said why sing all these songs, he would say, "Why not? Does anybody have anything better? To hear the young ones talk," Panko would say, "you'd think the English have better weddings."

Lena knows that her father thinks like she does. He came to Canada in 1903, and he thought it would have been foolish to try to bring the Old Country with him. Mike was happy to be rid of the Polish *pans,* and the priests, and he was eager to learn the ways of Canada. "Oh, it's all right to celebrate the way the district wants to celebrate," Mike would say. "Let Dounia sing all she wants." It's just that he's not going to make a fuss one way or the other.

Hryhori Budka drinks a glass of whiskey. For him this is a great honour, as if the brew is the blood of Christ. He motions to the priest. "The wedding!" he says. For Hryhori a wedding is next to God; the *kolach*, the braided bread, is Holy Communion, the body of Christ. On Easter morning on the grass of the churchyard, he proceeds on his knees, following the banners with the people and priest in procession three times around the church. In the aisle of the church he crawls on the floor to kiss the smudged picture of Christ on the small altar. The words of the priest, and anybody else of importance, are sacred for Hryhori. He will bow to everybody of importance, even bow to Panko.

"Come on," Danylo says, "Another glass, Hryhori." Sure, Lena thinks, encourage him to drink more. They love to see him drunk. This makes a wedding for Danylo.

Danylo will put up with the rest of the ritual if that is what it takes to get married, that is as long as Danylo doesn't have to do anything. He will take whatever is fun from the traditions, and that is all the men have ever had to do. They take nothing serious but a good time.

For the women it is different. All of the women, even Marusia Budka in a way, have the faith of Baba Dounia. They are rooted, swaying on their benches like the grasses in the meadow. Every word of every song is as vital to life as every drop of rain. Old Dounia would say that English is like poison on the land, and if the true spirit of the Ukrainian soul will be broken, it will be the men to blame. It's the men who buy the radios.

NINE

Four years ago, at the festival of *Petra,* Lena had her First Communion. The priest travelled from Sifton to serve the Ukrainian Catholic parishes, including Gruber and the church at Fishing River. Lena's religious instruction coincided with the summer *praznyk* at Fishing River. It wasn't often the Melnyks got the opportunity to attend church, maybe five or six times a year, or whenever the priest made a visit. At Easter they'd go to the church at Gruber, and again in September to the week-long mission, when they celebrated a *praznyk* for the blessing of the fruit. *Petra* was an opportunity to visit people at another parish.

St. Peter's Day was at the start of hay cutting, always on July 12th. It was an exciting event because the Melnyks stayed overnight at Uncle Peter's farm. Lena always thought the *praznyk* of *Petra* was a celebration for Uncle Peter.

The Gruber people assembled on the road a short distance from the Fishing River church. Everyone sang. Their hosts met them. Men, women, and children from each parish bowed to those in the other. Already the sun was hot and there was not a cloud in the sky. A breeze kept the mosquitoes away, and the air smelled fresh from a rain during the night. The groups formed together at the church gate where they met the priest.

Bohdan Kobzey had his Holy Book in the crook of his arm, and with his brass-plated censer he shot clouds of incense over the people, on the gates, on the church doors, and then he led the procession around the church. The priest sang solo in a deep voice, then the people sang. Priest, then people; priest, then people. Lena and Nellie and two girls from Fishing River carried the wood-framed icon of the Virgin Mary. Three times the procession circled the church in the direction the sun travelled across the sky. At each corner the people fell to their knees, heads bowed beneath the flapping church banners.

Once inside, the men stood on the right, women on the left. There was no possible way that everyone could get in. The older people sat in the few rows of pews in the front half of the church. Lena and the other first communicants knelt at the very front, boys on one side, girls on the other. Behind the pews people were packed, standing all the way out to the steps and into the yard.

When Paraska and Panko entered the church, heads turned. Married women wore *babushkas,* girls went to church bare-headed, with hair braided into a *kosa,* or more recently with their hair worn loose over the shoulders. But Tata Paraska was wearing a hat. Where she got the idea to wear an Eaton's hat to church, who could even imagine. The women's side of the church was a garden of *babushkas*, with Paraska's hat standing out like a weed. Voices murmured *"Kapeliukh! Kapeliukh!* Look! A hat! She wears a hat!"

Maybe Tata Paraska had simply decided to buy something for herself for a change, but she got more than she had bargained for. "Look at Paraska," they whispered. There it was on her head, a navy-blue hat with a yellow silk flower stuck in the brim.

"Look," Baba Dounia said, "she put a flower yet!" She pursed her lips and frowned, as if to say how could Paraska flaunt herself in the church with a yellow flower on her head? Even the men turned their heads.

After Mass, only Lena's father defended her.

"What is wrong for a woman to wear a hat?" Mike said. "Don't we live in Canada?"

But nobody else supported her. Even Panko criticized. "I never could tell her anything," he said.

Mass continued for three hours, the priest's deep chant answered with high-pitched women's voices and the low drones of men. *"Hospody pomylui, Hospody pomylui, Hospody pomylui,* Lord have mercy...."

The church grew hotter, more humid, and more steeped with incense and the aromatic smell of the sweet basil bouquets many of the women held on their laps. Marusia Budka sat beside Lena's mother in the back pew. Her dress was wet down her side from perspiration.

The discomfort prepared the people for the sermon

they knew was coming. Not often did the priest get the opportunuty to lecture his flock, five or six times a year, and for this *Petra* not everyone had gone to confession. They knew they would hear about it. Some people went to confession only at Easter. What if you died before next Easter? You would go to hell. For the sermon, the people in the church had melted into submission. At least those in the pews could finally sit, and those standing could but imagine what it would feel like to sit. Men nursed hangovers from the night before because *Petra* was a two-day celebration. When you visited overnight there was not much time for sleep. Some hadn't slept at all. They leaned on the walls, against the back pews, on the unlit stove, on the stairs leading to the choir loft, on one leg, then the other. Only the boys outside leaning against the bell tower could walk around and breathe fresh air.

In his sermon what sins the priest hadn't heard about in yesterday's confessions he borrowed from the confessions of last Easter. "Gluttony and home-brew. Is that all you men do with your time is get drunk? How many of you are guilty of eating meat on Friday?" Is there anything a priest can't preach? The Ukrainian Orthodox priests marry and have children, but the Ukrainian Catholic priests, at least in Canada, are celibate. This didn't stop Kobzey from referring to certain rumours. He talked about adultery in the district. There was not a scraped shoe or a hint of a cough in the church. Even the boys outside stopped talking.

"Even old men," the priest said, "old men lusting after adulterous women." Marusia Budka squirmed in her seat, wiped the sweat from her brow with a hand-kerchief. She leaned to Lena's mother. "You know," Marusia said, "I shouldn't tell the priest everything."

THE DAY BEFORE THIS SUNDAY SERMON, in the priest's confession room, Lena had knelt under Kobzey's stare. While kneeling in front of the priest she had a sudden thought that just three weeks ago she had had her first period. She didn't know what it was and had waited two days to ask Rose, had waited until she was pretty sure she wasn't going to die. Why did she think of this now? The next moment she was conscious of the priest's black whiskers, a face with the texture of sand-paper, hearing the rasp of his hand rubbing the bris-tles on his chin.

Lena had stayed at Uncle Peter's the entire week before *Petra*, learning her catechism. Other children came from the Gruber district, even Nick Semchuk. She had spent the week memorizing the routines of the confession: *Bless me, Father, for I have sinned...* and *I am heartily sorry for these and for all the sins of my past life, and I beg pardon and absolution from you, Father.*

The priest heard the confessions in his room behind the altar. Lena knelt at her pew waiting her turn, biting at her fingernails, the cuticles torn and bleeding. Fingers still in her mouth, she gazed up at the flying angels on the ceiling. How many were there? Six? Angels painted on the light blue backdrop of the nar-row tongue-and-groove boards. The church was painted in the colours of white, blue, and gold. The painting of the blue-robed virgin gazed over the stand of brass candle holders. On the other side of the altar St. John the Beloved looked at his candles. In the Fishing River church the men lit candles on one side of the altar, women lit on the other side. The procession banners on long staves were mounted two on each wall.

If Lena was nervous, it didn't appear that Nick was. He performed at the side of the altar. He drew his hand to his forehead, thumb and two fingers together: *In the name of the Father,* then his arm extended to the altar. He gazed around for approval, grinned, then brought his hand back to his forehead, the *Son, Holy Ghost, Amen.* Twice more. He hadn't been in the confessional any more than thirty seconds. What a liar he was. If he told all his sins he'd be in there for the whole afternoon.

On his way down from the altar Nick crossed himself rapidly, ten or eleven times, grinning at the boys sitting in the front pew, and then he stuck out his tongue at Lena.

She waited until he was kneeling, mouthing his penance. Then she got up from her seat, snuck quickly by the altar, hesitated, then made the sign of the cross three times. She could hear Nick laugh, but didn't dare look back. The door to the back room was partially open, and she heard the cough of the priest. He sat on a chair, turning his head to face her as she stood at the doorway. He nodded, then frowned straight ahead at a Holy picture on the wall. Lena stepped forward and knelt at his foot. She thought about her period. She had heard that the Roman Catholic Church in Topolia had private booths for confession, the priest in one, and you in another. But here she was; right at the priest's foot. She could hear him rubbing his black whiskers.

"Bless me Father for I have sinned..."

"Wait, my child. Wait." The priest reached back over his shoulder and pulled his outer garment forward, a flowing robe, dark red, embroidered with gold thread. He draped it over his head and down over Lena kneeling at his feet, his face inches from hers beneath what became a dark and private place.

"Hmmn," he said. "Tell your sins."

She told him about trying to get out of doing the supper dishes, about not saying her prayers every night, about yelling at her sister Rose, about eating a piece of chicken on Friday. His face touched hers, moving. She could feel the prickles of his whiskers.

"Have you had sex, my child?"

"Huh?" She didn't know what he meant and had no idea what she should say. "No," she said. She could hear his breathing. Smell his sour breath. Thinking she might faint, Lena moved her head, lifted the edge of the garment to get some air.

"Have you touched yourself? For pleasure? Your private parts?" She didn't understand, only her period, and then speechless, she remained motionless, head hanging, then swaying side to side. What kind of sin was he talking about? She looked straight ahead in the semi-darkness beneath the robe, at his knees. "Rubbing yourself here," he said, and pointed to his groin. Her head dropped and she whispered.

"No."

Nothing was said for at least ten seconds. She wanted to get out from under the cloth. Raising it again to the side, she took in more fresh air then blurted out her memory work: "*I am heartily sorry for these and all the sins of my past life and I beg pardon and absolution from you, Father.*"

The priest rubbed his whiskers again, raised the vestment back over his shoulders, and cleared his throat. "For your penance," he said, "Five Hail Marys, and three Our Fathers." He mumbled a prayer she couldn't make out, and finally, "Go, my child," he said.

TEN

On this night before his wedding Danylo stands off by himself, drinking a beer and tossing pebbles into Panko's well. "God-damn," he whispers, why does he feel an urge for Marusia Budka, not Nellie? How does this happen? It's not that he feels guilty, he will marry Nellie tomorrow, but he feels bewildered, as if he's flying in the wind.

Ten minutes ago he had been standing in the door-way, and Marusia was sitting with the other women, all of them talking and passing around those wreaths. She had caught his eye.

A lone figure walks across the yard towards him. He drops the pail in the well, leaning over and jerking the rope, tipping the bucket so it will sink and fill with water. Waiting for Marusia, he can smell the moist coolness of the well, and as she draws nearer he feels more and more excited. He imagines her smell, the smell of sweet basil, the lake.

"Are you going to jump in?" she says. Her head is level with his at the rim of the well. "For what are you looking?"

"For nothing." He straightens up, turning towards her, and for a few moments neither one of them says anything. She steps up closer to him, just inches from touching.

"What if I dump you in there?" he says.

"Why would you want to do that?" She leans closer, her body pressed to his, then reaching around him she grabs the rope. He takes it from her, pulling the pail to the top. Each of them drink.

Marusia lowers her head to the well. *"Halloo, halloo,"* echoes from the water. She presses herself against Danylo's hip, squirming like a cat on a boy's pantleg, and Danylo pulls her to his waist.

"A nice night for a walk," she says.

"It's dark. Hard to see."

"We have the moon." She takes his hand from her waist, pulling him along, leading him. "Darker in the bush. I know a place."

They grope their way through the trees, following the path to Panko's shed.

"Here?" Danylo asks. "The still?"

"You like the stink?" she reaches to his nose, pinching it. "We go further. Just come with me."

They pass by the shed and emerge from the bush onto a field. In the moonlight, piles of branches and uprooted stumps appear as black ghosts. This is Danylo's field. His father will give it to him for a wedding gift. Danylo has been scrubbing out the stumps here for two years. As good a place as any, he thinks. Danylo caresses the soft flesh of Marusia's hip but she laughs and pushes at his chest.

"Wait," she says. "Wait."

She takes him to the road all the way to the little bridge. From there they follow the creek to a meadow. In the distance they can see faintly in the dark the tops of spruce trees outlined against the sky.

She leads him through a tangle of shrubs and tall grass at the edge of the bush, parting willows and red birch, feeling in the dark with her feet not to trip on the spongy hummocks of grass on the uneven floor of the bush. They break into a clearing, the bent stands of swamp spruce surrounding them. An outline of branches above their heads is drawn in the light of stars. The growth is like in the legends, *Where firs nodded their boughs overhead, like bears waving their paws.*

"I like to be here," she says. "It's so quiet, and the smell of the spruce is like perfume." She sits down, spreading her dress on the moss, brushing aside fallen cones and needles. Danylo stands with his hands in his pockets.

"You are young," she says, "and so handsome."

"Not so young. I am twenty-five." He wonders what Nellie might think. What about the men? Can he think of any other man on his wedding eve who has been out in the bush with a woman like Marusia Budka? Nellie doesn't have to know. He can say he was out drinking and lost track of the time. And so what if she does? She had better get used to knowing who's boss anyway. Marusia holds out her hand. "Lift me up." Before he knows what has happened she has pulled him down to her, embracing him.

"Oooohh," she says, and laughs. "You fall on me."

She clasps her hands on his neck and rolls over him. Her breasts move with a heavy softness against him. She plays with his belt buckle. Her hair falls across her lips and Danylo's lips. *"Phhh,"* she blows at the strands of hair, tosses her head to the side, sweeps the hair away with her hand. She kisses his neck, her body undulating. "Mmmm, Danylo," she says, moulding into him. And then she pulls away, gently, gets up on her knees, opens the buttons on Danylo's shirt, his pants, opens her dress, brassiere. Then she nestles to him, flesh to flesh. He strokes her hair and feels it matted with spruce needles.

A clear and sudden sound startles them, twice in the silence: *"Hooohh! Hooohh!"* Lit by the moonlight an owl perches on a branch of a dead spruce.

Marusia squirms and darts her tongue into Danylo's mouth. They roll over and over on the cones, locked to each other. Danylo is running his hands on the back of her thighs, his face between her breasts smelling of sweet basil and a trace of her sweat. Her fingers reach down his body. At that moment a voice calls like a gunshot in the trees. "Danylo! Danylo!"

His motion stops, even his breathing. After a moment he gets to his feet, still listening, pulling on his trousers.

"Danylo? Where are you?"

It sounds like Nick Semchuk. Danylo buttons his shirt, and leaving Marusia lying down, he runs to the voice. He finds Nick just outside the trees. Danylo spits on the ground.

"Is there a fire? Somebody die? How did you find me?"

"I followed."

"Why don't you mind your own business?"

"They want you at the house. You have to try on your myrtle wreath for tomorrow."

"Myrtle wreath?"

"You know. The little ones they make for wearing at the altar? Don't you ever go to church? The priest puts it on your head."

"Hooohh, hooohh." The owl calls then flaps its wings to perch yet higher on another tree. Danylo cups his hands and mimics the sound: *"Hoooh, hooh."*

But the owl does not answer. Instead like echoes from the well the answer comes *"Halloo, hallooo,"* and then laughter, *"ha, ha, ha, ha."*

ELEVEN

Lena loves weddings. Food. Dance. Music. Ukrainian weddings. But if it ever comes to her own, she will plan it. Nobody else. Even Nellie insisted; no one told her she had to marry Danylo; she decided herself. Lena can't imagine marrying a man of her mother's choosing. Yet it used to happen, was even tried in her own family; an arranged marriage for Rose.

Lena knew there'd be an argument. She knew that nobody would tell Rose what to do. She would pick her own husband. She said she was going to marry Yuri Belinski and that was that, no matter how they ridiculed. She used to get furious when Danylo and Nick would mimic Yuri's Old Country love talk, the quoting of Ukrainian poets, *my bright star, my spring flower.* Did Rose really love him or had she simply been standing up against Mother?

As things turned out, the more that everyone else spoke against Yuri, the more Rose seemed determined to marry him. He was different from the other young men. Lena can remember dancing, the feel of his hands when he came to their school to instruct Ukrainian dance for concerts, soft teacher's hands. Everyone would notice him, tall, straight, handsome, his speaking in English educated and refined, not farmer talk.

He had left Lviv in 1935, had come to Winnipeg where he quickly learned English and studied to become a school teacher. Rose met him at a schoolhouse dance at Fishing River.

You'd think that at least the old people would see him as a good match for Rose. He was always talking about Taras Shevchenko, and Ivan Franko, and some writer named Kotsiubynsky. Lena didn't think anybody but Panko had ever heard of them. He was a true master at dance, teaching the old folk classics and explaining their meanings, speaking in Ukrainian, which the young people didn't like and the old ones did.

For some reason, even Baba Dounia thought Rose was being foolish to want to marry Yuri. Lena could understand an old woman thinking that parents knew better how to choose a mate for their children, though she didn't agree. Maybe her grandmother could have thought that Yuri was too much a Ukrainian. Maybe somebody like Yuri would have been a right choice for a young Dounia in 1903, but not today. If a girl wants to get ahead today she has to marry a man who is more Canadian.

"How can you marry him?" Danylo had said. "Have you seen him on the hay rack trying to drive the team?" Danylo would shove his arms out like sticks, pumping them up and down, his elbows stiff, imitating Yuri.

Rose shouted at him. Just before turning on her heels and stomping away, she had said in Ukrainian, "A pumpkin to your mother, *Harbuz Mami tvoyii.*"

Such a dumb saying, yet everybody used it, old and young alike. Lena's grandmother said it had to do with weddings. If your mother doesn't get you the bride, she brings you back the pumpkin.

Rose wanted Yuri; she wasn't going to have Mother arrange any marriage for her. Lena could see that with her sister it didn't matter what anyone thought. No one could change her mind, not Mother, not Danylo.

One Sunday on Lena's eleventh birthday the *Pan* Andreychuks from Sifton came to visit. Lena's mother was excited. This visit was a business deal and both families would be shrewd at all costs. Andreychuk was rich, like a Polish *pan,* and Mother would pay him respect. This was bred into her. Who knew when you might need the favour of the *pan.* Respect the *pan* whether you like him or not, and if nothing else, Ukrainians were good at pretending.

The Andreychuk's purpose for visiting wasn't Lena's birthday. In fact, when they came to the house the birthday was forgotten, if anybody besides Lena even knew about it in the first place. The Andreychuks came to ask that Rose be the wife for their oldest son. This wasn't a small matter to Mother. *Pan* Andreychuk owned half the country. *He* was respected.

Pan Andreychuk's wife sat in Mother's rocking chair. "Our garden is not doing good. So many bugs. I don't know what to do." The men didn't seem interested in potato bugs. Dad decided that he and

Andreychuk should go for a walk. "What you say, *Pan*, we go to the pasture and see my cows. Let the women go to the garden and talk about cabbages."

And the women did go to the garden and talk, about this, about that, even cabbages, then poppy seed, mushroom picking, weddings in the district. Only when the men returned did Mother say, "How is your family, Mrs?" Mrs. Andreychuk did not answer the question.

"Oi, oi, oi," she said, "Look at this yard!" She bent over a flower bed, breathing in deeply. "The sweet williams! How lovely the smell! And look how bright the marigolds are starting!"

"Come into the house," Dad said. "Have something to eat." Mother motioned for Rose to go to the cellar for a jar of strawberries, and then led the Andreychuks into the living room.

"You get the berries," Rose whispered to Lena, then vanished out the door, running up the hill to the old house. Lena didn't mind because she wanted to hear what the Andreychuks had to say.

Again Mother said, "How is your family?"

"Oh, they are fine," *Pan* Andreychuk's wife said. "You know." She rocked back and forth in Mother's chair, hands clasped on her lap, face pinched in its perpetual frown. "Sometimes the little ones catch this, catch that, but they are fine."

"And the older ones?"

"Oi, oi, oi," she said. "You know what it is on the farm." Her eldest son worked too hard. It was time her Fred considered a wife. He was farming three

quarters of his own land. She did not say that she had birthed two families, that Fred was a son from her first husband in the Old Country. But everyone knew this just the same.

Mother nodded her head. Lena could see her excitement. This was the perfect catch for Rose. "Yeh, yeh," Dad said, his eyes squinting. He held up a bottle and poured into a shot glass. "Hey, *Pan*, a little drink."

"My Rose is getting to that age," Mother said.

"They would make a nice couple," *Pan* Andreychuk's wife said.

"Oh, yes," Mother said.

"Does your Rose like to cook?"

"Oh, yes. And sew."

"Does she make these flowers?" *Pan* Andreychuk's wife pointed to the wall of holy pictures, their wooden frames decorated with paper flowers.

"She is learning," Mother said.

As soon as the Andreychuks left, Rose appeared back in the house.

"What good fortune," Mother said. "*Pan* Andreychuk's son wishes to marry you."

"So that is why they were here." Rose said. "Do you know how old he is?" No one said a thing. Twenty years earlier it wouldn't have mattered if the man was old enough to be a girl's grandfather. But the time had changed. Even Mother must have known that. And for Dad it wouldn't have mattered even if the time hadn't changed things. He would have done what his daughter wanted, if he could convince Mother.

"I want to marry Yuri Belinski," Rose said.

"Phaa," Mother said. "Belinski!" There was fire in Mother's eyes. She did not like to be contradicted. Did not like to lose. "Don't you see? Andreychuks are rich people. The son is rich."

"If you like him so much," Rose said, "Why don't you marry him?"

Dad laughed, and Lena could see that for him the issue was settled.

Rose had escaped from Andreychuk. The glint in Dad's eyes may as well have said that *Pan* Andreychuk's son *got a pumpkin*. Then after a minute or two, though Lena could never before have imagined it to happen, a sheepish glint of amusement came to Mother's eyes. It was as if she too saw that the Andreychuks *got a pumpkin*. Mrs. Andreychuk was not going to be able to take Rose home to her son. Instead she would take him a pumpkin; *Harbuz Mami tvoyii*. In any case, the issue had been settled; nothing more was ever said about arranging a marriage for Rose. How was it she could handle Mother so easily? Lena would have been beaten with a stick.

But Lena remembers that it took Mother more than a while to get used to Yuri. She wasn't fussy to have an Old Country school teacher. For one thing, she didn't want to lose Rose. Mother wasn't eager to try getting Lena to take over the housework. Fortunately for Yuri, he was Catholic, not Orthodox. In Mother's eyes the Orthodox may as well be Bukovina Gypsies.

As far as Lena knew, the only difference in the churches was the pope, and how the churches made their crosses. The Orthodox cross had a slanted bar at its foot. Panko told her it was slanted because of Christ's agony. He kicked so hard the bar twisted. He said that some Ukrainians in the Old Country were Catholic because of their dealings with the Polish. Some changed the endings on their names, even Yuri's grandfather, from Belinchuk to Belinski just to gain favours from his landlord. It's always been like that... go cap in hand. For Yuri the name change was simply another reason to hate the Polish.

If Lena's family questioned Rose's choice of husband, it was because he was not a farmer. He was a good school teacher, and a wonderful dancer, but men would say what is a man if he can't harness a team of horses?

But time healed things, and it hadn't been many months after that Lena's parents found out that Yuri Belinski wasn't that bad to have around. Before a year had passed, before Mother hardly had time to figure out what was happening, she was preparing a wedding. Rose and Yuri were married, and not only that, he got along half-decently even with the men. He played crib with Dad and Danylo. Even beat them sometimes.

TWELVE

At midnight Lena walks home alone from Panko's. She had seen Marusia and Danylo leave from the well. Should she have told Nellie? Maybe not. Why spoil her wedding? Nellie will have more time than enough to be unhappy after she is married to Danylo. Most of the crowd has left already; tomorrow is another big day. She knows the road so well, even in the dark: the large meadows on each side, the strawberry patches, the hermit's shack, the creek.

The frogs croak in the cat-tails. In a school book the frog prince.... She smiles, thinking of reading books. Books save her here. Books take her away. Dream of turning into a princess. Will she have a prince? Here? For sure not here. Winnipeg? Anywhere?

How excited Nellie is with this wedding, and for what? Everybody has a good time for three days. That's what they all live for, a good time at weddings. And even her father, after this wedding is over, will sit at the table holding onto his head, and he will cite proverbs blaming his misery on something other than himself. *Ukrainians were created by God to suffer misfortune and poverty.* Who suffers? The women suffer. Nellie will suffer, and the men will chase after Marusia Budka and laugh at Hryhori. That's the way it is. Things are as God ordained, at least here.

Lena has a sudden urge for a cigarette. She stops on the road and takes her package of Black Cats from her purse. She strikes the match, smelling the sulphur in the clean night air. The paper from the cigarette catches on her lip. She inhales the smoke, then hears a shout and a laugh coming from Panko's; the heavy drinkers will stay at it all night, then settle their stomachs with Tata Paraska's borshch at sunrise.

Nick asked if he could walk her home. "I can find the way by myself," she said. Why did she say that?

Her garter is pinching. She unclasps it, pulling down her stocking. As she does this she gets the odd sensation that something is close by. She doesn't know why she feels this; she hasn't heard anything, only the frogs. But it's the frogs that give it away. She had noticed that when she got close to them, the croaking stopped. It started again after she passed them by. Behind her just now the croaking has stopped. Someone is back there.

She's not far from the turnoff to the hermit Gregorovitch's place. Is he behind her? Was he snooping around Panko's? Gregorovitch never goes to weddings, but he's known to snoop around. She had seen him on his bicycle in town. People say he's always mailing away for things. She doesn't know what things. She knows he sells seneca root. Nick used to dig with him.

She tugs at her stocking, does up the clasp, and starts to walk – one, two, three, four, five, six, seven steps – and then she stops to listen. She hears a shoe scrape on the gravel, then nothing. She walks again, and it's the same thing. Whoever's there stops when she stops.

"Who are you?" Lena says. "Is that you Mr. Gregorovitch?" He doesn't answer. "Who is it?"

"Did I scare you?"

"Damn you, Nick! Why are you following me?" She reaches out to touch him, her hands sliding down the arms of his suit jacket, then pushing him back a step.

"Danylo is passed out. Sleeping in the barn."

"Serves him right."

"I thought I'd tell you. Have you got one of those cigarettes?"

"I have only three left," she says, automatically snapping open the clasp on her purse.

He takes the package from her. "One is plenty for me. Where are you going?"

"Where do you think I'm going? I'm going home." She lights a match for him and he leans forward puffing at the cigarette.

"I'm going to Vasylko's. Want to come?"

"At midnight?" She wants no part of it.

"Come on. You never know what you'll see at Vasylko's." Lena has never been to his shack, she'd always been too scared to go. What a time to pick, the middle of the night

"Sure, come with me. I'm taking him a drink. Feel this." He takes her hand, pressing it against his chest.

She can feel a bottle in his suit jacket pocket. "Look," he says, "a light in his shack. He's awake."

Gregorovitch is seated at his table. He holds a jack-knife in one hand and an ornately carved length of wood in the other. A kerosene lamp, woodchips, and various papers cover the table. Besides his table and chair, the shack is furnished with a tin woodstove, a cot made with poplar poles, pin-up calendars and orange-box cupboards stuffed full of papers and magazines. They say he has stayed away from other people on purpose, not trusting them, but always watching, that he taught himself to read from calendars, sardine cans, anything at hand until he could discover the English world of mail order. It could be anything at all he reads now.

He doesn't seem surprised to see Nick, but it's obvious that he didn't expect Lena. The first thing he does is stand up and take off his bent wire-rim glasses, attempting to clean the lenses with a rumpled hand-kerchief. He then dumps some papers out of a box in the corner and arranges it for Lena to sit down, sitting himself again on his chair, facing her and staring.

"You're Danylo's sister. I've seen you hang clothes on the line. I can see from the road." His eyes dart around the room; he gets to his feet and sorts through more boxes, taking out wood carvings and laying them on the table. He has a horned owl, a figure of the Virgin Mary holding the Baby Jesus, a carved frame with a picture of Rita Hayworth which he sets on the table then changes his mind and puts back in the box, wooden puzzles he has carved.

"That's enough," Nick says. "Vasylko is a wood carver. He wants to show you some of his work." Lena tries to smile, and she's conscious of her cheeks tightening at the corners of her mouth.

"Would you like to learn? I could show you. Don't you think so, Nick? A lady carver?" Vasylko Gregorovitch picks up one piece and sets it down, then another, and another. Then he puts all of it back into the boxes. His glasses sit at an angle on his head and bounce as his nose twitches. They sit at an angle because he has a large bump on his left temple.

"Get me a glass, Vasylko. You need a drink from the wedding." Nick takes the bottle from his pocket and sets it on the table.

Nobody ever sees Vasylko at a wedding, but Panko has said that the hermit knows more than you think. He knows everything that goes on at weddings and everything else. He doesn't go to church, but he knows all of the icons, maybe still from his mother having taught him years ago. The priest had asked him to carve a nativity for the church in Topolia. Vasylko said he might ride in on his bike to have a look. It's been many years since anyone has seen him in a church, but he did carve something for the Gruber church. Kobzey talked to him one day at the country store. He wanted a candelabrum for twelve candles to place before the icon of Saint John the Beloved. Kobzey would pay him five dollars.

"I think I know what you want," Vasylko told the priest.

With the handkerchief he used to clean his glasses, he wipes a glass tumbler that he takes from a basin of murky water sitting on another of his boxes, and quickly hands it to Nick. "Maybe the girl would like a drink," he says.

"No, no, I've had too much already," Lena says, "And the wedding tomorrow."

"Yes, the wedding," Vasylko says, "That is tomorrow. And tonight at Panko's. The Budkas there?"

"Of course," Nick says. "Hryhori falling down."

"Marusia is his wife." Vasylko's eyes glare like two black beads reflecting lamp light.

"She was there," Nick says. He fills the tumbler to half and the hermit drinks it down at once, as if it is a much needed medicine. He's not known to be a drinker, but when he swallows nothing flinches on his face, only the bump on his temple.

He continues to look about, his glasses bobbing more than usual. "You should eat," he says.

Nick could have predicted that Vasylko would feel he must have something for them, and in fact would have nothing, so he came prepared. He pulls a sausage from his pocket along with two buns he brought from home. Immediately Vasylko takes his jackknife and slices the meat.

"Here," Gregorovitch says to Lena.

"No, no," she says. "I've had plenty to eat."

"Come on, come on. Eat!"

She sees that he will not let up so she takes a piece of sausage and puts it in her mouth. Vasylko sits down, crosses his arms, and smiles.

IT'S TEN PAST THREE IN THE MORNING when they leave the hermit's place. They are walking on the road, approaching the spot where the creek flows under the small bridge. Lena remembers Baba Dounia's Rusalka stories. She remembers how she would sit at this bridge waiting for the Rusalka to appear, only to wait a long time. She saw scurrying tadpoles, minnows, and now and then a jackfish. Never Rusalka, but Lena imagined her hidden somewhere under the bridge.

"Hey," Lena asks. "Do you think the fish are running?"

"Don't you know they come only in the spring?"

"Yeh, I guess I know. But I can wish it all the same."

"And anyhow," Nick says, "How could we see a fish in the dark?"

"Let's follow the creek," Lena says. "It will be light soon." They climb through the barbed wire fence, her dress getting snagged and Nick having to free it from the wire. The back of his hand just for a moment touches her leg above her knee. Starlight and the moon reflect on the water. They can see to walk into the pasture. Beside a pool sheltered by a poplar bluff they sit down beneath branches reaching over the water. The air has stayed warm and it's filled with the smells of the poplars, the bulrushes, swampy grass, and the mud where cows have walked at the water's edge. Lena wonders about the fish. Where do they spawn? The little fish are born and swim back to the lake, but not all of them. Some don't make it back. Where do they go? Do they just dry up and die?

"Will you stay in the army, Nick?" She lies on her

back, gazing up at the Milky Way. She hears the hum of mosquitoes, but they don't seem to be biting.

"Do you think I want to get shot?"

"What?"

"The army. Am I going to stay in the army?"

"Are you?"

"That's what I said. I said do you think I want to get shot?"

"But after the war?"

"After the war, if I don't get shot, the hell with the army. I got a letter I had to go. That's all."

"Will you come back here?"

"I don't know. Do you think you'll spend your life here?"

Lena doesn't say anything. Instead she stares down at the dark water, and wonders about sitting out here alone with Nick. What's going to happen? What does she want to happen? The Devil wooed Rusalka in the water.

She didn't think much of Nick when he was still in school. He used to watch her constantly, and it didn't matter whether she was at her desk or outside on the playground. There he was, with his moon face and fat lips, either gawking or grinning.

She can't forget the time he caught her with the Christmas candy. The school board had brought ribbon candy and chocolate bon-bons, a large box of each to dole out at the Christmas concert still a month away. She knew about the candy because her father had gone to Topolia for it. The teacher had the boxes hidden behind the library shelves in the cloakroom.

Who would notice if she took a chocolate when nobody was around? She got out of bed earlier than usual, milked two cows, gobbled her breakfast, and ran the half mile across the pasture to school. She was there even before the teacher came to light the fire. She took a handful of the ribbon candy, and resisting the temptation to eat it on the spot, she looked for a place to put it. She had no pockets. The only place was in her bloomers. Sure, why not. Lots of room. And then a handful of chocolate bon-bons into her pants with the ribbon candy.

All morning all she could think of was how good the candy would taste. Where could she eat it so nobody would see? The toilet in the yard. That's it. She could latch the door and be all by herself. At recess she waited while the other girls went out and then after she was positive nobody would be at the toilet any more, she put on her felt boots and went outside into the snow to the outhouse. She pulled down her bloomers and sat looking at her treasure of candy along her thighs. She noticed that some of the bon-bons had started to melt, and then she heard a thump against the door. Then another, twice: *thump, thump.* She stood, hearing someone talk outside. She began pulling up on her bloomers. *I know what you've got,* a voice said. Immediately she froze, every muscle in her body tensing, her stomach tensing unable to control herself. A warm liquid trickled down her thighs. She had wet herself, and all the candy. Damn that Nick Semchuk. Who else would trick her? Talk like that in his sneaky voice, *I know what you've got?*

Lena waited until she was sure he had gone, then dumping all the candy down the hole, she walked home. She had to change her clothes.

"I have a bottle," Nick says.

"What?" Lena grips her fingers together, hugging her knees. Thinking of winter made her feel chilly. "Didn't you drink the home-brew at Vasylko's?"

"Sure, the home-brew. But in the other pocket. I have something only for you. I bought it in Dauphin. Orange Gin." He hands her a flat bottle from inside his jacket. So he bought gin. Sure, she knows what he wants. But she doesn't mind. Her first time. Maybe it's the night's effect on her with the smells of the marsh grasses, the mud, the poplar trees, and the water, or else the ancient Ukrainian ghosts are talking to her and she doesn't realize it: *Without foolery this world has no taste; it might just as well be without the wind.*

"Come on," Nick says. "Here. You try."

She sips, tasting it on her lips. The liquor is sweet and sticky, and easy to swallow.

"Go ahead," he says. "Drink more."

They will sit out here and wait for the sun to rise.

A gust of wind rustles through the poplar branches. In the legends a poplar tree is Rusalka weeping on the banks of the river. Her wet hair extends down to the water. Rusalka walks on the marshes searching for her child. Rusalka drowns at night, and rises at dawn to search again.

The Devil kissed her on the cheek.

"Oh, you have burned me!" the enchantress said. "You smell of brimstone! If you must, let us slip into the water,

else you would burn me with your hellish love."

*The moon covered as with silver Rusalka's white body,
which looked as if it were carven, and her braided kosa,
twisting like a serpent, crossed over her breasts, twined
round her slender waist and fell to her knees.*

"Turn the other way," Lena says to Nick. Pulling
her dress up over her thighs, then undoing her garters,
she peels off her cotton stockings, placing them carefully in her purse. She'll wear her Kayser rayon stockings tomorrow. *Be wiser, buy Kayser.* And she'll wear
her *Stardust* shoes. She stands up, hangs her purse on
a branch, then steps forward, planting the imprint of
her bare foot into the black mud. Holding her dress to
her thighs she wades into the water, feeling its chill as
it reaches her kneecaps, then halfway up her thighs
until she retreats back up the bank. Her legs are
colder now than they were in the water.

"Any more gin? I need something to warm me up."

"Here." He holds the bottle for her, sitting close, his
arm around her neck. She nestles closer to him.

She lies on her back. Above her head the quivering
leaves glow red with the first rays of the sun. She looks
towards the meadow and sees the flash of the sun's
light peeping over the horizon of spruce trees, all at
once bright, penetrating with power and splendour
suddenly from night to morning.

Her head buzzes like a warm spinning round and
round from the gin. She thinks of Nellie's black silk
lingerie, and her own plain white cotton brassiere.
She'll wear her Bestform bra tomorrow. Nick's fingers
fumble with the clasp.

On the grass. Bare legs shivering, warm hands. Fog rising from the pool. Morning dew. He tugs at his trouser buttons. Under her dress his fingers slide her panties down over her thighs. She feels the cold of the empty gin bottle against her hip. What if she gets pregnant? Does she want to sit in the bush all her life like Nellie will? She could end up as Paraska's daughter-in-law and Nick could be killed in the war.

His knee parts her legs. He kisses her on the neck. Kiss again. Then, as she knew would happen, a sharp pain. She tries to lift her head to glance. She feels him inside. He presses, falling and rising. Another fall and rise, another, and she lifts to him. Buzz like warm spinning round and round in her head. *Rusalka rises from the waters.*

Nick groans. She feels the sudden jerk and shudder of his body rigid for moments. If he could stay like that. But what if she gets pregnant?

His body goes limp, collapses on her. Please, Nick, please. She feels a wetness on her thighs. He turns away from her muttering something unintelligible.

She rolls the other way, lying on her stomach pressed to the ground, the side of her face rubbed into the meadow grass, her bare arms spread, fingers digging. She hears her own breathing, feels her torso touching harder each time she draws a breath. Her eyes are closed. Birds chirp. She knows they're only sparrows. She tries to relax, smelling the tang and morning freshness of the grass at the water's edge.

THIRTEEN

Shortly before eight Panko is still in bed, thinking of the proverb that says, *Pain is natural to life*. It seems that he has just fallen asleep when Paraska digs her elbow into his side and shouts in his ear, "Do you want Melnyks to find us in bed? You lie there snoring when it was your idea to have the wedding in July. You don't have to cook. You don't have to keep the meatballs from spoiling."

Yeh, yeh, Paraska, Panko thinks. Enough shouting. He covers his head with his feather pillow. Why doesn't she yap to Nellie? It is Nellie who wants the wedding. What do I care. Nellie wanted tiger lilies on the tables. Where would you find them in the winter time?

In one half hour Panko and Paraska are sitting outside on the bench waiting for Nellie. Panko holds the *kolach* on his lap, two flies buzzing around it. Panko licks his finger, touches the loaf, then licks again. Paraska swats him on the chest.

"Easy! Easy!" Panko says. "Do you want to knock me off the bench?"

"Stupid time for a wedding," Paraska says. "Middle of July."

"That's what she wants," Panko says. "Paraska, it's all right."

"All right? How all right? Don't you know this is the middle of haying?"

"The hay can wait." Why are we sitting here, he thinks? Do we have to practice? He's tempted to pinch off a piece of the bread, but Paraska is all steamed up about the food. It's the wrong time for him to try something foolish.

"Cabbage rolls! How can we keep the cabbage rolls from spoiling? Why can't we have the wedding in January? At least November like everybody else?"

"No tiger lilies in November. Don't you think it's too late now to complain?"

"That's all you care about the wedding!" She shouts to the doorway. "Hurry with that combing already. Before people come. And you have to be at church before ten o'clock."

"Shh," Nellie says, her headpiece and ribbons poking out the door. "Do you want them to hear you in Topolia?"

TWENTY MINUTES LATER Lena is standing by the side of the house straightening Nellie's headpiece, her fingers lingering a while on the coloured ribbons, stroking them, letting the pretty lengths fall flowing down the back of Nellie's gown.

"I'll be right back," Lena says. She leaves Nellie,

hurrying to Panko's well, dropping the bucket tied to its rope, and draws up the water. It's clean and cold, washing out the remnants of sweet gin in her throat. She wonders if Nellie's a virgin. Probably everyone is wondering the same thing. This morning Lena had to wash blood stains from her panties from last night. She thought of the blood this morning when she saw Paraska's red beet borshch boiling on the stove, remedy to nurse a man's hangover. The best for the stomach after celebrations, Panko says. Hot borshch like her mother's pan of pig blood from the butchering. She gags thinking about it and quickly takes another drink of water from the pail, letting the dribbles run down her cheeks.

The people think of a virgin only about a girl, not Danylo. It's the opposite with him. How many girls has he slept with? The more the better. They think that if he hasn't there is something wrong with him, or that he simply doesn't have a way with the girls.

She thinks about Nick, and her stomach tightens. She wants her period to come quickly. Last night she had combed out Nellie's braid, unravelling the virgin *kosa*. What would Mother say if she knew about her and Nick? Nobody has to know; Nick won't say anything. She runs back to Nellie standing as pretty as the sweet peas on the fence.

Paraska yells at them, "Come, Nellie. Hurry up." Lena straightens a ribbon and gives Nellie a hug. Baba Dounia enters from inside the house carrying an embroidered linen cloth. She spreads it on the ground at Panko and Paraska's feet. Nellie kneels before them. Baba Dounia stands aside and sings:

> *Say not that you are taking all,*
> *Pray you have no fears.*
> *Upon the linen cry and leave your tears.*

Panko touches Nellie's headpiece with the *kolach*. This has been done many times, far back to Panko's childhood. In Ukraine his own sister bowed to her father. Panko repeats the words: *By the sweat of thy brow thou shalt earn thy bread.*

Why does it have to be so sad, Lena wonders? Is it because she thinks about the blood on her panties? Like a butchering? But also it is sad because Nellie is submitting to a life in the bush.

AT THE HALL ACROSS THE ROAD from the Melnyk farm, Lena dances holding her bouquet pressed against Hryhori Budka's face. The tiger lilies don't match her shoes, but who cares? Nick is laughing, turning away when she looks at him, strumming the *tsymbali*. She turns her shoulder into Hryhori's chest. Does she have to hold him from falling on his face? Maybe she can steer him towards her father. He's with Panko pouring whiskey near the hall entry. Hryhori would never refuse a drink.

"Hey, *Pan* Budka!" Panko says. He pours from a blue enamel pot. Lena's father pats Hryhori on the back, extends the glass to him and sings:

Oh who drinks, pour them some more.
Those who don't, don't give them any.
But I will drink, and I beg God
For our good health
And the health of our mother
Who taught us to drink
Very slowly.

Lena escapes out the door, taking deep breaths of night air as if she's been holding her breath for the last five minutes. She sets her bouquet beside her on the steps and massages her feet. As much as she likes her *Stardust* shoes they pinch, and rub at her heels, forming blisters.

The buzz of voices, the laughing, the stomping, the *Hie! Hie! Hie!* of the orchestra grated on her nerves, but now the sounds seem pleasant. Even the smells – cabbage rolls, home-brew, gas lamp, and sweaty bodies – are not as overpowering out here on the step.

A cool breeze soothes Lena's wet face. In the sky a haze of cloud fuzzes the full moon, then passes over, and the moon's exposed like a beacon. She looks the other way to a darker sky and sees two stars, and other fainter ones behind thin clouds.

She loves a wedding, but right now she'd rather be sitting out here, and not dancing with Hryhori Budka. She said no, shook her head, but he grabbed her by the waist anyway. She didn't want to make a commotion with everybody watching.

The music has stopped, and Lena hears table legs scraping on the wood floor. She puts her shoes back on and goes to join Nellie and Danylo being seated at the front of the hall. Rose puts wine, sweet cider, her mother's elaborately braided *kolach,* and a collection plate on the table. Dounia sets down a small evergreen. Its branches are trimmed with ribbons, red, pink, yellow, like Nellie's ribbons. Bits of coloured wool, and small clusters of green highbush cranberries are tied to the branches. Dounia sings:

> *The great raid is coming!*
> *They will fight, they will rob us,*
> *They will take me with them –*
> *The little one, the young one,*
> *Like a red cherry.*

Lena hears another voice. Marusia Budka stands in the corner at the back of the hall, hands clasped, a curl of hair escaped from her yellow babushka, her voice a high-pitched wailing, clear and shrill:

> *See my friend, the sky*
> *See, the cranes on high;*
> *Wing to wing they fly together,*
> *Fading as they fly.*

Yuri Belinski walks out of the crowd to meet her. He's wearing the black pants and white shirt of a country school teacher, but around his waist he's tied a gold-and-blue striped sash. A man standing straight, thick eyebrows, black streak of a moustache, bending his arms, extending his hands to Marusia. He joins her singing, the sound deep and heavy, swelling up from his chest:

> *Croo, croo, croo,*
> *Though the wings are true,*
> *We may perish on the ocean*
> *Like some weary crew.*

No buzz of talk, no shoe scraping, no laughter from the crowd, only a gentle tinkle of the *tsymbali*. Yuri grows straighter and taller with the song. Above the rest. Alone from the rest. The gas lamp sputters, pulsing unevenly, dim then bright, dim then bright.

He says one word, *"Holubchyka!"* and a cheer erupts from the wedding guests. Across the floor he dances, squatting and kicking out his feet.

Somebody yells "Nick, play the *tsymbali*. Yuri is dancing *Holubchyka*." Like a Cossack he stands before Marusia and gestures with his arm. The *tsymbali* plunks one note. Yuri leaps three times, feet spread wide, shoulder high, then offers his arm to Marusia. She steps back, one arm in the air, the other resting on her hip. She moves to the slow tempo of the *tsymbali*. The two dancers face each other.

"Holubchyka!" Yuri says again, and the music starts to build. The crowd hushes, forming a wide circle, slowly clapping.

"Hiee ya!" Nick says. The hammers of his *tsymbali* strike faster and faster, and faster plays the accordian. The couple spins round and round. What holds them from flying apart? Everyone is clapping, urging them,

the dancers as delicate as hummingbirds and flying just as fast.

"Hiee ya!" How much can they speed before they fly out the window? Clapping, clapping, clapping, the crowd moving them. Round and round the dancers twirl, as if pulling everyone down into the whirlpool. Nick's *tsymbali* sings with pain, straining to the limit, tighter and tighter ready to break. The accordian crashes down a final chord and Marusia and Yuri fall to their knees, facing the table.

All at once Hryhori comes staggering towards Lena, passing the kneeling dancers and crashing onto the collection plate. The evergreen tips on its side to the floor. Red cider splatters on Nellie's dress. She screams. "Asshole!" Everyone looks around for Marusia. Where is she? As if by magic she is gone, and where is Yuri?

All is quiet, a jumbled circle of people staring back and forth, from the *kolach* and spruce tree in its ribbons on the floor, to the open door and darkness outside. A car drives off. No one makes any move to follow or chase. Rose grabs a corner of the fallen table then drops it, her hands hurrying to her face, muffling a cry. She runs out to the road, stops, then continues across the ditch and through the gate to her mother's garden.

Nick, Lena, and the bride and groom straighten the table. Baba Dounia bends to pick up the *kolach,* and her husband Metro takes the decorated spruce. He walks with it to the doorway and outside to the hall steps, where he peers out into the darkness at the disappearing car lights.

FOURTEEN

Two dragonflies, the colour of the sky at its deepest blue, stuck one on top of the other, land for a moment on Panko's knee. The next moment they fly off in the breeze, vanishing like the dancers at the wedding. Panko blinks three or four times, then rubs an irritation away from the corner of his eye. He looks left, then right, raising his torso from the bed of hay he has shaped to suit his own comfort. On this hay meadow a few of Mike Melnyk's neighbours and relatives are shaking their heads while they eat their lunch, several of them trying to be very serious about the disappearance of Marusia and Yuri. Everybody has questions, but with Rose present, some people are hesitant to ask. How should they console her? But at the same time Panko knows that each person is thinking about what the runaways must be doing. As sorry as they are for Rose, how can they not at the same time be excited with the scandal? They think that Marusia Budka must be a witch! Of course the district is in shock. Where did Yuri Belinski go with this Marusia? Which one is to blame?

Only Panko notices Metro Zazelenchuk behind a haystack taking a leak. He passes his water in dribbles, and then of all things, when he finishes he puts his hands on his hips as if to do a jig. He tries to bend at the knees, but winces and rubs the small of his back. His right arm stretches up and out, and he begins turning in a circle. He must think he's a Cossack dancer. At one time Metro could dance, but not now. Not for twenty years. Not Ukrainian dance. He better be careful turning or he'll lose his balance and fall on his rear-end.

"Ah," Panko says, "Only poor Rose suffers. Everybody else has something to talk about. Don't you think so?" Nobody is listening to him. He takes off his cap and uses it to wipe his wet forehead. Sure, he thinks, the runaways have given something for the people to gossip, or like Metro, something to think about. Maybe Metro is thinking to buy Marusia something else besides shoes. He motions with his hand. "Paraska! Pass me a jar of beer before it gets too warm."

They sit on the grass like their Ukrainian ancestors who sat the same, generation after generation, century after century, each season on the meadows, relaxing at noon. Each face shows an on-again, off-again strained look. These labourers show little outward sign of any fascination over the wedding incident, their brows carrying only the painful frowns of worry, real or feigned, even Metro when he returns to the group.

Panko watches his wife Paraska sort through the food, handing out pieces of chicken, bread, and boiled eggs, with Dounia beside her on her knees slicing dill pickles.

Panko feels sorry for Hryhori Budka. The poor man stands chewing a crust of bread, hesitates a moment as if he can't make up his mind, then paces to another spot a few feet from where Lena sits on the ground. She moves aside, a foot or so, fussing with her headscarf, fixing it on her forehead to shade her face from the sun. Mike and Metro appear almost as relaxed as Panko, elbows on their knees, quietly rolling cigarettes.

Panko listens to their conversation. Then dozing off time and again, he can no longer concentrate. The hay is so soft, and smelling so sweet. Looking up to the sky he sees dragonflies, butterflies, horseflies. At this moment life is a perfect comfort, but then he thinks that the next moment he could be bitten by a horsefly. And such is life, of course. Just when you think you are on top of everything, the Good Lord brings you down.

"Another drink of beer," Panko says. "The beer, Paraska." Dounia has brought two jars of Annie's beer and two of water to the hay field. They are wrapped in wet cloth. For the second time Paraska passes him one of the jars.

Before he takes a drink, Panko notices Dounia taking the lunch basket to Rose who is off by herself, forking hay on a stack thirty yards away from the group. Rose is paying attention to nobody, concentrating on her hay fork, each succeeding swipe at the hay more savage than the last. The old lady goes to her, Panko watching and listening.

"Ah, Rose," Baba Dounia says, "Maybe it's not Yuri's fault. What do they say about Marusia Budka? Could it be she is a witch?" Rose takes off her headscarf, shakes it, and wipes her face. Tears come to her eyes, but quickly she shrugs her shoulders and drinks from the water jar, then reaches to the lunch basket for a cucumber.

"Yes," Dounia says, speaking to no one in particular, slapping a mosquito on her forearm. "Maybe a witch."

Panko takes another drink of beer from the cloth-wrapped jar.

"Wait," Paraska says. "Here is a glass. Do you think all this beer is for you?"

"Ah," Panko says. He looks to make sure that Rose is out of earshot, and then speaks with a sigh. "Yuri Belinski." Panko has a grin on his face, the grin of a day-dreamer, which of course he is. "Yuri Belinski can't even drive a team of horses." He shakes his head. "But then again Marusia Budka is no horse."

"Yeh, yeh," Metro says, his tobacco-stained teeth showing in a grin. "Marusia is no horse. But a thoroughbred, don't you think?"

Mike Melnyk stands up, turns his back, then stoops to pick up his hay fork. "Good lunch," he says. "I'll help Rose with that stack. Then I go for the horses. We have enough stacks built to start pulling them together."

Panko has noticed that Mike has eaten nothing at all. Rose has always been Mike's favourite and his Anna has been rubbing it into him that they let her marry Yuri Belinski. But Rose is a fighter and she'll get Yuri back, whatever she wants him for anyway. Panko could not figure out why.

For a time Panko chews on a slice of buttered bread and digs into a jar of jellied chicken. Then he lies back, the glass of beer in his hand, and he looks skyward to Hryhori, talking to him. "In the poolroom in Topolia I heard that someone saw them in Dauphin."

"Dauphin?" Hryhori says. "I've been to Dauphin. Last summer." He is eyeing Panko and his beer. Paraska takes the beer glass from Panko and pours it full for Hryhori.

"Thank you," he says. He drinks it down and hands it back to her. She then pours for old Metro. Metro is gazing around, looking at the stacks, and counting.

"They'll find out they're not in heaven," Paraska says. She straightens and rubs her back. "Wait and see him running back to Rose like a puppy."

"Ya," Panko says, "that's true. Too much is too much. Whiskey, or women."

FIFTEEN

Vasylko Gregorovitch has a secret treasure left to him by his mother. He does not like to think about his mother, so long has she been dead. He was fourteen. Only one year and a half in Canada, and then her violent death. He won't think about it, only the gold.

She brought it from the Old Country sewn into her clothing. She had found the coins one day while cutting grain in the Polish landlord's field. She had stopped to have a drink of water in a nearby stream. The landlord was a rich man. He had a reputation of being sober and upright at nearly all times, but once or twice a year he went on wild sprees and could be dead drunk for several days. As it happened, here he was sprawled beneath an oak tree dead to the world, snoring like a bear. Vasylko's mother, a widow, had by necessity learned to be sly. She spotted the landlord's leather purse on the ground beside his leg. She looked around. There was nobody to be seen but the sleeping man. She put the purse into the folds of her skirts and hurried back to the fields. The purse bulged with gold, ancient gold from the time of the Empress Maria Theresa. A treasure. But she would have to keep it hidden. The landlord ranted for days about his missing coins, his twenty-two 10 ducat gold pieces, but the peasants knew nothing. Vasylko's mother kept the secret to herself. One day with all the excitement of villagers emigrating, she went along to Lviv and saw a Jew, in secret giving him one of the coins if he could arrange for her and her son to also come to Canada.

Vasylko kept them in a pint jar; twenty-one coins, each having on one side the queenly profile of the Empress, on the other, the double eagle. He did not keep the jar in his shack nor bury it in his yard. It was too dangerous. Vasylko Gregorovitch was afraid of what would happen if the authorities found him with these coins.

Instead he brought them to the spruce forest on the edge of the big meadow close to the lake. This was not far from his place, maybe half a mile. Nobody goes to the spruce forest because it is said that giant snakes have been seen, ten feet long and thicker than a man's wrist.

At least he thought no one came to the spruce forest until this afternoon. When he digs up his treasure just for the pleasure of playing with his coins, he hears a singing voice, shrill and haunting, resounding through the forest, the voice of Marusia Budka.

"Little bug, little bug, seven, eight, nine...." She counts the dots on a ladybird beetle she holds in her palm. Vasylko watches, hidden beneath the boughs of a swamp spruce.

From the shade of his hide-away his view is clear of the figure of this woman who steps through the yellow potentilla shrubs, her hand parting the taller growth of willows and red birch. As careful as a deer, Marusia's feet light on the spongy hummocks of grass. She emerges from the willows not more than seven or eight yards from Vasylko. She wears a yellow babushka with white silk fringes, a green skirt with a wide embroidered belt, and a white blouse with the same embroidery, gathered at the neck. She wears five strands of red corals, running the beads through her fingers. How lovingly she plays with them. She lets the beetle fly away, kneels on a patch of moss, and picks up a twig, touching it to a large grey toad propped on a rotting tree stump, on wet moss that has grown and died, turned brown and mingled with crumbling wood that fills the stump's hollow, the combination giving off a mouldering odour. Marusia sits at the stump, her legs extending out together, the toes of one foot rubbing the other ankle, the skirt lifting above the knee. A few feet away stirs the constant work of an anthill.

The swamp spruce trees are not cathedral straight like giant firs, but bent, the boughs askew, the tallest and thickest hiding Vasylko with his jar of coins. A distant wind off the lake rustles the leafy branches of poplars, sounding with the hum of Marusia's song.

The toad blinks at her. Long ago Vasylko's mother told him about these toads. In the Old Country such a toad as this was certain to be a witch. What is this woman doing talking to the toad? Is it her sister? A lover she has bewitched? What if she finds Vasylko hiding under this tree and turns him into a toad?

She has such full and upright breasts tugging at her blouse when she breathes. When a witch becomes old her breasts can hang to her waist, pendulous breasts, and when she flings them over her shoulders she is able to fly through the air. Can this beauty fly?

Vasylko can see the curve of her legs exposed below the skirt. Her toes wiggle back and forth. This Marusia is more beautiful than his mail-order pictures, even the ones without any clothing whatsoever. He feels the bump on his temple throbbing against his glasses.

She takes off her yellow babushka and her hair falls to her shoulders. She holds a strand of this hair to her lips, tickling them. The sun breaks through an opening in the trees, which makes her hair glisten the colour of gold, and the light falls on her shoulders and the red beads. She squirms as if enjoying the warmth, and the corals and her breasts jiggle.

Vasylko rubs his groin. What does she say to the toad? Is the toad Hryhori? He has always thought there was something strange about Hryhori. She never pays any attention to her husband. Maybe only when it's times like this do the two of them come together. It all makes sense. This is the place of the giant snakes. She brings a young man here, lures him with her laughter, seduces him, then tickles him to his death. Would Vasylko like her to tickle him?

But what did she do with Yuri Belinski? Were they here? Has he bought her these red coral beads? Maybe this toad is Yuri Belinski.

Vasylko takes a coin from his jar. Never has he parted with a single one of them. Never has anyone seen his treasure. He will go to Budka's tonight. Leave the coin with a note somewhere so that she can find it. But where? He will have to think of a place where he can leave the coin.

Marusia sings again. He listens, and watches closely. From a pouch hanging on her belt she takes a small package, a cloth tied with string. "Salt," Marusia sings, setting it on her babushka spread out on the ground. Then she produces a bread roll and a piece of black cloth. What is she doing? She lifts her coral beads from her neck, pulling the necklace carefully over her head and setting it beside the bread and salt then wrapping the three articles in the black material. Not only does she doff the beads but also her blouse, belt, and skirt. For a second she stands exposed to a ray of sunlight, her brown nipples, her pubic darkness, exposed to Vasylko. She brushes the hair from her face and falls to her knees, arms across her breasts, head turning this way and that, peering into shadows, stopping for a moment, gazing it seems right at Vasylko. She fondles the package, picks it up and holds it on her lap, all the time glancing around. She whispers, "Bury it. Bury it."

Marusia gets to her feet, and with her black package cupped in her hands, approaches the anthill. She drops again to her knees, scoops the loose earth, sticks, white eggs, and scurrying ants, and buries her bread, salt, and beads.

Vasylko wants to touch her clothing strewn on the ground, to smell her skirt and blouse, but he dare not move from his hiding place. She peers about again, as if startled like a deer at the snap of a twig. Vasylko hasn't moved. She hasn't seen him. But she shivers, rubbing her arms, then quickly dresses – skirt, blouse, belt, and babushka – and scurries through the willows, the red birch shrubs, and potentilla out of the bush and across the meadow.

Vasylko remains hidden half an hour after Marusia leaves. During this time he puts his coins back into his hole in the ground and covers the dirt over with spruce needles. He can't erase the sight of Marusia's naked body. How can he get a coin to her? The mail. What could be safer and more dependable than the post office? What could be simpler? Mail it to her. Put it in a match box packed with paper and mail it to her.

What about the note? This will take longer to plan. He won't have it figured out for several days; this he's sure of.

AN HOUR LATER Vasylko Gregorovitch sits on a stump in front of his shack. He's taken the front tire off his bicycle and is now sanding the inner tube. He is seemingly concentrating at his work, not looking up as Nick and Lena walk the path through the tall grass into his yard.

Nick wants to hear what Vasylko thinks about Yuri and Marusia. Lena would rather not hear anything. Lena wishes she was away some place where she wouldn't have to hear about Yuri and Marusia. But Nick insisted she come. It doesn't matter; Vasylko's quite harmless. She won't catch a disease or anything like that.

"When are you going to cut your hay?" Nick asks him. Vasylko sets the tire tube down and stands up.

"The hay. I should cut the hay." He doesn't have a cow but every summer he takes his scythe and cuts the small meadow between the road and his dwelling. But haying appears to be the last thing on his mind at the moment. He looks at Lena. "You're Mike Melnyk's girl. That right?"

Lena nods.

"The one who hangs clothes on the line?" He speaks quickly. "You were here the other night. Last week, wasn't it?"

"The night before my brother's wedding."

"Danylo. That's your brother, right?" It's easy to see that Vasylko has to have things clear in his mind. He doesn't want any uncertainties at all. Too many things are uncertain in this world. Lena sees that he is more nervous today then he was the other night. His temple throbs a deep red and the sweat beads on his forehead.

"My garden. You want to see my garden?" He talks to Nick. "You come too," he says to Lena. He takes them behind his shack and around a small clump of poplar trees.

"See these potatoes?" He digs under a plant and pulls out a potato the size of a baseball. "Not bad for the 25th of July?" He has two rows of potatoes, a row of onions, and the rest of his garden is made up of cabbages. Dill weed and rhubarb grow wild around the edges. "What else would you like to see?"

Nick takes out his tobacco pouch and rolls a cigarette. "Did you hear about Yuri Belinski and Marusia Budka?"

"What do you say? Yuri Belinski?" Vasylko turns his head away from both Nick and Lena. "Wild raspberries are thick this year. Bunch growing along the edge of the bush, right there." Nobody says anything for a moment. Vasylko takes off his glasses, bends one of the arms and puts them on again, glancing here and there as if checking his adjustment.

"Yuri Belinski and Marusia Budka?" He still does not look at them.

"Took off together," Nick says. "Night of the wedding at Melnyk's."

Vasylko leads them back around to the front of the shack and picks up his rubber tube.

"Got a flat tire." He stretches the rubber and sets it down on the tree stump. "Should be good once I fix it." Again he peers around in all directions, scratching his knee. "They took off together? Marusia Budka? Yeh, I did hear something. Can't remember who told me." Vasylko takes two steps towards the door of his shack, then turns around and strides towards Lena, rubbing his fingers over his mouth. "Yuri Belinski married to your sister?" He says this with his head not six inches from Lena's.

"Yeh." Lena fiddles with her hands, and before she knows it she picks up the inner tube.

"Got a hole in it." Lena jumps back as if Vasylko is

pointing at a snake in her hands, and she throws the tube to Nick. It drops between them. Vasylko picks it up again and puts it on the stump.

"Something to eat? I got sardines...."

"No," Nick says, "We better be going."

"Yeh," Lena says, "We...."

"Just a short walk from here to your place." Vasylko leads them on the path into his hay meadow. "A mile to Melnyk's? Nick's home is across the bay." The hermit's eyes shine, as if he's about to smile. "I know that Panko. Your father, Nick?"

"Of course, my father," Nick says. "Let me know if you hear anything about Yuri Belinski." Vasylko Gregorovitch waves, then disappears into his shack, shutting the door behind him.

SIXTEEN

That's him! Lena thinks. That's Yuri's car turning into the yard. She climbs down from the garden swing and runs around the side of the house to the summer kitchen. Rose is separating milk. Should I tell her, Lena wonders? God, I don't want a pail on my head. She hurries for the house.

"Rose?" He knocks on the door.

Lena stands inside the porch, talking through the screen door.

"In the summer kitchen," she says. She'd like to hear what he has to say, but that's her sister's business. Lena wants no part of this squabble, and the sooner she can get him out of her sight the better. But he doesn't go away. All he does is stand there on the steps.

She points. "Over there, if you have to know. Separating milk." It's on the tip of her tongue to ask him where he's been all week. Half the country would like to know. At least he's got the courage to show up; that's more than Lena thinks she could do. She watches him walk away from the house. How can he go back to teach at Fishing River with all the talk? How will he patch things up with Rose? Does he think the two of them can start up again as if nothing has happened? When he's far enough away she goes out on the step, curious to see what will happen at the summer kitchen.

Yuri turns around, catching Lena watching him. "Has she said anything?"

"Huh?"

"You know.... Where I've been...."

"Find out for yourself." Lena slams the screen door. "Maybe you can help her turn the separator."

He walks further away across the yard, his steps hesitant, as if he's testing the firmness of the ground. At the side of the building, away from the door, he runs his fingers through his hair then swings his jacket from one arm to the other.

Yuri's hand is in his pocket, his fingers rubbing the pearl broach he has bought for Rose, not nearly as expensive as Marusia's red coral beads, but a gift all the same. He rounds the corner to the open door, gazing in and seeing her fitting the bowl to the top of the separator. He's positive she knows he's there, but she doesn't look at him.

"Rose...?"

She takes a cloth, forming a strainer, clipping it to the rim of the bowl with clothes-pins.

"How are you, Rose?"

She doesn't answer, but instead lifts a pail of milk and pours it carefully through the cloth into the bowl. He takes one step.

"Don't come near me." She grabs the separator crank with both hands and begins the slow turning, one revolution, then another, each one a little faster than the last. "So you're back!" she says.

He sets his jacket on the bench beside him and sits down. "You won't believe what I'm going to say...."

"Then why even say?" The crank continues round and round, a bell on the handle tings on each turn, the hum of the rotor slow at first, faltering, momentum building more and more, the hum raising its pitch, becoming steadier with each turn of the handle until the bell stops and the machine is ready for the milk to run through. Rose turns the thin metal rod reaching up in the middle of the bowl, opening the valve.

He stands up, his voice hushed, yet resonant, like passing over still water. "Marusia Budka's song...." At the mention of her name Rose speeds up even faster on the crank. Milk is pouring from the larger spout into the pail on the floor, then a trickle of cream from a smaller spout splashes on the cast metal tray extending from the separator.

"Give me that!" Rose says. "Quick!" She points to a glass jar beside Yuri on the bench. He hands it to her and she places it on the tray to catch the spilling cream.

Yuri paces two steps each way, the sinew in his neck taut, hands clenched behind his back, turning away from Rose. "I was enchanted. Taken to the shadows of forgotten ancestors...."

Rose lets go of the handle, looks up at him with her mouth open.

"God!" Her upper lip twitches. The flow of the milk narrows, the cream drips. Yuri glances over his shoulder.

"The wood nymph casts a spell...."

"A spell! Your great Ukrainian literature and its spells, like Goldilocks and the Three Bears. I wondered if you'd come up with something like this."

"You don't understand." He turns from her gaze. "I was enchanted. The next thing I knew it was days later and we were in Dauphin."

"Of course." This time she laughs out loud, and resumes the turning, the bell tinging again, *ting, ting,* until the speed returns, the flow of milk widening. The drips of cream form again into a steady trickle.

"I did come back."

All the milk has passed through the separator. Rose removes the pail of skimmed milk, setting it aside, then pours the other pail into the bowl. She stands facing him, her hands on her hips. "Do you want to do something, Yuri? Well?"

"Sure," he says, and steps forward.

"Sit down! Dad has some scrubbing on the other side of the pasture beside Semchuk's. Hitch a horse. Go pull stumps, and let the mosquitoes eat you!"

He drops the brooch on the bench and leaves. Her body shakes, and she backs away, fingers gripping the rim of the separator bowl. He gave her pearls at their wedding, said he knew she didn't want anything old-fashioned, didn't want an embroidered linen to hang on a wall.

A potato bug crawls up the bench leg. She flicks it

off and squashes it on the floor with the toe of her shoe.

PANKO HAS NEVER SEEN A MESS LIKE THIS. The poor horse, lucky he hasn't broken a leg. The animal snorts and neighs, shaking her head back and forth, eyes bulging. It's good Panko went to check his home-brew mash after supper. Otherwise he wouldn't have heard all this commotion. He takes out his knife, then shakes his head. No sense to ruin good harness. It takes Panko a while, but he's able finally to calm the horse. Soon he has unfastened all the snaps, freeing it from the harness and the stump chains. The horse jostles to her feet and stands quivering, shaking off dust.

"Come on," Panko says. "Let's get away from these mosquitoes. We'll go to my shed and have a drink."

Panko lifts a two-quart sealer off a small table, unscrews the lid and smells the contents. Every time he opens a new jar it is a unique experience for him, maybe not because the whiskey is so different every time, but his mood can be, what's on his mind can be different. He's curious about the love affair. Because of this, the whiskey has the sweet and sour smell of armpits. He knows this is just in his imagination. He hasn't seen Yuri since the wedding and he wants to know what has gone on with Marusia.

But he sees that the young man is worn out from fighting the horse. "The mare is all right," Panko says. "She's in the barn chewing oats. What better life for a horse?" He wonders what Yuri was doing out in the field in the first place. At least in the brew shed they aren't eaten alive. "Come in, come in and shut the door. The mosquitoes."

This shed is Panko's special project, and he is very fussy about it, even had Vasylko Gregorovitch on the construction, trimming logs because of his skill with wood. When Vasylko lays the logs there never are cracks, but the trick is getting him to do it. He doesn't trust anybody. Panko bought a wire carrier basket for Vasylko's bicycle, filled it with Paraska's donuts, and took these presents to him. "I need your help," he told Vasylko, and he came just like that.

"Do you have cigarettes?" Panko asks Yuri.

"Yeh, sure." Yuri tugs a package of Players from his shirt pocket. Panko lights a match and each man drags deeply several times before another word is said.

Panko fills the glass. "Take," he says. "You need it." Yuri wipes his brow and rubs the side of his face. He nods, accepting the glass.

"To your health." He holds the glass forward, then drinks.

"So," Panko says, "that Marusia, she's some woman." Yuri puts the glass in his left hand, lowering it to the level of his waist, then he steps to the side, glaring at Panko. He grabs the sealer and pours another drink for himself, downing the whiskey, and then another. He takes a deep breath and lets it gush out. Lifting his head to look at Panko, he opens his mouth, then hesitates. He looks up to the cobwebs hanging from the roof, throws his cigarette down, grinding it into the dirt with the toe of his boot.

"Does your wife believe in you?" He places the jar of whiskey in Panko's open hands, walks to the door and steps outside into the trees. He calls back to Panko. "Does she?"

Panko's lips tighten and he hunches his shoulders, screws the lid on the jar. He has never thought of such a thing as Paraska believing in him. What is there to believe or not believe? Panko is Panko. Does Paraska believe in Panko? The man must be crazy from the mosquitoes in Mike's field, or crazy with Marusia. Yes, Marusia.

Yuri stands in the open doorway, holding out his glass. "I heard Marusia sing. She did enchant me, as if I was in the legends. Kotsiubynsky's wood nymph was luring me into the shadows of the forest."

"Maybe you've had enough to drink."

"You don't understand." He wipes his mouth, puts his hands in his pockets, and stares at the floor. His lips begin to move, quoting poetry, quietly:

"They strip naked, and splash about in the stream like forest creatures that have never known shame....wolfbane shimmers and monkshood berries hang down like blue slippers...frogs croak sadly...."

"Yes. Yes. My mother told me when I was a boy, or was it my father said? Something about forest creatures." Panko twists the lid off the sealer. "You teach that at school?"

"It's our culture, Panko."

Panko pours a drink for himself, sipping it, smelling its rawness.

"No culture. I would like it, but there's no use. Not here."

"You play the *sopilka,* Panko."

"Shit! Big deal, *sopilka.*" He shakes the sealer at Yuri, the whiskey spilling on his plump fingers. "What will your poetry prove in Manitoba? Do you think anybody gives a damn about this Kotsiubynsky? Do you think I'm stupid? Do you think I know nothing about your bullshit?" He pauses, head shaking, lips quivering, and then he's suddenly aware he's holding the sealer and the glass. He sets them on the table. "Wait a minute. I got something to show you from the house."

He comes back with a photograph. A man carries a flagstaff with the Union Jack. He's marching on a Canadian city street, between the streetcar rails. He wears jackboots, breeches, a military coat, shirt and tie, and a pillbox cap with a Ukrainian badge and a short peak pointing at his nose. He leads a procession of twenty or thirty other men in uniform, playing tubas and trumpets and beating a drum. Two women carry a wreath. A black hearse follows, and behind it a trail of people.

"My brother's funeral," Panko says. "He was one of those who dreams of liberating Ukraine. Can you imagine a Ukrainian army in Oshawa, Canada? The Seech Brotherhood, is that what they call it? Do they think they are Cossacks fighting Turks a hundred years ago in the Crimea? Instead my son is in the Canadian army."

"Let me see." Yuri grabs the photograph, running

with it outside to the light, absorbed in study. Panko catches up to him, and standing on his tiptoes he peers over Yuri's shoulder and points down to the hearse. Yuri turns away, shoving at Panko with his forearm.

SEVENTEEN

At seven in the morning Lena squats on her milk stool, her head pressed against a cow's flank, her head covered with a plain babushka. She's wearing a pair of Danylo's old dress pants, the cuffs rolled up and pinned, and a pair of rubber boots too large for her feet. Why wouldn't Rose help? Just because she's married and moved away from home doesn't mean she can't milk a cow when she spends the summer holiday at the farm. She'd have something to do instead of feeling sorry for herself. But would that really work? Lena has no trouble milking and feeling sorry for herself all at the same time.

A grey-and-black-striped cat stares up at Lena as the two streams of milk ring into the pail. She aims for the cat's face and it swats at the milk with its paw. It licks, preening itself and tasting the milk on its fur. All at once the cow tenses and lets go with a gush of soupy dung, liquid from a summer diet of green grass. It slaps its wet tail in Lena's face.

"Whore!" Lena says in Ukrainian. She stands up, pail in one hand, looking for something to strike at the cow. Teach it a lesson. Lena grabs a lantern from the manger and crashes it down on the cow's head, breaking the glass. In the commotion a chicken squawks and flutters down from the loft. Lena takes a rag from the pocket of Danylo's pants and while she's wiping her face she notices bare legs descending. A woman. Lena backs out of the stall, the rag still held to her face. The legs belong to Marusia who is standing in the manger, her finger on her lips.

"It's only me."

Only Marusia. As if it's a common thing for young women to inhabit barn lofts. In her hand she holds her yellow babushka, and she laughs, tying it to her head. "I'll help you with the milking," she says.

Lena doesn't know what to say, what to do, only to hand over the pail. The next moment Marusia is singing and milking. The cow chews its cud and its tail hangs limp.

Finally Lena asks her, "What are you doing here?"

"Milking," she says, and hands the pail full to Lena. "Not a good answer? Okay. Is it all right for me to tell you that if I can't sleep I like to walk at night?"

"To our barn?"

"I might find somebody. I found you."

IT ALL HAPPENS AS IF Lena was Alice in Wonderland. Across the pasture the dew on the grass glistens. The five measured notes of a meadowlark call in the stillness, wait, then repeat. The sun warms, drawing out the scent of sage. Lena follows Marusia along the creek all the way to the plank bridge at the road.

Pulling off her rubber boots, and rolling her pantlegs up over her knees, Lena wades into the creek. Marusia sits on the bridge, her legs dangling to the water. Suddenly she points. "See the crayfish?"

"Where?"

"By your toe." Marusia jumps into the water and reaches down, scooping the lobster-like thing wiggling in her hand, its claws like scissors opening and closing. Lena examines it from a distance. "Here," Marusia says, tossing it to her, letting it plop into the water.

"Don't!" Lena jumps back, almost losing her balance. For a moment it's all she can do to catch her breath. Marusia is full of the Devil. Lena swipes at the water and Marusia runs laughing up the bank.

She doesn't know Marusia, has seen her only in church and at weddings, and the day she went with Nellie inviting guests. All she knows about her is that she's poor, and that all the men chase after her. Yuri chased her, but she's not at all like Lena expected. She's like a schoolmate, the two of them on their way home, stopping to sit at the bridge watching for a fish.

"Will you talk with me?" Marusia asks.

"What about?"

"Anything." Marusia bends around, gazing into Lena's eyes. "Have you been to Winnipeg? What do women do there? Is it like Dauphin? I've been to Dauphin."

"I know you have. No, I haven't been to Winnipeg." Marusia's excitement is catching. Lena tugs at her pantlegs, at the knees, Danylo's pants, lifting the material like tents, and suddenly both women are laughing. "You look so young, even younger than me."

"I will always be young. You know, I've never been to school, but I read. I teach myself. Hryhori doesn't know how." She puts her fingers to her mouth, and looks the other way. "I'm sorry my husband bothered you at the wedding."

Lena puts her hand on Marusia's shoulder. "No, don't be sorry. It was nothing."

Their eyes meet. "He drinks too much."

"Don't worry. Everybody knows a wedding is a wedding."

Marusia blushes, blurts her words out all at once.

"You wonder about me and Yuri. You think I'm a whore?"

"I don't know what to think. You ran away with my sister's husband. He says you put a spell on him. In a way it could even be funny if it wasn't for my sister." Lena bites her lip. "Whore? Don't say that. It's not a nice word for a girl to say."

"Or be?"

"No, Marusia. I don't know what you are. Why should I judge?"

Marusia plays with the white silk fringes on her babushka.

"Yuri, he's nothing special, you know. I thought he was. He's an educated man. I was curious, and how he could dance. A summer night you just forget everything...." She tosses a pebble into the water, ripples spreading in circles. A mudhen swims, startled, only for a moment.

Lena remembers her night with Nick. Her period should have arrived a week ago.

Marusia drops another pebble. "After a while can you believe I missed Hryhori? I missed chopping wood and cutting beets. I'm not a Hutzul goddess the school teacher wanted me to be, some magic fountain he drinks from. I never went to school. How could I answer his fancy words? And Lena, I'm sorry I did this to your sister. I have to tell you. I'm too ashamed." The women sit looking at each other, then down to the water, tears forming in their eyes. The mudhen dives, a long time under before it comes up.

Marusia jumps to her feet and picks up a stone. "Who can throw farther?"

"I can," Lena says, hucking a rock overhand far into the pasture where it lands splashing in the creek. Marusia grins, and dropping her stone into the water, she runs, crossing to the edge of a bluff on the other side of the road. Lena joins her, stepping through waist-deep grass into the intermittent shade of the poplar bluff. Sunlight speckles the leafy ground. Nettles grow, along with raspberries, red birch shrubs, and yellow-flowered potentilla. A clump of mushrooms has broken through the leafy ground.

"Look!" Marusia says. "A morning glory!" She bends down, taking the flower in her hand, and with the tips of her fingers she touches its blue-tinged white petals. The stem winds into the branches of a potentilla. She pulls at the stem, stretching its coils, snips it with her fingernail, and holds the flower to Lena. It's no longer free to wind its slender stem around a raspberry cane, around a twig of yellow potentilla. It no longer curls where it pleases. Now it can only wilt.

"Do you know that the flowers and the trees have souls and can speak to each other?"

"No," Lena says, "I don't know that." Marusia's remark makes her think of the barn animals talking on Christmas Eve. How silly. She bites at the nail on her little finger.

They stand face to face, each studying the other. Lena's hands go to her face, pulling off her babushka, her barn babushka with streaks of shit from the cow's tail. She laughs for the second time, and Marusia joins in, taking her scarf off too, the yellow one with the white silk fringes. Marusia places the morning glory in Lena's hair.

EIGHTEEN

The very next morning Lena gets a visit from Vasylko Gregorovitch. He wants something, but she can't imagine what. In fact she still can't imagine even after he's done with the visit.

Vasylko's been struggling with the writing of his note to Marusia Budka. He doesn't know if he should sign his name. Could he provide a clue like "a friendly neighbour"? Or say nothing, but simply mail the coin? He wonders if maybe Lena Melnyk can help him. He doesn't know how to write letters to women. Can he ask her without revealing the existence of the coin, and that it is intended for Marusia Budka? He must confide in her alone, and carefully.

For three mornings he rides his bicycle on the road past the Melnyk farm, and on the fourth morning he sees her beside the garden, hanging wash on the line. Vasylko places his bicycle against the willow fence and walks through the gate into the garden. The clothes-line is on the other side of the fruit trees, and he can just see Lena, reaching to the line, holding a white sheet and taking a clothes-pin from her mouth.

"Lots of plums this year!" He shouts through the trees.

Lena should be startled, but she's not. She recognizes him at once, first his bicycle, then his awkward stride through the garden, his glasses and the bump on his head. She's reminded of a circus clown appearing from nowhere, sad and seemingly lost in the woods. He peers up at the loaded branches of a plum tree. She wonders what he wants coming here? He must be looking for Danylo or her father.

He turns towards her, wrinkling his forehead, and fingering the plums, moving his hand up and down as if weighing them.

"Take one," she says.

He lets go of the branch.

"No, no," he says. "Green. They're green." He wipes the palms of his hands on his pant legs then glances towards the house. He whispers, but it's a loud whisper, as if he is forcing the air from his lungs all at once. "Do you write letters?"

"What?"

"Do you ever write letters? A boyfriend, or something like that?"

"You have a girlfriend, Mr. Gregorovitch?"

"No, no!" he says. "No! But do you ever write to a boyfriend? At another school or something?"

Lena lays the empty clothes basket down on the path between them and sits on the swing. What can he want? He wants to know if she writes letters? To a boyfriend?

"No," she says, biting at a fingernail. She notices a

drop of blood then wipes it on her dress. "I've written letters, but to my sister, not a boy."

"No good," he says, "Not to a sister." He puts his hand over his mouth and pulls at his lips. Vasylko looks as if he has not shaved for three days, and Lena imagines she hears the rasping of his fingers on his beard, like the rasping of the priest Kobzey. He makes a sudden move away, towards his bicycle, but then stops and turns back. "Let's say you wanted to send a gift to someone, but didn't want anybody to know."

"Couldn't you mail it?" Lena asks.

"But you don't want the person getting it to know either."

"Send it anonymous," Lena says.

"Anonymous? You mean not put a name?"

"Yeh."

"But then the person won't know."

"Isn't that what you want?"

"But not forever. What if Anonymous wishes to see her." Vasylko looks around while he is saying this. His knees are bent and his hands are on his thighs.

Lena thinks for a minute. What an odd man this Vasylko Gregorovitch is. "Why don't you write a note telling a time and place to meet. You could say: *If you would like to meet the sender of this gift meet me at such and such a place at such and such a time.*" Vasylko lifts his cap and scratches his head for a moment. Then his eyes brighten and he smiles.

"That would work," he says. "Your father's pulling stumps up at the scrubbing, eh?"

"He was looking for some more help. Someone to

help Yuri pick roots." Lena jumps off the swing and picks up the basket.

"Oh, no," Vasylko says. "I've been awful busy lately. I see you've got to get to work too." He scratches his head again, then goes out the gate and picks his bicycle off the fence. "See, I got it fixed." He gets on and pedals off down the road.

THE GOLD MARIA THERESA NESTS in crumpled newspaper stuffed into an Eddy matchbox. On the table beside the coin is one of his pictures, a nude brunette wearing a cowboy hat. She has one foot resting on the lower rung of a rail fence. Her hands cup her breasts. He got this picture last winter through mail order from Chicago. Beside it is an open can of sardines. Some of its oil has spilled on the photograph.

There's more where this came from, he writes in pencil. Then he puts the pencil down. He knows the meeting place: by the anthill. A fly buzzes around the sardine can, but Gregorovitch pays it no mind. A fly-strip hangs above his table, covered with flies. He takes a calendar down from the wall. This is Monday, he thinks. We should meet Saturday morning, but not this coming Saturday morning. That won't allow time for the mail. It will have to be the next Saturday. Better yet, he should give her a longer time to think about it, to feel the gold, let it sweat in her hand. She may not come unless that feel can sink in and she can't stand any longer not knowing. Give her a month to wonder. He examines the calendar. The Saturday he wants is the fourth one. "That's it," he says. "The fourth Saturday in August."

Should he allow for a second date? The fly lands on the bump on his temple and he brushes it away. Then it buzzes around his nose. Still it does not bother him because he is concentrating so hard. No, a month is good enough. *"There's more where this came from. If you would like to meet the giver, come to the anthill in the spruce forest at 10 o'clock, the fourth Saturday in August."*

That's all he will write. He folds the paper and places it on the Maria Theresa. Then he slides the matchbox shut. With another sheet of writing paper he starts to wrap it, but realizes he needs string. There is some string in the box where he keeps his pictures.

Finally the gift is wrapped, addressed, and ready for mailing. Vasylko, sitting in his chair, digs out a sardine and lays it on his tongue, then chews, slowly. He picks up the picture of the girl with the cowboy hat, but then he stands up and puts it away in the apple box with the rest of his treasures, things now paled in the light of his venture.

He has his plan made, a meeting with Marusia alone at the anthill. He will wait till the fourth Saturday in August. In the meantime he will act as if nothing has happened. He would like to see Marusia, not talk to her, but just see if he can notice any change. See if he can notice whether she has received the gift. She often comes for the mail at the Volga store.

Vasylko won't use the Volga post office to mail the coin. That would give his secret away. Old man

Stupych would make sure to see who he was mailing to, and he would blab it to every customer who comes to his store. Vasylko will send his parcel from Topolia, just like he does most of his mail-order business from Topolia, except sending away box-tops for free gifts. He always buys his groceries at the store, sells his muskrat pelts and seneca roots, and he gets his cheques sent there. He'll wait a week or so, and then he'll hang around the store waiting for Marusia. She often comes there.

SIX DAYS AFTER HE MAILED THE COIN he's at the store, leaning against the pop cooler watching Panko Semchuk and Metro Zazelenchuk play cribbage with Ivan Stupych. Panko shuffles the cards then holds the deck tightly in his palm, tapping it three times with his index finger. "You read in the *Ukrainian Voice* about Dieppe?" Ivan asks.

Metro rubs his nose and then his chin. "What is Dieppe?"

"On the French coast. Soldiers in boats from England. Canadian boys. Some kind of landing experiment. Many of our boys from the prairies shot on the beach. The Cameron Highlanders from Winnipeg, and the South Saskatchewan Regiment that was training at Shilo two summers ago. Remember they were running around in the hills south of Dauphin?"

"Yeh," Panko says. "Nick is training with the Camerons. If they are going to fight Hitler, they need more than experiments. I think Churchill is leaving it up to the Russians."

"What can they do?" Ivan says. "The Germans are cutting through Ukraine like a knife through cheese."

Panko pauses deep in thought, the other two men watching him. He shuffles the cards once again and taps the deck on the counter. Ukrainians can fight better than Russians when they have to. But like it always is, the Ukrainians are on both sides, or better yet, on neither. Yes, more like neither.

"Stalin is no friend of Ukrainians," Panko tells Ivan, as if the matter is settled. The people must wonder can Hitler save them from him? Then they must wonder again, can Stalin save them from Hitler? That's how it is with Ukrainians, some of this, some of that.

Panko points his finger at Ivan, finalizing what he has to say. "But you see, many Ukrainian boys fight in the Red Army. They will have their backs against the wall at Stalingrad. There they will stop the Germans." Panko is just grateful that Nick doesn't have to be there. He could go to France maybe, but not there. At Stalingrad the English would learn what it is to fight. Panko starts dealing out the cards.

"I would like to count another twenty-nine," he says.

"Another?" Metro says. "When did you get a twenty-nine?"

"I did." He continues dealing, nodding at Metro. "Ask Danylo when you see him. The two of us had a game in my shed this spring. Three fives and the Jack of diamonds. I cut the five of diamonds! Honest to God!" Panko sets the remainder of the deck on the counter top beside the cribbage board. "Here, Metro, cut them."

"Shit!" Ivan says. "A nine! And here I threw a six into your crib."

At this moment the little bell above the front door tinkles. Marusia Budka walks into the store. Vasylko moves quickly to stand off by himself beside the old couch and three empty pop cases where men often sit and smoke when they are not playing crib. He takes a new horse collar down from a peg on the wall, and examines it.

Marusia appears even more jolly than usual. "Ivanka," she says to the store-keeper, bending over the counter, one hand on Panko's shoulder, the other on Metro's, peering straight across the counter at the store-keeper. She tickles Metro's moustache. Panko stares at her feet. She is wearing the shoes Metro gave her at Easter. Panko winks at Ivan and points at the floor. The store-keeper's eyes gleam. Eighty years old with no teeth, and bent like a dried apricot, but he straightens up as if he is a twenty-year-old Cossack.

"Have you got chocolate-covered cherries for Marusia? I like chocolate-covered cherries."

"I will ask the Jew when he comes from Winnipeg." Ivan leans forward, head to head with Marusia. "The Jew will know. I've never had such a thing in this store, but I will get them."

"Did you buy a horse?" Metro yells to Vasylko.

"Ha, ha, ha." Marusia Budka raises her hands in the air then presses them to her cheeks, puts her lips to Metro's ear. "Maybe Vasylko wants the collar for himself. He can put it around his neck."

Vasylko does not hear her, but he's sure that she smiled at him. So she likes chocolate-covered cherries. Maybe that's what he should have sent instead. He'll have to check his mail-order catalogues for chocolate-covered cherries. From her appearance he cannot detect a thing about the coin, just that she is happy. And one more thing. The way she talks to that old man Ivan it's certain that she likes to have presents. Perhaps she will want another Maria Theresa.

NINETEEN

Lena bangs the mop on the floor outside Nellie's door, and hears a voice responding from the bedroom.

"Come in if you want."

Nellie sits gazing at her dresser mirror, her hand lifting the black silk nightie from its pink box, then dropping the spidery garment, lifting, then dropping. Lena watches from the doorway.

"Did you wear it?" Lena asks, and then she wishes she had kept quiet. What a silly question to ask. Does a bride talk about a honeymoon?

"Did he even notice?"

"Did you stay at a hotel?"

"Of course!" Nellie doesn't smile. She jams the lid on the cardboard box, and holding it with both hands, turns around and faces Lena. "A honeymoon is not like the magazines. And now I have to live here with your mother."

"Where is Danylo?"

"Went to town, as usual. Says he wants to talk to Armstrong about hauling fish to Winnipeg this fall.

Always an excuse to go to town."

"Should I mop in a different room?"

"Oh, don't mind me, Lena, and for goodness sake you don't have to clean my room, but..."

"I can come later. It's no trouble...."

"No, no, Lena, I'd rather mop it myself. But don't leave. Come in and sit down."

Lena hesitates, grips the mop handle with one hand, then grips with the other, hand over hand to the top. "You've been crying, Nellie." She sets the mop down, and sitting on the bed, glances at the lingerie box clutched in Nellie hands, then up to her eyes. "What is the matter?"

"Would you like these?"

"Your lingerie? Nellie!"

"It's nothing. What good are such things here? Better for you to put away. Some day you might go to live in Winnipeg, or even Toronto. You are my friend. I'd like you to have them."

"Not for me. It's not for me. I'd feel silly wearing a black brassiere and panties. And silk yet. Who knows, maybe if it was red. I like red. But keep the lingerie to wear for your anniversary. See what Danylo says a year from now. Even if he only laughs."

Nellie shoves the box back into the dresser drawer then takes out a black babushka coloured with red and yellow flowers and green leaves.

"This is more the style for me now to wear to church, like all the other babas." Nellie drapes the shawl over her shoulders.

Last week at the wedding, Lena had watched Baba

Dounia tie a babushka over Nellie's bridal headpiece, not this flowered babushka, but a plain white one to wear entering her husband's home. It was to be stored in the *skrynia,* not to be worn again until her death when she could wear it at her funeral. Lena's mother said to put it away and she gave Nellie the floral one. Nellie is now a married woman covering her head. She is a baba. God, what an awful sounding name for a woman, *baba, baba, baba.*

Facing the mirror again, Nellie ties the cloth on her head, covering her forehead and the sides of her face. She stands up, and grabbing the mop from Lena, she pokes it between Lena's feet and under the bed. Then she hops about the room riding the handle as if it's a witch's broom.

"Hey, you silly," Lena says.

Nellie sits on the edge of the bed, takes off the babushka, then sprawls face down on her quilt, her hands on her chin and legs kicking up.

"Did you go to a movie in town?"

"Nick took me last Saturday night. *Gone with the Wind.*"

"Clark Gable and Vivian Leigh. Rhett Butler and Scarlett O'Hara. I have all my magazines under the bed." She leans over, tugging out boxes, then leafing through each box until she finds the issue she wants. "Right here. I don't throw any of them away. Pictures from the movie. And it has write-ups. I've kept it for two years, and finally *Gone with the Wind* has come to Topolia. I wish Danylo and I could have seen it."

She gives the magazine to Lena, then rolls over on

her back, clasping her hands behind her head. "It must have been exciting!"

"I don't know...." Lena puts the magazine down and picks up a pillow from the unmade bed. Setting it on her lap, she begins puffing up the feathers.

"Hey," Nellie says, "let's have a smoke! Do you have any?"

"Nick gave me a new package, but Mother's downstairs...."

"An old hen with you under the wing?"

"Wait," Lena says, "I'll be right back." She grabs the mop and runs down the stairs and outside to the summer kitchen. On a high-up ledge is her new package of Black Cats and a small box of matches, hidden beside an old cigar box. Her father had bought cigars one Christmas, and when the men had smoked them all he gave it to her. She used it to keep her precious things, if she had anything precious. The next Christmas Panko had given her a shiny new nickel. He must have noticed how down in the mouth she was. Danylo had played a trick on her Christmas Eve. She had hung up a stocking like English children and in the morning all that was in it was a lump of coal. The nickel was the only treasure she had in the cigar box all that winter, but by the time spring came she had spent the money on candy from the Volga store.

That June, on her way to school, by the short cut across the south pasture, she had found a blue feather, a delicate light blue like the sky. All that day at school she kept it in the pages of her Grade Four reader, putting it in the cigar box when she got home. The very next morning she found another blue feather, and an orange one, and so she began looking all summer for different coloured feathers. She collected a yellow and black feather of a goldfinch, a red cardinal feather, a blue and black of a blue jay, several more sky-blue bluebird feathers, the orange and black of an oriole.

Her treasure of feathers in the cigar box had sat on the ledge in the summer kitchen since that summer, kept from Danylo so he wouldn't smash it, or put something bad in it. She forgot all about the box until yesterday when she hid her cigarettes. When she found the box and opened it the feathers made her think of a mouse nest and not a treasure. She quickly closed the dusty lid and left the box on the shelf.

Lena puts the package of Black Cat cigarettes into her dress pocket and hurries back into the house and up the stairs. A voice comes from the east room.

"What are you doing?"

"I have to shake the mop." Her mother always has to know everything. Yet she spends so much of her time alone in her east room with her crafts, always making flowers with crêpe paper, wire, and hot wax. She decorates Easter eggs, drawing wiggly lines and circles and stars. For days she can withdraw from everything, talking to no one, neglecting the cooking and washing, not caring if the men don't get supper. She expects Nellie to take over with the cooking, as if what else is a daughter-in-law good for? If Nellie doesn't know how, Rose can show her. Rose will have to show Nellie how to bake. Nothing will stop Mother from making flowers – wrapping green crêpe paper around a wire, forming pink rose petals with more paper, and dipping her flowers in melted wax. When she decorates *pysanky* she dips the eggs in wax. A candle smokes heating a tin cup filled with the wax of wild bees. She frames the Holy Pictures with her flowers, with old *pysanky* shells she has saved, and with pussy willow twigs. The Holy images in these frames gaze down from three sides of the room. It has always been like this with her mother.

When Lena gets back to the bedroom Nellie is sitting in front of the mirror experimenting with different ways to wear her babushka.

"Do you want to be a baba?" Lena says. Only married women wear babushkas. Lena's never going to wear one, only when she does dirty chores, never a dress-up babushka, not even if she gets married.

"How does it look this way?" Nellie says. "Tie it at the back? Or is it better at the side? You know what the old people say? They say you can tell where a woman comes from in Ukraine by the way she ties her babushka."

"You're not really going to wear one of those things, are you?"

Nellie throws her headscarf at the dresser, the material landing half in and half out of the open drawer. "Let's have that smoke," she says. Lena opens the window, and the warm wind flaps the curtains. They sit down on the floor, face to face. Nellie takes a deep drag and all at once she's gagging, bending forward, Lena pounding her across the back.

"You shouldn't have inhaled," Lena says. "Is this your first time?"

"It's those stupid Black Cats!" Nellie gets off the floor and lies face down on the bed, coughing into her pillow. Lena goes to the window, takes a few drags of the cigarette, then butts it out carefully and puts it back in the package.

After a moment or two Nellie lifts up her head and says to Lena, "I don't think Danylo would ever move to Winnipeg. Do you think so...? Hey, anything serious with you and Nick?"

"Serious? What do you mean?"

Nellie's eyes light up. "You know."

"No, I don't know." Lena's face is red. "Nick's okay. He'd do anything for me. Not like...."

"Danylo?" Nellie laughs. "Danylo is no Nick. That's for sure. Would you marry Nick?"

"I'm too young."

"I'm not?" Nellie says.

She wants to tell Nellie about something that is bothering her like nothing else has ever bothered her, something about the night with Nick. Wants to tell somebody that she missed her period. Does that mean she is pregnant? If only she could talk to Nellie about it, but she can't. She can't tell anybody about what she and Nick did. What if it got around? What would her mother do? Maybe it's nothing. Surely she's not pregnant. And if she isn't and she talks to Nellie, who knows that it might be blabbed around. Best for Lena to keep quiet and just wait and see what happens.

She directs her attention to the ticking of the alarm

clock on Nellie's apple-box night table. It is twelve minutes after ten.

"Mother will wonder if any work is getting done."

"At least you don't have to stay here," Nellie says. "I wish Danylo would go away for a job."

"You know, Nellie, I've been thinking."

"No kidding."

"About Yuri. Don't you think he's...that he's acted like an ass?"

"Sure. But what do you expect with a woman like Marusia Budka. I feel sorry for Rose."

"Me too. But I feel sorry for Mrs. Budka too."

"What? A witch?"

"She's no witch. Not Marusia."

"But she's something, I tell you."

"Ahh," Lena says. She takes the babushka hanging from the dresser drawer and tries it on herself, making faces in the mirror. "Hey, you know what? Rose and I are supposed to pick strawberries this afternoon. She can stay and bake bread, and you and I can pick berries." She leans forward with her chin propped on the mop handle, then with a shrug pulls off the babushka, putting it in the drawer, and starts mopping at the top of the stairs.

The men said yesterday that the field where they were scrubbing stumps was loaded with strawberries, big red ones ready to pick. Lena hated this chore when she was a child, but it seems to her now to be more of an outing than something she had to do.

"Bring a jar," Nellie tells Lena. "We can fill it at the well."

Carrying milk pails for the berries, they leave the house. Nellie's wearing her white wedding babushka. "I dug it out of the *skrynia,*" she says. "If I wait till I'm dead the moths will eat it."

Picking the berries will be a picnic compared to picking roots. The field was to be ready for seeding next spring. Danylo had spent the winter cutting poplar. He hauled the cordwood to the station in Topolia; the Jew paid him two dollars a cord. The willow he hauled to the yard. Mother always said that nothing was better than willow fire to heat up the *pich* for baking bread, nothing better than willow to smoke sausage.

But Lena was glad she didn't have a husband who earned his living scrubbing bush. "Goddamn stumps!" Danylo would say. "What can you do with a stump? Leave it rot for a year then burn it to hell!" That's what Danylo would say. Along the road the girls notice berries in the ditch so they stop to pick them. Their pails are a quarter full before they leave the ditch and cross over into the scrubbing. At the edge of a poplar bluff on the west end of the field Yuri Belinski is picking roots and stacking them in a pile. Hryhori Budka works with him. Danylo stands with the horse beside a woman on her hands and knees. "Hey," Nellie says. "Is that Marusia Budka picking?" She bumps Lena with her pail. "There they are alone, Danylo and that woman."

"Hryhori is there too," Lena says. "And Yuri."

"Sure! Yuri!" Nellie says. "You can trust Yuri Belinski? And do you think that stupid Hryhori will keep his wife off them?" Nellie hurries over the rough ground: the roots, stumps, holes, and clumps of dirt. Lena follows.

Marusia Budka's little pail is half full and her lips and teeth are red with strawberry juice. Danylo is smoking a cigarette.

"Where did your father go?" Nellie asks Danylo.

"To Panko's to sharpen his axe," Danylo says. Marusia gazes up at Nellie and Lena.

"You bring some water," she says. "I would like a drink of water. See, Danylo, I said they would have water and you wouldn't have to run to Panko's to get some for me." Nellie hands her the jar. Lena can see that she's tempted to throw the water in Marusia's face, but she doesn't. Marusia drinks, the water trickling down the side of her mouth, wetting her blouse. A gold coin hangs from a string around her neck.

TWENTY

Before sunrise on the fourth Saturday in August Vasylko hides under the spruce tree. He told Marusia ten o'clock in the note, but so filled is he with thoughts of her that he can't sleep at home. The crisp morning air carries the clean scent of spruce needles and the lake. The sun rises behind him over the open water on the other side of the trees. He hears the croaking of frogs somewhere out in the boggy places in the big meadow, and he thinks of Marusia's toad. From the lake he hears the quacking of ducks.

Perched on his knees Vasylko opens the buttons of his pants and urinates, aiming the stream as far away as he can. He feels something pinching on his knee, and digging at the ground he pulls out a jagged piece of rock that fits in his hand like the head of an axe. He tosses it aside.

Streaks of sunlight begin to penetrate through the trees. He sees sparkles of light glint off the heavy dew on the meadow grass. He's cold, and thinks he should have brought a coat.

Should he show her all of his coins? He digs in the

loose soil for his jar, handling it with care, rolling it gently in his hands. When he sees Marusia coming will he crawl out from under the tree and greet her with the jar of coins held behind his back? He waits minute by minute. The noises of flocks of birds lifting from the lake increase then die away as the minutes turn to one hour then another.

Vasylko's patient. How long has he been waiting? She's late, eleven o'clock, and the sun is almost directly above the trees. Most men would have given up, but not Vasylko. His plan to meet Marusia is clearly etched in his mind and he can't allow doubts to cloud his purpose, not when the moment of meeting her is so near.

What is the time now? He takes out his watch again. Twenty minutes to twelve. She will come from the north-west across the open meadow. He follows the second hand on his watch, playing a game to pass the time. For thirty seconds he holds his breath, then forty, forty-five, a minute, working his way up to a minute and a half.

This morning it has not entered his mind that she might not come, though he has had these thoughts on previous days. He has considered that she might be afraid to walk out here alone and not know who it is she is to meet. Would he come under the same circumstances? And he is a man, not a woman.

The sun has dried the moisture from the grass. The morning chill has long ago disappeared and his discomfort is different now; he's hot, not cold. A sense of betrayal begins to take hold of him, his hands trembling such that he backs away from the rock and the jar, afraid that he might bump them together and break the glass. Five after twelve and there is no Marusia. He is seized with a realization he has had many times. Circumstances begin to make things brighter in his life, and he starts to feel better about himself. He could ask Marusia to come to his house for tea, and he could show her his carvings. Dare he show her the one he's doing of her? He convinces himself that she will come out here to him, and yet his old doubts will not allow him to let her know that her admirer is Gregorovitch.

There will be no Marusia this morning. At least no one else but Vasylko himself knows of his humiliation. He will never tell anyone, not even Nick Semchuk. Can he be trusted anymore? Before he went away to the army he was a good friend. He still is, but he doesn't visit as often as he used to. Maybe it's because Nick has a female friend.

Vasylko is to the point of admitting defeat when he notices something. Out in the meadow fifty feet away the grass is rustling. Something is moving because the grass is moving. He doesn't want to imagine that it is Marusia lying in wait of her gift giver. But could it be her? No, he forbids himself to think of such a thing. First he will bury his coins, and then he will investigate.

To be safe he picks up his piece of jagged rock. As he stalks into the meadow the movement in the grass ahead of him has ceased, but just as he reaches the spot where he had seen it move, he hears something, a slithering. There it is, at his feet. A giant snake writhes, an evil thing longer than a man is high, and as thick as Vasylko's wrist. He has never seen one before, but the stories are true. There are such snakes by the spruce forest. Without even thinking, he steps hard with the heel of his boot, pins the Bull Snake at its neck. Again and again he crashes the rock on its head, pounding it to mush.

TWENTY-ONE

Soldiers are everywhere on the dance floor, and they stand at the entry, a mass of uniforms, both army and air force. The orchestra plays modern music with brass horns; three saxophones and a trumpet, accompanied with a piano, drums, a clarinet player who sings. Lena feels so Canadian to be away from the bush country, to be dancing at the Mallard Lake Pavilion. Mother said she was too young to be going that far to an English dance, but Father said she could go. "Why not?" he said. "How could she be in safer hands than to be with a soldier like Nick?"

This has to be the happiest day in her life. Her period came last night. She's not pregnant. She'd like to tell Nick, but she hadn't told him about missing her period in the first place. She wonders what he would have said.

Another blister has formed on her ankle, but she won't let the irritation stop her from dancing in her *Stardust* shoes. She imagines her feet light as air on this dance floor, and Nick a handsome prince in his army uniform. She wonders what it is to be in love, or is it only the romance of an evening that she feels? Is it a magic in the air from the sounds of music and the scents from Mallard Lake and the raptures of lovers? Nick is a wonderful dancer. Is there a magic land at the end of a rainbow? Will she find someone different than Nick? Someone who is not Ukrainian?

It's one of those summer nights where a person feels full of everything good, overflowing with life, a princess dancing in the Hollywood palaces of Nellie's magazines. Lena and Nick dance in a star world among all the slowly moving bodies, hearing the sounds of the drummer's brushes, the cry of saxophones, the trumpet; smelling the lake breezes coming through the screens on three sides of the dance floor. And she's not going to be stuck at Panko's farm with a baby, and a husband off to the war. Sweet sixteen. She couldn't feel better. She doesn't feel out of place among the soldiers. If anything she should tell Danylo and Nellie to slow down. Don't be a hill-billy, don't be a bush-bunny. Lena likes the slow dances. She drifts off, her head on Nick's shoulder. The clarinet player sings. Lena sees moonbeams and dreams little dreams. Prince Charming is her theme.

"You are a wonderful dancer, Nick. Where did you learn?"

"I learned where you learned. A dance is a dance. That's all." He leads her through the swaying bodies and across the floor, as smooth and unassuming as two fish in water. The man she'll love will be big and strong. To dance like this is life without babushkas. Sophisticated, romantic. The dance floor is in semi-darkness; over their heads Chinese lanterns glow red and yellow; leather-soled shoes swish in rhythm on the hardwood floor, as if the entire hall gives way to the music, until the number is over.

Lena and Nick stand among the other dancers waiting for the music to pick up again. How out of place a Baba Dounia would be at Danceland. This is no place for a *tsymbali*. Danceland defines a new Lena, what she wants to be. Danceland is the home front seeing the soldiers off to England. She is one of the girls in a smart dress and high-heeled shoes. She's wearing the ones she bought for the wedding, her red *Stardust* high heels, and her Kayser hosiery. *Be wiser, buy Kayser.* Nellie has curled Lena's hair into gentle waves; a single curl falls down the right side of her forehead.

When You Wish Upon a Star. Another song. There is so much room for so many dancers, space above the coloured lights, the criss-cross rafters curving under the round roof. Ten Ukrainian halls would fit inside this one. Lena is happy not only for herself, but for Nellie. Danylo had said he'd take them to the dance at Mallard Lake, take them to Danceland because he and Nellie had missed out on seeing *Gone with the Wind.* This dance is even better than seeing the movie because they're not just watching something, they're doing it. Danylo seems even more at home than Nick at these English dances. It's probably because he's been running all over the country going to dances as long as Lena can remember. And not just Ukrainian weddings.

It's good to get her mind off Yuri and Rose, though Lena knows that Rose would have loved to come to the dance. But it's hard for her to go anywhere with Yuri because she thinks people will point them out, whisper about the affair with Marusia Budka. It takes a long time for these things to go away, and one thing about Rose: she's proud and won't stand to be laughed at. But Lena didn't come here to worry about her sister.

The tenor sax player leans back, swaying with his instrument, his fingers running up and down the stops, the golden brass gleaming, the long and slender goose neck bending to his mouth. Lena watches him, her head resting on the coarse fabric on Nick's shoulder. All at once Nick says, "Maybe you should marry me?" Lena straightens up, looking at his face. His expression keeps changing from a smile to a frown, and back to a smile, his lip twitching.

"You mean after the war is over?" Lena says.

"I don't know."

"Who knows where each of us will be by then. Are you going to come back to the farm?"

"What's to farm? Maybe fishing."

"I'm going to Winnipeg when I finish Grade Eleven," Lena says. "Let's wait and see what will happen after the war." For a moment they stand there. The set of three numbers is over and people are moving off the floor, seeking new partners, some relieved to be, some not.

"Come on," Nick says. "There's Danylo waving. He's telling us to come outside for a drink."

The air coming off the lake tempers the heat from the dance hall, a mixture of scents that Lena can almost taste: perfumes dabbed on necklines, hamburgers and frying onions, potato chips and vinegar, beer drunk out behind automobiles, weeds raked up on the shore of an English lake with cottages, not a lake dark and uncontrolled.

A cool breeze touches Lena's face, the air a tonic she breathes into her lungs. They stroll on the boardwalk built out over the water. Danylo stops and reaches under the wood decking, pulling on a rope to which a burlap sack is attached. He has stashed beer to cool, and untying the rope and opening the bag, he takes out four wet bottles.

The strings of lights outlining the dance hall reflect off the water rippling up against the boats tied to the wharf. The sounds of *Star Dust* carry from inside the hall through the screens and across the water. Laughter echoes from a crowd of people standing out front mingling about the cars angle-parked along the curb. The stars of the Milky Way are thick across the sky, a stroke of spattered paint. Lena swallows a drink of beer, then another. The after-taste of yeast comes back up her throat, not unpleasant.

All at once Lena has a thought that it's good to be alive and young with the rest of the night ahead of her, days and years ahead of her if things could be just like this...filled with song at twilight time.

With shoes and stockings off, Nellie and Lena sit on the end of the wharf dangling their feet in the cool water. The blister on Lena's ankle has broken and she lets the cold soothe it. Danylo and Nick have gone to watch a fight breaking out by the parked cars. Lena swishes her feet in the water, then hugs her knees, letting them bounce against her chin. She listens to the singer's voice carrying over the water. Lena sees garden walls and bright stars.

"Isn't it fun?" she says to Nellie. Why couldn't it always be like this? Next week the priest comes to Gruber church for the mission. "Aren't you glad we came, Nellie?"

"Yeh. Sure. But I'd rather see *Gone With the Wind.* Got a smoke?"

"Sure." Nellie never has her own cigarettes, but then she doesn't smoke much. Only when she's alone with Lena.

"You know, our men are better dancers," Nellie says.

"You mean Danylo and Nick?"

"No, I mean Ukrainian men."

"Oh," Lena says, and she lights Nellie's cigarette. Ukrainian men. Next week the priest Kobzey will come to spray Holy Water on beets. Baba Dounia will crawl up the aisle to kiss a picture on the altar, her knees and forehead dragging on the wooden floor. The priest will spread smelly smoke all over the place.

TWENTY-TWO

In the middle of the week, Wednesday at mid-afternoon, Marusia walks to the church for confession. She wears her yellow babushka with silk fringes, and when she gets to the church she will take it off and put on a black one. The way the weather has been it's too hot walking to church wearing the black shawl, and, also, wearing black in the sunshine is too gloomy for Marusia. There's enough time to be gloomy inside the church.

This is the week the priest Kobzey preaches every day, preparing for the Sunday Blessing of the Fruit. In Ukraine the celebration is in thanksgiving for the harvest, but here it hasn't started yet. The people buy oranges and pears from Ivan Stupych who brings them from Topolia. On Sunday they will take these fruits in baskets to be blessed at church.

Marusia stops by the side of the road, crossing the ditch to sit on a stump. She can feel a pebble in her shoe. She takes it off, dumps the little stone on the ground, then massages the ball of her foot. She holds the shoe to her face, rubbing the soft leather against her cheek. She continues sitting, thinking about what to say at confession. Panko told her that life is like eating, and you should enjoy it. However, the more you enjoy, the more you fill with corruption and have to dump it out. She knows that confession will make her feel better, and she's not afraid to tell the priest she has committed adultery. He wants to hear that, for what else can he have?

She grips the coin tied around her neck, examining the profile of the crowned woman for at least the hundredth time. Someday she'll discover the sender. No sense to worry about it.

As she walks by the Volga store she remembers the chocolate-covered cherries, and she decides to go in and see if Ivan Stupych bought them for her.

The men discuss the latest events of the war, Yuri reading headlines from Ivan Stupych's *Ukrainian Voice* mailed weekly from Winnipeg, Danylo browsing through the *Dauphin Herald*, while Panko, old Metro Zazelenchuk, and the storekeeper agree that you should not believe everything you read in the papers. Will they ever open up a second front, instead of the English pretending to land at Dieppe, and sending Canadian boys to die with nothing to back them up? In Ukraine the Germans have crossed the Dneiper before the end of June. They're pushing to Stalingrad.

The new Russian tank will show them a thing or two. Ivan brings out a clipping from *Life* magazine his brother sent from Chicago. The men in the store have mixed feelings about Russia. The Ukrainians have been oppressed for three or four centuries, but then again, the Germans also oppress, and more efficiently.

The article says: *The Russians will do literally anything to win, will crouch all night in the swamp or snow, deepen and camouflage their trenches in their spare time. They take to swamps like muskrats, to forests like bears, to desert steppes like coyotes, to snow like ptarmigan. This infuriates professional German soldiers who like to do a neat killing job.*

"Many Ukrainians fight side by side with the Russians," Panko says, "But enough with fighting. Look who comes in the door."

He will offer Marusia a drink. Why not? Panko considers it necessary to make pleasant things in life into celebrations. Make the best of an occasion, and the presence of a beautiful woman is high on his list for pleasant situations. Yuri had told him about libations, as if a Ukrainian has to be told.

"Is that not right, Yuri? You studied the gods at university in Lviv. You told me Bacchus." He reaches under the counter producing a bottle and holding it forward. "Is that not right? Libations? We drink to the gods? Hey, Danylo. Grab a Coca-Cola from the ice cooler. A small drink, Marusia. To God!"

"No, are you silly?" She takes a step back, fingers of both hands curled at her mouth, her eyes a-sparkle.

"How you mean 'silly'?" Panko says.

She tells Panko that she is going to confession. What would Kobzey think if he smelled home-brew on her breath? She can't stomach home-brew anyway. She looks at them in turn, eye to eye, winking at old Metro, moving her right foot side to side, showing her shoes.

"What brings you to the store?" Panko asks.

"Handsome men."

"You must be at the wrong store."

"Yeh, yeh," Metro Zazelenchuk says, tobacco-stained teeth showing in his grin. "I have a story to tell I heard from town." He's talking to the men, but it's apparent that he's directing his message to Marusia just the same. He scratches his arms and at the side of his trouser legs. "Should I tell it? Maybe the lady will blush."

"Oh?" Marusia says. "What makes you think so? Do you think Marusia is afraid to blush?" Not one of them says a thing. Ivan takes a rag from under the counter and starts dusting tins on the shelf, Danylo begins rolling a cigarette, and Yuri shuffles his feet, looking down to the floor.

"You like to make a woman blush?" Marusia asks, touching Metro's moustache with her little finger.

"You go to the priest? I tell you something good to hear before confession."

"Why not? But do you have my chocolates, Ivanka?"

"Chocolates? Yes! Yes!" the storekeeper says. He takes the gift from under the counter and hands it over. "Two pounds. I got from Winnipeg."

She holds the box, all the time smiling at Metro as he wipes drool from his mouth with the back of his hand. He begins.

"A rich Pole walked on a road with his wife and daughter, and all the while he is boasting that there is not a man anywhere in the world that he is afraid of."

Ivan stumbles off his footstool. "The Cossack?" The

stretched parchment skin on the old man's face colours red.

"You've heard?" Metro says.

"Not me," Danylo says. Metro leans back against the counter, his fingers pulling at his suspenders.

Panko sits on a Coca-Cola box, rolls a cigarette, but doesn't light it. He watches Metro.

"A Cossack comes riding up on his horse, a big man with a musket slung across his shoulders, and a sabre at his side. He jumps off the horse and shouts to the old lady, 'You old whore! Take off your babushka.'"

Marusia smiles, and tearing the paper wrapping from the box, she opens it.

"Mmmm," she says. "They are delicious. Have some." She holds the tray open to Yuri. He takes one of the chocolate-covered cherries and nibbles slowly, his face red from her gaze, quick to hide again behind the open pages of his newspaper. Each of the men take a chocolate.

"What happens then?" Marusia says.

"The woman takes off her kerchief. 'Lay it on the ground!' the Cossack says. She does this and he leads the horse to stand with its hooves on the kerchief. 'I don't want my glorious Ukrainian Cossack horse to dirty his hooves in the dust.' And then he tells the old man, 'You stupid Polack son of a bitch. Hold the reins so the horse doesn't run off.' The rich man's fingers tremble like aspen leaves, reaching for the reins. Then the Cossack tells the daughter, 'Lie down and spread your legs!' And to the old woman he says, 'You old witch, there's my Cossack honour to defend. When

I'm on your daughter you hold me by the testicles, for your daughter's a Polack and she isn't worthy to have me bouncing her on the rear with my testicles.'"

All the men look at Marusia to see if she's blushing, but all she does is bite into another chocolate and lick her lips. Her eyes twinkle. Panko rearranges himself on the Coke box, rubs his hands on his knees, reaches into his pocket for a match, and lights his cigarette.

"Well," Metro says, "After a while when the Cossack gets heated up and carried away, the old woman can't hold on at all. Like a madman was he taking that girl. She lets go, letting the testicles bounce. The Cossack finishes his business then rides off on his horse without even a thank you.

"The man with his wife and daughter resume walking down the road, no one talking for a long time. Finally the old man says, 'Shame on such a Cossack hero. Do you know that the horse kept stomping his feet more in the sand than on the babushka? If he were a good Cossack he would have cut off my head with his sabre. He didn't even touch me!'

"The old woman says, 'Husband, don't even think about that. He didn't want to bang our daughter on the rear with his testicles. Why he moved only a few times before I let go, for I couldn't hold on. When he began flopping on her rear with those little testicles, it was funny even for me.'

"Then the daughter says, 'You know, Mother, I also deceived him. Every time he shoved at me from above, I would go twice from below. I showed him I could push at him more than he could at me.'"

Before Marusia can say anything, the little bell above the front door tinkles, and into the store comes Vasylko Gregorovitch. She takes her box of chocolates from the counter.

"You missed the story, Vasylko, but you can still have a chocolate." She strolls towards him, holding the box forward as if mocking the Ukrainian tradition of welcome with the bread and salt. He stops, staring straight ahead and not responding to the offer of candy, as if he doesn't see it. His glasses waver from the throbbing of his temple. For a moment Marusia trembles. He is staring at the neckline of her blouse. Men have stared before and this has never bothered her. This is what she usually enjoys. But Gregorovitch is looking at her gold coin. She knows he is the gift giver. Thank goodness she didn't go to the spruce forest. His stare lifts to her eyes and she must glance away. He knows that she knows. What will he do?

His lips move but the sound doesn't come out. "Come here," Panko says. "Marusia! Bring those chocolates. What are you doing? Hoarding for yourself?"

"No," she says, trying to laugh, but the sound chokes in her throat. She turns and hurries to Panko. Gregorovitch leaves the store just as quickly.

To get to church it's half the distance taking the path around the swamp. She has never been afraid of Vasylko before; why should she be afraid of any man? Even the priest. But now with this coin what should she do? Should she be walking out here? Hryhori says that witches live in the middle of the swamp, on an island of reeds. Marusia sees clouds of smoke from the peat fires hovering over the water, and where there isn't smoke, the mosquitoes swarm in a thick mat, humming like a motor. In thunder-storms late at night Hryhori has seen fireballs rolling across the water.

The reeds are like long green onions with clusters of brown seeds at the tops. In places thick patches of bul-rushes grow with fat brown cat-tails sticking up. Hryhori says there is quicksand. Cattle have been lost in the swamp. Marusia fingers the coin at her neck, wishing she had her coral beads. To bring her luck she had planned to return to the anthill for her treasures. Vasylko Gregorovitch must have seen her bury the beads. His note mentioned the anthill. Should she go tomorrow and get them?

The ground is stony with yellow-flowered potentilla shrubs spotted here and there among the stones, moss, grass and snail shells. Blackbirds flit bouncing on the reeds at the shoreline. In places along the path circling the swamp, the willows extend to the shore, allowing only a narrow trail the walkers have beaten through. Behind the willows is a solid mass of poplar bush.

Marusia comes to a place on the path where two posts stand in a clearing. A rusted iron brace hangs from a nail on one of the posts. Off to the side are three graves overlooking the muskeg. At one time the people gathered here, but they changed the location when they built the church. The first two years when the people came to Manitoba they held services in this clearing, walking to the sound from the bell hanging from the posts. Everyone came to worship, and it was sacred ground.

But now for a long time the ground is no longer sacred. No one talks anymore about this place; they don't want to remember. A witch was stoned to death here: Vasylko's mother.

Marusia doesn't remember the old woman, only stories about her. She was apart from the other women, just like her son is apart from the men. She was a widow and people only guessed about her doings. They guessed that she kept terrible secrets.

Marusia also is different from others. What do those women know? How would they like it to be married off at age thirteen to an old man everyone laughs at? All she knew at age thirteen was to work here and there for anybody who would take her in. No mother or father, only an old aunt who wanted to be rid of her, gave her to Hryhori in return for a goat he must have stolen from somebody. At age thirteen what did she know about sharing a bed with a husband? And what kind of a husband did she have to teach her? What could Hryhori teach her? On her wedding night she lay rigid as a stick on his hay-filled mattress, saying nothing, hardly breathing. He sat at the foot of the bed smoking cigarette after cigarette, also saying nothing. It was a credit to him that he wasn't drinking. She thought maybe he had no whiskey in the house. Finally he blew out the lamp, took off his shirt, pants, boots, and stockings and snuck into bed.

"Are you sleeping?" he said.

"No." She saw the darkness of his hand reach out above her stomach. She tensed even more and he drew back his hand without touching her, then covered his mouth as he coughed. They lay motionless and silent. In the next while he turned to her twice more touching her the second time, his finger on her shoulder, and she flinched. Shortly after that Marusia went to sleep.

In the morning she woke early and, turning on her side, she watched her sleeping husband for a long time. He was snoring. His nose was long and narrow with two or three hairs showing from each nostril. His skin on his narrow face was stretched and red lines appeared through it on his cheekbones. He had a nick on his chin from a razor cut, but no other mars or wrinkles except at the corners of his eyes and on his brow, as if he was frowning because of a dream. Every once in a while his upper lip twitched. She reached out her foot and brushed against his leg, gently at first, and then repeated several times until she kicked him. He grunted, then opened his eyes wide, mouth open. He slid out from the bed, sitting upright at the edge, then reached under it, groping until he produced a bottle.

Later on following evenings, she became more familiar with the presence of Hryhori beside her in bed, his breathing, his inadvertent poke with an elbow, familiar and more comfortable with his smell after she told him to wash. After all this she began feeling curious. One night after another she waited for him to reach out and touch her. She lay flat on her back, squirming a little now and then to let him know she was awake, but he remained motionless. She couldn't figure out why he married her. For her it wasn't as if she was developing a desire for him, but she wondered whether or not she could be desired, as if there might be something wrong with her. One night she touched him. With the tip of her fingers she brushed the angular bone of his hip. She thought she felt him shudder to the touch.

"Oh," he said, and he rolled over, careful not to weigh on her, mounting over her. But he wasn't able to do anything more. Was he frightened? Intimidated by her? She was only thirteen, but she wasn't timid. She reached down, caressing him, but to no avail. Was it that he had drunk too much home-brew in his life so that alcohol kept him limp? He pressed down five or six times on her but nothing would happen. Poor Hryhori. Good only for chopping wood. A husband by name, but more of a child. She could love him as a child, care for him, but they never loved as man and wife. The times he later tried, he was hopelessly drunk, and his efforts remained hopeless. At least he wasn't mean to her.

The three graves by this swamp remind her of the church and her wedding. He didn't drink at their wedding. At every one of them since their marriage the men have laughed at Hryhori being drunk, and they laugh at him when he is sober and doesn't know how to tell the time on a pocket watch.

Maybe he is stupid. Of course he is, so why does she have to live with him? What is so wrong for her to dance with men? So what if she ran to Dauphin with the school teacher. She'd had enough of mosquitoes at home, enough of milking a cow with shit on its tail. Why can't she have nice things like other women? Should she spend her life making sure that Hryhori keeps his axe sharpened, spend her life learning only things like how good the borshch tastes when it's made with young beets? Look at the woman on her gold coin; did she have to cook borshch for a man? Why shouldn't Marusia be free to run as the wind in the meadow? At weddings how those other women sneer at her. Let them sneer; they are jealous.

She fingers the coin between her breasts. How excited she was to receive the gift in the mail, as if it was dropped from heaven for her. Hryhori drilled a hole in it so she could hang the gold on a string around her neck. Then she discovered it was sent by Vasylko.

Marusia makes the sign of the cross three times at the graves, then takes off walking, every so often breaking into a run. Never before has she been afraid to walk this path, but coming from the meeting with Gregorovitch in the store she can't stop herself from looking back over her shoulder. When finally she is in sight of the Gruber church it's as if she's in the arms of God. She holds her hand to her heart and feels the pounding.

Inside the church two old women wearing dark babushkas are kneeling on the floor, preparing to confess. Marusia exchanges her yellow babushka for the black, then kneels to pray. She likes the inside of the church, the paintings on the walls, the holy saints and angels up high on the ceiling as if their spirits are descending from heaven. The saints in the paintings are bearded and stern, and the Virgin Mary is so lovely and gentle. A wood-framed picture of the Virgin hangs on the wall by Marusia's head. The Sacred Heart of Mary pulses red flames and a dagger pierces through the centre. Marusia doesn't know what the dagger means, but it must be that the Queen of Heaven suffers.

The priest darts out from his little room beside the altar. He swings his censer with quick short strokes in three directions, making the sign of the cross at each turn. He looks to see the three women in the church, nods to them, then returns to his room.

When it's time for Marusia, it's as if she has turned into a little girl and Kobzey is the Holy Father. The room is small, less than eight feet by eight. Against the wall sits a trunk with metal straps, and across from it stands a high table with two silver candlesticks, a Bible, and two small glass pitchers, one with wine and the other filled with water.

Kobzey sits on a chair. He holds a small wooden cross in his hand. There is no place for Marusia but to kneel at his feet. No longer does he drape his red robe over his head, like he used to do. Hryhori said that Mike Melnyk was on the church board and he told Kobzey the practice was old-fashioned. He didn't have to do such a thing in Canada.

"Bless me Father for I have sinned...."

She does not dare look up.

"My last confession was Easter..."

"Yes, my child."

She will tell him about Yuri Belinski, about the sin

of adultery. Should she mention not always keeping the Friday fast, in the same breath as adultery? What should be first? If she starts with Yuri the priest will be interested in nothing else, so she better save it for the last.

"...And I have committed adultery."

"How many times?" She can hear his fingers scraping on his black bristles. He lifts one leg over the other under his black gown. Marusia hadn't thought to count.

"Ten," she says.

"With the same man?"

Doesn't he know, Marusia thinks? Everybody else in this district heard about it. Maybe the news didn't get to Kobzey at Sifton. The priest wasn't at the dance, only at Panko's house and the church.

"Yes, with the same man." She tells him about Yuri Belinski, about Danylo's wedding. But if Kobzey hasn't heard about her running away with Yuri....

"Ten times?" Kobzey asks.

"Not at the wedding. We ran off and were gone for a few days."

"Yes, yes, I see. This is a grave sin indeed." He shifts again on his chair, crossing his legs the other way. He waits a long time without saying anything – only his breathing she hears – and Marusia wonders if he wants her to provide him with more details. What can she say?

"This is not the first time you have confessed the sins of adultery to me, Marusia Budka. Think of your poor husband. Think of the wife of the man you have sinned with." Marusia looks up and is startled. Kobzey is gazing at her chest. Her hand clutches the Maria Theresa and she holds it to her breast.

"Yes," he says, with a sigh.

What does he mean, "Yes."

"Are you sorry?" he asks.

Marusia says what she is supposed to say. "Yes."

He mumbles his prayers and gives the sign of the cross over her head. She has forgotten to say the Act of Contrition, and he doesn't ask her.

"Ten Hail Marys and ten Our Fathers," he says. "Your penance. Go in peace."

TWENTY-THREE

Before the start of Holy Mass women talk outside, carrying baskets of fruit and vegetables to be blessed, each basket covered with a white linen cloth, and set carefully in rows on the grass in front of the church: a building as if dropped from heaven into a clearing in the bush.

Men stand in groups smoking, laughing, and speculating on the whereabouts of Marusia Budka. Where has she run to? No one has seen her since Wednesday, and simple Hryhori has been walking from farm to farm asking for her. When she had run off with Yuri Belinski at least Hryhori knew who she was with, but this time he knows nothing. Since Wednesday he has not even come to the church to ring the bell, so obsessed is he in his wanderings to find her.

Even this morning Hryhori tramps through bushes and meadows, through the tall grass that grows in the large meadow on the south-east side of the swamp. He's lived with Marusia long enough to know that she wanders in many places picking flowers and searching for mushrooms. Across the meadow a wall of poplar trees looms as dark as the shadow of night. He knows the swamp is on the other side; he's searched the path, but not the poplars, not in the willows. His feet drag through the wet grass, his pantlegs soaked from his boots to his knees, walking lengthwise and sideways across the meadow, combing his way to the far side.

Marusia could pick mushrooms in the trees at home. Why would she bother to hunt for them in other places? Often he has picked with her, but it's no use for him to pick by himself. He hasn't paid attention to how Marusia cooks the mushrooms, so what would he do with them?

He's halfway through the bush when he smells it for the first time, something not pleasant like mushrooms, but an odour like his bloated calf last summer, dead already a week.

The smell leads him to where he finds a fragment of cloth, an iron bar.... Further on, tangled in willow saplings, a bare foot protrudes.

AT THE CHURCH what started as a hot morning of a hot week gets hotter and hotter inside. Through two hours of the Mass the air turns thick and heavy, humid and scented with incense. In procession around the altar, Kobzey halts for a moment, swinging his censer back and forth three times, wafting clouds of aromatic smoke over the people. A drop of sweat, then another and another, escape from the wrinkles on his brow, forming a rivulet rolling down his nose. He wipes the moisture away with his sleeve.

He stands behind the forward altar, the small table where at Easter the glass-covered picture of the Christ in his shroud is kissed by everyone entering the church. A white-bearded man and three women including Baba Dounia drag themselves forward on their knees up the centre aisle, crossing themselves, then bowing their heads to the floor.

They crowd towards the priest to hear the Word of God. But something is missing. Never before has this group been without Hryhori Budka. Always he is the first one to hear the sermon on his knees. Even the Sunday after the wedding when Marusia ran away with Yuri Belinski, Hryhori was on his knees crawling to the altar.

At the back of the church people turn to someone shouting at the door. Hryhori appears, but not on his knees. He lurches up the aisle, at the same time making the sign of the cross over and over until he reaches near the front. He whispers in Mike Melnyk's ear. For a moment Mike is still, then his head snaps around to look Hryhori in the eye. Mike rises to his feet and goes to Panko. They whisper something to the priest, then turn to leave. A pathway opens for them. Baba Dounia follows.

"By the swamp! By the swamp!" Hryhori Budka runs far ahead, then runs back as Mike and Panko cannot keep up. It's so hot Panko can barely breathe – all week, one hundred above. He doesn't remember any year with heat like this during the week of the mission. The heat will bring a storm, he's sure of it.

Hryhori leads them along the edge of the swamp

overgrown with reeds and bulrushes. Baba Dounia stumbles far behind.

"The priest warned of the Evil Eye," she mumbles. "The woman wasn't in church. She has given herself away, and now her foolish husband leads them to her, to the evil place."

Hryhori stops. "Here," he says and points away from the path to the tall grass, willows, and poplar trees. "I would have seen nothing," he says, "but I could smell, and then I stepped on this." He digs in his pocket and reveals a piece of white cloth embroidered with red and yellow silk. "Her sleeve," he says, and then he reaches to the ground. "This iron bar...."

"Don't touch that!" Panko says. Hryhori looks back over his shoulder to Panko.

"I see her black babushka, and a box in the grass. Chocolates. Here the grass is trampled where he dragged her. I find the yellow babushka, then one shoe, and then the other."

Marusia's body is sprawled in the willows, head down, legs apart at her knees, the soles of her bare feet spread even wider and tilted upwards. Her dress is thrown forward, revealing her buttocks crawling with maggots.

Panko doesn't know what to do. He looks back and finds the two babushkas, walks to them and folds them, setting them down on the grass.

"She went to confession," Hryhori says, "Four days ago. Never came home." He falls to his knees. "But God bless, she is free from sin."

"Son of a bitch," Panko says. He doesn't know if he

should be looking at the body. God, he thinks, Marusia was one time beautiful, and now look, bloated like a dead calf thrown on the manure pile. He doesn't want to breathe the stench. He shakes his head. Who did this? Mike and Panko look at each other. Are they going to leave her like this in the trees, head down, feet up? The police will want to see, so maybe they should touch nothing. But anyway, how could they touch?

They hear something from the path. "Are you there?" a voice says.

"That's you, Dounia?" Panko says. "This way. Behind the willows." He has never in his life felt such horror. Marusia Budka is dead. Someone has killed her.

Hryhori prays on his knees, sobbing, and then his hands clutch the grass and his head drops to the ground, down and up, down and up.

"Oi, oi, oi." Dounia makes the sign of the cross. She stares at the maggots. The old woman's expression slowly changes back and forth, as if she is making up her mind. She goes from a look of pain and horror to wonderment. "Look at the worms," she finally says. "Dear God. Dear God."

TWENTY-FOUR

The policeman rests his clipboard on his knee, with his foot propped on a Coca-Cola box. He takes off his hat and sets it beside the cribbage board on the counter. A second Mountie, younger and without a moustache, stands at attention behind him, breaking his pose only to hand a pencil to his superior.

"You say she was in the store Wednesday?" Both Panko and Ivan Stupych nod their heads.

"Yeh, that's right," Panko says, "Wednesday, I think so. A few days ago."

"Was she going back home, or...?"

"To confession," Ivan says. The officer hands the clipboard and pencil to his assistant then goes to the door and looks outside.

"She walked around the swamp?"

"Yeh, yeh. To church. Big *praznyk* all week. The Blessing of the Fruit."

"What was the woman wearing?"

Panko butts in. "The same clothes." He thinks that he better speak out before the old man gets everything mixed up. "The same skirt and blouse as we found her in the willows, and the same shoes, but they were off when we found her. A yellow babushka she was wearing in the store, and a black babushka in the trees. Why two, I don't know."

The storekeeper, rubbing the side of his face and nodding, speaks directly to Panko in Ukrainian: "The shoes. Should I tell them about the shoes?"

"What do they care about that?" Panko says, sticking with the language. "Are you crazy?" He stops talking in order to light a cigarette. He sucks in the flame, breaks the matchstick in half, and drops it on the counter. He can't let himself get worked up. Who knows what trouble these police can create? Panko picks up his cribbage hand and sorts through the cards. Their cribbage game was interrupted when the police came. Hmmm, a good hand: three sevens, two eights, and a nine. And it's his crib. He won't let the police bother him, won't step to their every bidding. He can't let them think they control everything. Panko doesn't get excited and all mixed up like Stupych. That's no way to win at cards. He will throw in a seven and an eight, and see what Stupych throws.

"No," the senior policeman says. "I'd like to hear about the shoes."

The Ukrainians stare, first at the officer, then at each other.

"How do you know...?" Ivan asks.

"Why do you think I was transferred to Dauphin?"

"The shoes are not important," Panko says.

"I'll decide what's important, and what isn't. Go

ahead. I'd like to hear what you have to say about them. Tell me everything you know."

"He knows nothing," Panko says, "An old man bought her shoes."

"When?"

"I don't know. A few months ago. Easter time."

"You say an old man? What's his name?"

Panko glares at the storekeeper. "Just an old man. He lives far away in town. Metro Zazelenchuk his name is. Nothing to do with this business."

"We'll decide that," the policeman says. "Who was in the store besides the two of you?"

"Yuri Belinski," Ivan says. "Yeh, and Metro was here. Metro Zazelenchuk."

"No," Panko says. "Not Metro. When was he here? What's the matter with your head?" Panko turns to the officer. "The other man was Danylo Melnyk. We were playing cards. And then...." Suddenly Panko remembers something else. "Wait," he says, "I remember something she was wearing. Around her neck. A gold coin on a string. I wondered where could she get such a thing." Panko pauses for a moment, drawn as he has been over and over to the image of the bloated body. He concentrates as he must to recapture the more pleasant Marusia.

"She was always getting things. Don't you remember Ivanka?" He smiles and mimics Marusia, "Have you got chocolate-covered cherries?"

The storekeeper picks up the two pieces of Panko's broken match and drops them into an empty can. "The coin. I saw it too," he says. "I saw the same once in a book. An Austrian coin. Very old. From the time of Maria Theresa."

The policeman turns to his assistant. "Nothing on the body... no coin around the neck."

"The murderer must have took it," Ivan says.

The policeman takes a crumpled note from his coat pocket and shows it to the old man.

"There's more where this came from. If you would like to meet the giver, come to the anthill in the spruce forest at 10 o'clock, the fourth Saturday in August."

"Hmmm." Ivan screws up his face. "That's just last week. What do you think, Panko?"

The police are thorough workers. Only yesterday afternoon they got to the swamp and already this morning they've been to Budka's and come with this note. What are they looking for? What spruce forest? The big trees by the lake? Such an evil mystery the district has never seen. Panko had made sure to come early to the store. He thought the police would come. Always when there is government business in the district it is handled from the Volga store.

What does he think? How would he know handwriting? He doesn't run the post office. Panko sets his cards down and looks at the note, shakes his head, and gives it back to the storekeeper. He asks the policeman, quietly, "Do you think this has something to do with the gold?"

"I have seen such writing," Ivan says. "This hard pressing with the pencil, and shaking. The writing is Vasylko Gregorovitch. Yeh! Don't you remember, Panko? Marusia wanted to give him chocolates. How he stared. As if the Devil possessed him."

METRO ZAZELENCHUK COMES into the store shortly after the police leave.

"What for are you coming out here from town?" Panko says. "You could get a stroke walking in this heat."

"Strawberry pop," Metro says to Ivan, digging a nickel from his pocket and placing it on the counter, then lifting the lid on the cooler. "Why don't you put ice?" he says, fishing in the water-filled tank through the assortment of bottles.

"Go to the icehouse and get some if you want it."

Metro wipes the bottle on his sleeve. "Where is the opener?"

"On the side of the cooler where it's always been," Ivan says. "Are you going blind?"

Metro opens the bottle and takes a long drink. He turns his attention to Panko, who is standing by the window looking out to the road.

"You found her upside down with her bare ass in the air?" Metro says, his lips wet and tobacco-stained teeth showing in a smile, eyes gleaming. Panko ignores him. The old man takes another long drink, finishing the bottle.

Ivan leans forward over the counter and whispers. "The police were asking when you bought the shoes. They wanted to know if you were here the day Marusia was."

"What did you tell them?" Metro says, bending to put his empty bottle in the pop case on the floor, hesitating, then standing upright, the bottle still in his hand.

"I told them nothing!" Panko says.

"Should we tell him about Gregorovitch?" the storekeeper asks Panko.

Metro cranes his head towards them. "They suspect Vasylko?"

"All we know," Ivan says, "is that they have a note with his handwriting."

"Baah!" Panko says. "How should I know who they suspect?"

"What kind of note?" Metro asks.

"Ivan doesn't know what he's talking about. Just a note. It's nothing."

"It wouldn't surprise me that Vasylko killed her," Metro says.

"What does your wife say?" Panko asks, walking in behind the counter and reaching under, his hand emerging with a bottle of home-brew. Ivan gives him a glass.

"I didn't ask her," Metro says. Panko pours for himself and drinks. The storekeeper does the same. Then Metro.

"At least I gave her nothing," Panko says.

"What do you mean?" Metro asks.

"You gave her shoes. Ivan gave her chocolates."

"The police don't suspect me, for goodness sakes!" Ivan says.

"How do you know?" Panko pours himself another drink, and then a third.

"What are you doing with that whiskey?" Metro asks. "It does nothing."

"How about three-hand cribbage?" Ivan says.

Panko shakes the remaining drops of whiskey from

the glass. "Too hot to play cards."

Metro starts for the door, then turns. "Have you seen Danylo?"

"Someone said he went to Winnipeg," Ivan says. "I don't know how long he's gone for. Fish hauling. Armstrong netted a late summer catch up at the north end."

"I thought I'd go to the farm and see how the crops are coming along," Metro says. "Did the police ask for Danylo?" He waits for Panko to say something.

The storekeeper answers. "I don't think they said anything. Did they, Panko? Did they?"

Panko doesn't answer.

TWENTY-FIVE

Vasylko has vanished and they say he's hiding in the swamp. Lena walks to Panko's to find out if there's any more news. As she passes by Vasylko's yard she walks faster, then breaks into a run, not stopping until she arrives at Panko's house where she finds Paraska and Baba Dounia inside with the priest. Kobzey has remained in the district to bless the homes, and Dounia travels with him to help the blessings with her singing. Tata Paraska rants on and on to Kobzey about evil spirits and pays him two dollars to rid them from the house. Never has the blessing been more needed than now.

Sitting on the bench beside the house, Nick is talking to his father.

"No," Nick says, "Vasylko is afraid of police. They should have had me go see him instead of driving up with the police car."

"I agree! I agree!" Panko says. Under his breath he mutters, *"Shliak trafyv."* He says the curse not with anger and not with jest, but with incredulity. *"Shliak trafyv! May lightning strike you!"* Maybe they all could be struck. Maybe they should be. He picks up his *sopil-ka* and plays three notes, as if calling people to mourn, then he turns it slowly around in his hands before setting it back down, leaning the slender wooden instrument against the bench. It is as if these three notes did beckon to others, because the next moment the women appear from inside the house. Baba Dounia is saying that Gregorovitch has killed Marusia Budka and has turned himself into a toad.

"Not a murderer," Nick says. "Vasylko is afraid of his own shadow. Do you think he's a killer, Lena? Huh? What you think?"

Lena shrugs, then turns her attention to the chanting of the priest as he comes out the door. He carries his cross and a jar of Holy Water which he sprinkles on the door posts. The frown on Kobzey's face warns that this task is by no means to be taken lightly. His bass monotones are met by the shrill replies of Baba Dounia. She walks with the priest around the house, to the barn, and even to the garden.

Panko lifts his *sopilka* to his mouth and starts playing again, the same three notes. He is grateful to have the priest at a time like this. As much as he sometimes questions what Holy Water can do, he doesn't mind that Kobzey sprinkles it all over the place, and when the priest returns from the barn, Baba Dounia following behind, Panko makes the sign of the cross three times and bows his head. Just before Baba Dounia goes back into the house, she turns and quietly says to Panko, "You found her upside down."

"Baah!" he says, glaring at her.

Just what the old woman likes, Panko thinks. This murder adds years to her life, and it takes years from mine. "Foolish." He says this to Dounia hoarsely, not a whisper, not a shout, and yet both. He does not want to listen to talk of witches, but if this is the case, why then does he play music as if he's serenading *Rusalka?*

"Upside down," Dounia says. "I saw on those willows." She shakes her finger and nods, then limps into the house.

Goddamn this talking of witches, Panko thinks. It's easy in 1942 to rave about witches because that's all that will happen, just gossip. What harm when everybody knows the police are here to deal with trouble. That's how it is in Canada. But doesn't old Dounia remember the first year? The second year? In 1904 nobody would think to go to the police. What did the people know? They knew to leave the Czars alone. That's what they brought from the Old Country. Damn right Dounia remembers, but she doesn't want to say. Nobody wants to say. Things too frightening, too horrible, disgraceful, to tell the children.

Panko was a young man not as yet married, but he and Paraska were both there in a circle of all the district people in the forest clearing around three graves and a church bell mounted on posts. The out-of-doors was their first church in the new country: grass floor, tree walls, sky ceiling. The people stoned Vasylko's mother to death. Dounia's first baby boy had just the week before died at birth, and Semchuk's cow had gone dry. The old women started mumbling about a witch's curse. Metro broke an egg into a glass of water and everyone saw the cloudy white lines to prove the presence of a witch. The cow had walked towards Vasylko's mother, a sign as sure as the kiss of Judas, and the people stoned her. The boy Vasylko ran into the trees. Even Panko and Dounia threw stones.

Nobody talks of this. So damn it to hell, there should be no talk of witches now when everyone should know better. It's not something to play with. Panko stands up and takes his *sopilka* into the house. Nick and Lena remain outside alone.

"Vasylko won't be hiding in the swamp," Nick says. "He's afraid of the swamp. Besides, he has many places to hide right at home. Come with me, Lena. We'll go see him."

Is she hearing correctly? Nick would go out there at night after Marusia Budka has been murdered? Is she brave enough to go along?

"Are you crazy?"

"Not me," Nick says. "He has no gun to shoot us."

"Are you sure?"

"He has no reason to harm us, and if we don't scare him"

"*Us* scare *him?*"

"Make sure we don't come up on him by surprise. Let him hear us. He's probably in the bush."

The road on the way to Gregorovitch's is dark. How fast the summer goes, Lena thinks. The days are getting short again. The only light on the road is from the stars and a sliver of moon. She hears their shoes crunching on the gravel, and the croaking of frogs somewhere out in the meadow.

"Vasylko!" Nick calls out as the two of them walk single file on the path through the tall grass to his shack. Lena turns, looking behind her, hurries her step and bumps into Nick.

"Watch where you're going," he says. "Come on."

"Vasylko! It's only me, Nick! Just me and Lena." He stops to listen, but all they hear are the frogs.

He shouts again. "The police have gone to Dauphin. They won't be back until morning, but they are bringing dogs."

When they get to the shack they find the door padlocked.

"Don't you think we should leave?" Lena says. She holds Nick's arm.

"Shhh. Something in the bush." A twig snaps, and then they hear the shuffling of grass. Someone walks towards them. A voice comes from the dark.

"Dogs? You say the police are bringing dogs?"

GREGOROVITCH LIGHTS THE COAL-OIL LAMP, turning the wick down so there's barely light to see, then making it brighter, then dimmer, then no light at all as he decides to put in more fuel. As he pours from a gallon can, his hands shake and fuel spills all over the glass receptacle and the table. The smell of the coal-oil permeates the room. When lighted up again, the wick smokes, blackening the lamp's globe with soot. Gregorovitch mutters under his breath and adjusts the wick.

"Needed filling," he says.

He seats his visitors and, retreating to the end of the table, peers at them through the lamp light, one to the other. He says nothing, and Nick says nothing. Is Nick going to ask him about Marusia Budka? Lena wonders if maybe she shouldn't have come. Gregorovitch might do anything, the state he's in.

"Well?" Nick says. Gregorovitch glances to the side, at the dark window.

"The police," he says. "You said they're coming with dogs."

"They want to talk to you about Marusia Budka."

He stares again, back and forth from Nick to Lena, as if suspecting them of knowing something they shouldn't.

"I don't know how she was killed, but it's better if you turn yourself in, Vasylko."

The lamp flickers and a shadow leaps across Vasylko's face, his lips twisting, eyes bulging, the bump on his temple throbbing. His arm twitches and a stack of papers falls off the table to the floor.

"She is dead."

"The police found your note, Vasylko. The gold coin...."

Gregorovitch pulls at the table top, nearly tipping the lamp. His hands grip the edges so that the boards creak. Lena thinks of him on his bicycle coming to the flower garden and asking her to help him compose a letter. She feels herself somehow implicated in these terrible happenings. The look Gregorovitch gives her doesn't help. His eyes suggest to her that she has betrayed him. The eyes are asking whether she has told anyone.

"I didn't tell anyone about writing a note," Lena says. "Just Nick."

"The police want to talk to you, Vasylko. Can you do that? If you hide, the dogs will find you."

Again no one talks. After a moment his fingers begin releasing from the table. There is no doubt that he is terrified, but maybe he is realizing he has no choice.

"You know about my gift?"

"Yes," Nick says. "She wore it around her neck, and it is missing."

"Oh," he says.

"Come to the store in the morning," Nick says, "Before the police come."

"Dogs," he says, and turns the lamp wick down till it smokes.

TWENTY-SIX

By midnight the priest Kobzey has blessed enough houses for one day. He stayed longer than he should have at Melnyk's, but how could he have gotten away sooner? Danylo was his driver. How many times did Mike fill the glass? "I make a toast," Mike said. "To the Father, Son, and Holy Ghost. Not every day can father and son drink with the priest."

After they finished the bottle Danylo had brought Kobzey to the churchyard. It is here where the district built him the small house that he stays in for five or six nights a year, and of course for this past week of the mission. He sits on the edge of the bed staring down at the hem of his robe. On the night table a lone candle flickers. A restlessness churns inside Kobzey. Through his small window he sees lightning flashes illuminating the church cupola, and he hears thunder rumbling, ploughing up the sky. He pulls off one shoe and, holding it on his lap for a moment, decides to put it back on.

The Budka woman is dead. Why doesn't she leave him alone? No matter how careful a man is, even a priest, a Holy Father, his temptation is that of Adam. What are the strange powers that wind their limbs around a man's heart? So much his mind has dwelled on her death. The old woman Dounia chants about the witch. The whiskey he's drunk, and the fears of the people mix his thoughts to where he senses the Evil Spirit looming in every corner, and he yearns to join with it, find this Marusia.

The priest leaves the house, striding across the yard into the church. The dark, time and again, is cleansed with lightning flashes showing the icons in the church, the angels on the ceiling, Holy pictures on the walls, the tall banners, and the Virgin on one side of the altar, Saint John the Beloved on the other. Kobzey falls to his knees, praying to the icon of Jesus on the Cross. A sudden flash reveals to him not the Christ, but the woman suspended on the willows, then Christ again. He hurries to the altar, his hand fumbling in his pocket for matches to light the candles at the feet of John, the beloved disciple.

He carries the candelabrum into his room beside the altar, and sets it carefully in front of the two small glass pitchers on the high table. From underneath, behind the linen cloth draping the table, he lifts out a gallon of mass wine, a quarter full, and sits on his chair, holding the jug on his lap. A long time he sits, watching the twelve candles burning, tipping the gallon jug to his mouth, wine spilling down the front of his cassock. He fills the two glass pitchers and drinks from them, over and over, like two Cossacks passing the evening in conversation. But instead of calming him down, the drink has further stirred his soul, heightened his pain. He fumbles through his trunk of vestments and, finding a bottle of rye whiskey, he tucks it in a pocket in his robe.

On the wall facing him hangs the icon of the Sacred Heart of Jesus. The icons are windows to prayer, he thinks. The Sacred Heart appears to beat against its girdle of thorns. It bleeds.

Marusia knelt at his feet just nights ago in this room, and now she's dead. Did she give him the Evil Eye? What power has he against the Devil? Against the Devil's bride? The more he drinks, the more he sees the image in the willows. A clap of thunder shakes the tiny room, and Kobzey staggers to his feet, and clasping the candelabrum he proceeds to the altar. Once more the flashes light the icons so their gazes glare down as fiery darts into his soul. He steps back, his heel upsetting a jar containing dried pussy willows left at the side of the altar still from the Easter celebrations. He reaches down for a twig, when again the church lights up and thunder shakes the windows and even the candle flames.

Kobzey had blessed the pussy willows at the Lenten service when women brought them, bouquets promising spring. He had blessed a tub full of water, and the women filled quart sealers to take to their homes along with the willows he had sprinkled with the Holy Water. The police used the tub. They took it from the bell tower and hired Paraska Semchuk to wash the maggots from Marusia's body.

Kobzey holds the pussy willow twig before the candelabrum's flames. The Roman church blesses palm leaves waving the entry of Christ into Jerusalem. Instead Kobzey's people wave pussy willows. Do they celebrate spring or Christ? Maybe both. During a storm when an old woman is afraid, she sets the willow branch on fire, then douses it with Holy Water.

The banner of St. Michael, the Archangel, beckons to him. He snuffs the candles, then unclasps the long wooden handle of St. Michael from the wall and stumbles out of the church, standing on the step, the banner high above him flapping in the wind. When the lightning flashes, the bush surrounding the yard looms before him each way he turns. The tree-tops sway, hissing like ocean spray hitting rocks. The black poplars groan and creak. He hears the crack of a tree splitting.

Bracing against the wind, Kobzey proceeds around the church, his banner held forward, snapping. Then at the bell-tower he tugs on the rope again and again. *Ding-dong, ding-dong, ding-dong,* pealing through the thunder, *Kobzey is coming! Kobzey is coming!* The wind lashes through the yard, whipping Kobzey's robe, and high up on the church a metal cross breaks from its mount and clatters down the cupola, tumbling off the roof.

Kobzey recalls the story of the Devil's night, that in times past the Devil schemed to capture the Good Lord. He built a flour mill, and within it devised a mesh-work of chains for a trap. But instead of catching the Lord, the Evil One entangled himself forever. Only on a Devil's night can he break loose and fly across the sky. On such a night the wind rips roofs from churches, crosses are swept into the air, following after him. Tonight the Devil flies to his daughter Marusia. Kobzey must go there too. Opening, then closing the churchyard gate, he stops and takes a long drink of whiskey before he leaves to find the path.

The reeds sway in the wind, their brown tassels nodding like millions of frantic little people. On and on Kobzey marches, keeping to the path, his banner high, forming prayers in his mind to bless the icon in the willows.

Soon Kobzey's entangled. He's in a narrow place where the willows cover the path, and he crawls in the wet on his hands and knees groping for his banner. He pulls at branches till at last he finds his staff. Rain falls in large drops, spattering more and more, and then, as if the warning given, it sweeps down in sheets. Kobzey ignores the rain. Supported by his staff, his shoes sliding in the wet moss, he climbs to his feet. Where is the icon of the willows? Is it gone to the island? The old woman Dounia says those black spirits dwell on the island of reeds. He reels with his banner, floundering in muck, stumbling out into the reeds, water to his knees.

A sudden lull in the storm brings a new sound to his ears, and he stops to listen. The lightning flashes again, and to his right in a clump of bulrushes an alabaster maiden stands singing:

> *They will take me with them,*
> *The little one, the young one,*
> *Like a red cherry.*

She dives into the water, and all he sees is the tail of

a fish. A bolt of lighting streaks down the sky, cracking the air, the very next second sounding like the splitting of ice. Reeds, bulrushes and trees stand as if frozen at attention. Kobzey slogs through the water, attempting to run to the woman, but his feet catch in the muck and he falls to his knees. Clinging to the staff of his banner, for the second time he pulls himself upright and waits. From far away something hisses, as if burning pussy willows are being doused in Holy Water. All at once a ball of fire spins towards him, then veers to the side, bouncing across the swamp, then another and another, three balls of fire dancing, bouncing, rolling every which way before his eyes.

Among these swirls of fire the maiden rises. She lifts her skirts to her waist and jumps again and again, the balls spinning to and fro between her legs. *"Ha, ha, ha, ha!"* Rising and falling she swoops over the water, further and further to the west, fireballs racing with her out of sight across the swamp.

TWENTY-SEVEN

Rose's marriage is not the same anymore. Their teacherage when they moved in two years ago, like a playhouse for her to fix up and decorate, when she could even put up with the rats in the porch, all of it seems to have lost its purpose. She's even thought of leaving, going home to her mother. All summer at the farm at least she had others to talk to. Here there's only so much dressing up of a home she can do, and for what? For Yuri? She had hauled orange boxes from the Volga store to make a dresser in the bedroom. Sewed floral curtains for the open fronts. Upholstered an apple box for a stool.

How often she sits here rearranging her things placed out on the embroidered linen dresser scarf. Her ivory brush and comb set, her jar of Pond's Vanishing Cream...(just spread a white, cool mask of the Cream over cheeks, forehead, throat)...Kolynos Tooth Powder, Du Barry Face Powder...(three months of beauty for a dollar), Angelus Lipstick, Odorono Cream, her pearl broach.... Yuri's never said another word to her about his so-called "enchantment," and they don't talk about the murder, though they both follow the story in the *Dauphin Herald,* and Rose got a letter from her mother: *Vasylko Gregorovitch has been arrested and put in Dauphin jail. Hryhori Budka is helping with the harvest but seems very depressed, who can blame him?*

She takes needle, thread, and a button from her sewing basket, and Yuri's trousers hanging from the chair beside the bed. He has only two pairs for school. The Depression's over. When are they going to start paying him a decent wage? He doesn't stand up for himself and speak out. She doesn't know how long she can put up with his brooding.

Someone's knocking at the door. She straightens the mirror on her dresser and walks out of the bedroom. At the porch she opens the door to be greeted by Hryhori Budka.

"Praise be to Jesus."

He appears unwashed, and he stinks with body odour. Why would he come here? Her mother wrote that he wanders all over the country more than ever, and now he comes here. What could he want? She doesn't let him in, but instead joins him out on the step, the trousers folded over her arm. "Button missing," she says, and drops them on the porch railing. He's holding a bulky paper bag up in front of his face.

"You want to see Yuri?" She doesn't wait for an answer. "I'll run over and get him. He's working at the school."

"Praise be to Jesus," he says again.

She leaves him standing on the step; she doesn't want

to be alone with him, though he must be harmless. Hryhori has never hurt anyone. But as she leaves, his lips tremble, and his hands shake gripping the bag, his fists clenching and unclenching, crunching the paper.

When she returns with Yuri, Hryhori shows no sign of his turmoil. In fact, he is smiling.

"I have something to show you," he says. "The police didn't find this." Hryhori sets the bag on the kitchen table and, still holding on to it, he looks up at the orange boxes hanging on the wall: Rose's cupboards decorated with floral curtains, the same material she has in her bedroom, the same orange boxes. Yuri takes a deep breath and reaches through the curtains for an unopened bottle of rye. As if he can afford to feed him whiskey, Rose thinks. She had wanted to save the bottle for Nellie and Danylo who might come to visit after harvest. Hryhori will drink it all if they let him.

"To God," Hryhori says, raising the glass and drinking. He licks his lips and is about to say something, but Yuri interrupts.

"He wants to talk to me alone. I think man talk."

Rose goes to the porch and gets the trousers, then to the bedroom, closing the door, nothing said in protest or question. Not a glance back.

"I went to Vasylko's house." Hryhori peers into the bag. "This thing was in a box under some papers. Should I take it to the police?" He looks questioningly at Yuri, eye to eye, as if they share some kind of secret.

"What have you got?"

Hryhori pulls out a wood carving of a woman

figure, nearly a foot in height, placing it upright on the table. It's a model of Marusia standing naked, gazing upward, the fingers of both the statue's hands lacing her belly, legs apart.

"Has anyone else seen this?" Yuri asks.

"I showed it to the priest, and you know what he did? He threw it on the floor. He said, 'Take it to Belinski!'"

Yuri stares at the statue. How can this be? The carving is no doubt a work of art, and the likeness is remarkable. But it's more. Is it a sign? Is she coming back to him? Lines from the literature feed the torment that never leaves him. *"The taut body, which had not known motherhood, and was as fresh and rosy as a gilded cloud filled with warm spring rain, sailed freely and proudly through the young grass in the meadow."*

If only he and Marusia could be born again in the mountain pastures of Kotsiubynsky's Carpathia. If only Carpathia could be reborn....

TWENTY-EIGHT

Nellie, just like Rose, spends a good part of her mornings at her bedroom dressing table. Danylo had been hauling fish for Armstrong. Too wet to harvest, so off he went to Winnipeg, without Nellie. He would never take her along when he goes on business. He came back with a new two-barrelled shotgun for hunting ducks. He's not satisfied with his old single-shot. Where does he get the money? He never tells her how much Armstrong pays him. He did bring back some apples; he knows how much she likes them from Ontario, and he brought her a tiny bottle of nail polish.

She'd like to move to Ontario. There are jobs at the factories in Toronto. It would be easy for Danylo. Others have gone, and they write how good things are there. But Danylo just growls when she makes a suggestion. He says his friends are here. Some friends. He had wanted to visit Vasylko Gregorovitch at Dauphin, but that wasn't the way he was taking the fish. He went the shorter east way through St. Rose. She had wanted to go with Danylo. She feels like a prisoner on the farm, afraid even to go to the bush to pick mush-rooms. What if the murderer wasn't Vasylko, and Marusia Budka's real killer was hiding out in a bush shack like one of those Demchuk boys hiding from the army? It's not safe for a woman to be out.

Danylo laughed. How crazy you are, he said. Do you think some monster hides in the bush? But then she wonders if the killer might have been someone from the bombing and gunnery school at the airforce base in Dauphin. Some Frenchman coming out here to hunt, and he ran into Marusia.

Nellie wishes she could be with her mother and Lena at the fishing camp. She could make some money. Imagine Lena putting off school just to be with Nick. He's supposed to be on harvest leave, and there he is on the lake fishing. He said no Dieppe for him. Lena thinks he'll be around till the spring, even if they come looking for him. Even if he has to hide. It would be such fun to be up there at the fish camp with them.

Lena is so lucky the way Nick treats her, and she's not even that good-looking. Her figure is nothing like Nellie's. Lena's too tall. She's heavy, and wouldn't fit into Nellie's lingerie even if she wanted to. Five foot seven, and one hundred and thirty-five pounds. Nellie has blond hair, and Lena's is black. But Lena has better legs, and Lena's not married.

Maybe it's good that Marusia Budka is dead. Nellie doesn't know who murdered her, and she doesn't care. She doesn't think it was Vasylko, not because she has any good reason, but she feels it can't be him. She shudders to think it might have been Danylo. Why would he kill Marusia? If he had been fooling with her, would he be afraid that she might tell somebody? Nellie doesn't think so. If anybody had the right to hate her it should be Rose. What an awful thought that Rose might want to do it.

Nellie takes her box of lingerie from the dresser drawer, setting it beside her on the bed, opening the lid, feeling the silk. She examines the cover of *Movie Stars Parade*. A picture of Deanna Durbin. *Why Deanna's Marriage Failed.* Page forty-two, *Wedding of the year, April 1941. 500 relatives and friends jammed the church.* She leafs through the ads. *Exotic Glowing Earrings, glow in the dark. Want longer, stunning nails? All-vegetable hair remover. Girls get your man, fascinating course in five booklets.* She puts her hand on her stomach, feeling what she thinks is the beginning of a swelling tummy, a baby. She senses that she's blushing even at the thought of putting on her lingerie for whatever reason she'd put it on in the morning when she won't wear it at night. She walks over to the mirror, gazing into it, and then at Deanna Durbin on the front cover. Nellie's blond shoulder-length hair is full and glossy, like Deanna Durbin's, only Deanna's is black. She looks at the cover closely. Are Deanna's eyebrows plucked? She's not wearing earrings. Her coat matches her lipstick.

Nellie brushes her hair one hundred times, and then decides she'd better go help with the dinner. What must the Melnyks think? She's sitting in her room at ten-thirty in the morning while Danylo's harvesting. Her mother-in-law will need help with the rhubarb pies.

TWENTY-NINE

Danylo hauls this load of wheat right to town instead of shovelling it into the bin. He's taking it off the threshing machine to the elevator, in order to get money to pay the threshing outfit. They have hot and dry weather again after a two-day rain. Nothing better to breed mosquitoes. As his wagon nears Vasylko Gregorovitch's place, he sees a man sitting at the roadside on the plank bridge crossing the creek. For a moment he thinks it must be Vasylko, but then Danylo remembers that Vasylko's in jail. Driving up closer he can see that the man sitting is Hryhori Budka. Danylo pulls on the reins, stopping the team at the bridge, the horses facing down to Hryhori.

"Where have you been roaming?" Danylo asks. Hryhori doesn't answer. He holds a handful of rocks, tossing them *plop, plop, plop,* one at a time into the water.

"They need you at the outfit," Danylo says. "Pitching bundles." He points to the clouds on the west horizon. "Who knows how long we can thresh?

The weather is going to change again. Maybe it will rain again. Maybe snow."

As if awaking from a stupor, Hryhori blinks and murmurs, "Praise be to Jesus." He makes no attempt to get up on his feet, but instead draws the paper bag on the plank beside him closer to his body.

"Praise forever," Danylo says.

Hryhori peers up at him, blinking several times before saying anything more. It seems that he's trying to determine who it is that's talking to him.

"The police came to my house last week."

"They talked to me also, Hryhori."

"Nick Semchuk said you went to Winnipeg."

"I came back."

"What do you know about Marusia?" Hryhori stands up and walks in front of one of the horses, a spotted grey Belgian. He takes a carrot from his pocket, then, lifting the wire-mesh basket off the horse's nose, he feeds the horse.

Danylo leans forward from his seat on the wagon, trying to see Hryhori, but the horse is in the way. "What did you say, Hryhori?" All at once he sees him step forward, fist raised in the air.

"What happened with Marusia?"

"How do you mean, what happened?" Danylo says. "How should I know? Somebody killed her."

"I don't think Vasylko would do such a thing."

"Vasylko is crazy," Danylo says. "Who knows what he can do." Danylo quickly points down at the planks. "What do you have in the paper bag?" Hryhori goes to it and pulls out a bottle of home-brew. It's three-quarters full. He shakes his head and mumbles something to himself, then, approaching Danylo on the wagon, he hands him the bottle. "Marusia made for me."

Danylo holds it, hesitates, then hands it back. "You keep it."

Hryhori squints, then puts the bottle back into the bag, this time pulling out the wooden figurine, offering it up. Danylo stares at the statue, at Hryhori's weeping eyes, and again at the statue.

The wood is polished smooth, beyond the beauty of ordinary wood, and it's oiled the colour of amber, all the curves and valleys of a woman's body, the likeness of a goddess. Danylo brings it to his nose, smelling the wood and the oil of Brunswick sardines. He holds the statue at arm's length. How was it possible for someone to carve the hair tossed about and touching her lips, as if she's exposed to the wind? "Where did you get this?"

"I'm taking it back to Vasylko's," Hryhori says.

"He gave it to you?"

"No."

"Take it back, Hryhori. Then go to the farm. The outfit is in the field west of the yard."

THIRTY

The priest is relieved that with harvest the people have no time for him. He's had his fill of their problems. Each time he goes to the Gruber church, the Church of the Nativity of the Blessed Virgin Mary, he is faced with just about anything. They come to him crying with disaster after disaster. *Protect us from our fears. Forgive us.* What benefit is there to forgive? If only Kobzey could undo the wrongs. Why should God forgive a murderer? Do repentance and forgiveness bring Marusia Budka back to life? No one has returned the washtub to the church bell tower. How could he bless Holy Water in such a tub when all he would be able to think about is maggots and the stink? Not even the police will haul it out of there for evidence. Let the washtub stay at the swamp to rust.

Kobzey sits in his kitchen dabbing his spoon in his soup. Limp cabbage swimming. A piece of pork. He recalls the gold coin on the kneeling Marusia's neck. The scent of sweet basil. How he yearned to lean forward to touch her breast. In confession he is the instrument of God.

He tastes his soup. Lukewarm. Dips bread in it, from a loaf given to him by the old woman Dounia. How she puts her faith in him, as if he is himself a Christ to carry the cross of the people's sins. He is the responsible one, the father confessor, giving them freedom to do as they please as long as they ask forgiveness. They must believe that when he's at the altar with the smoking incense from his censer that it purges the corruption of his flesh, and he's transformed to Holiness, God-like in his robes. But at his table where he sits spooning cabbage soup he wears trousers like any man. He can't fool himself.

From a bowl he takes an apple from those his housekeeper, the widow Sloboda, had brought him, and rising from the table he crosses over to the window. On the other side of the road the stump piles in the field are smouldering, the smoke curling upward in the evening stillness. He bites into the apple, carelessly, so that juice spills from the side of his mouth, trickling into the bristles on his chin. He lifts the window open, biting off pieces of the apple and throwing them on the ground, watching a sparrow peck and fly away.

There is not much for Kobzey to do this evening, other than pray, and when the time comes for him to go to bed he knows he will not sleep. In the morning he will have mass at seven o'clock for Mrs. Sloboda and three or four other old women. They are devout, but as for the other people, it is not easy for an educated Ukrainian priest to reach them spiritually. Fortunately on Thursday he will take the train to Winnipeg for a meeting with the bishop. The city will be a welcome change.

THIRTY-ONE

Panko has in the past discussed things with Kobzey, matters of lust, of all things. Usually they talk over a glass of whiskey. For a priest Kobzey knows a lot about lust. Of course it is his business to know about sin. He hears of it all the time from confessions. When Kobzey has had enough to drink, sometimes his tongue gets loose. It is one of Panko's pleasures to listen to the priest, not in church, but when the two of them can have a drink.

One evening after Marusia's death they talk of matters even more serious.

"I bring you Holy Water," Panko says, and hands the priest a two-quart sealer of home-brew. "Maybe we have time for a little drink." The two sit at a small table lit with a lamp Mike Melnyk had at one time provided for the cottage, and not for just a little drink, but many, for the duration of the night.

"What is the Devil?" Panko asks, and Kobzey tells the story of the angels fighting, Lucifer chased from heaven. He tells the story of Adam and Eve and the Serpent.

"No," Panko says, "I don't think it was so simple; a snake talking to a woman so that ever since then everyone of us has to pay. I don't think so." Then he tells the priest of bad things people do. How twenty years ago John Zwarichka poisoned Wasyl Demchuk's well. Wasyl had seduced John's wife in the barn loft and John found out. Each man would blame the Devil. Why not blame somebody besides yourself when you get in trouble? How else can people define the Devil? Has anyone been to hell and come back to tell what the Devil looks like?

"And God?" Kobzey asks, after many drinks. "What is God?"

"God is good things," Panko says. "That's all."

"No," Kobzey says. "Our people here know nothing of God." At this point Kobzey proceeds to tell Panko the strangest of tales. He begins simply enough, a religious point of view with no complications. "Without repentance, no salvation," he says.

"Of course not," Panko says.

"But what is true repentance?" Kobzey stares into Panko's eyes, as if searching there to find the answer.

What does Panko know about this question? When has he ever considered such matters? Confession is confession, after all. Is not the priest happy enough with this?

"In the Old Country is the mystery of the *Khlysty*," Kobzey says. He tells of simple peasants who seek salvation, living most frugally, touching no liquor, fasting, and when they were to have Holy services, they even abstained from what Kobzey calls carnal pleasures.

For these occasions the peasants would gather at

dusk, sitting on benches in a humble dwelling, women on the left, men on the right. In the middle of the room one couple sat at the table. When the sun set the window was covered with a blanket.

What do the *Khlysty* believe? Man is nothing, a filthy sinner, a clay vessel. His only hope is that somehow this vessel can be filled with the waters of the Holy Spirit. But he must first be reduced to nothing, the false ego removed from the clay jar. The *Khlysty* begin singing, calling for the Kingdom of Heaven, for the downpouring of these waters.

"The Blood of the Lamb," Panko says. "I remember this spring, it was Good Friday, you preaching about the Blood of the Lamb washing sins." Kobzey ignores him, so immersed is he in his story.

They have nothing in their houses. No pictures. No curtains. No *sopilka*.

Panko interrupts again. "Not even flowers?"

"Not even a poppy."

Panko knows a group of Protestants living north of Fishing River. For them life is simple: everything is either black or white. If you don't believe with them, you believe with the Devil. These people must have heads swelled even bigger than the Polish. They believe that because Adam and Eve ate the apple, everybody merits nothing. You'd think then at least everybody would be the same, but not so. They believe that they alone receive the waters of the Grace of God to drown the Devil. All the other people the Devil has speared on his fork.

The apple is more interesting for Panko. He wonders that if mankind were given another chance, if it were left up to him and Paraska, what would they do? There's no doubt in his mind. She would scheme some way to get him to bite. That's how she is, and then she would blame him for it. But even without Paraska, biting that apple would have been tempting. Just imagine how much has rested on that one decision – all of mankind condemned. Imagine even more that if the chance came around again, Panko would probably do the same as Adam. How can he explain it? He wonders if even the Protestants at Fishing River would choose to eat the apple again? Maybe for a different reason than Panko, who would bite out of curiosity. Maybe the Protestants would bite because they like to protest. Maybe they would bite because they like the scheme that they alone receive the gifts of God's grace; they want none of these others with them in heaven.

But sometimes two sides claim God's ownership, sometimes twenty or thirty sides, each saying the Devil plants seeds of false salvation in the hearts of all the others. The trick would be to find the authentic side, and surely, Panko thinks, it couldn't be these *Khlysty* that Kobzey talks about.

Panko wonders about salvation. The question is not really one of getting to the next life successfully, it's more a matter of getting through this one. It's why the people need the priest. You have to have rules to keep things together, and a priest to keep the rules up to date. Is Kobzey worried that the young people are straying to the movie houses and the English language? Is he talking of these *Khlysty* because he's searching for a stronger book of rules?

Most people follow rules, and life goes on. The trouble with these times is that some are beginning to think they can choose. The rules are all mixed up with everybody else's, and life is becoming a patch quilt.

But *Khlysty?* Maybe in some village in Ukraine, in secret like communists meeting in somebody's basement in Winnipeg, but not Topolia. But then why not? What better place for hidden gatherings than the bush?

Panko can't believe what the priest is telling him. Kobzey says that throughout their evening services the singing of the *Khlysty* becomes more and more inspired, more jubilant and ecstatic, and gradually one after another the peasants disrobe, and replace their clothing with white muslin gowns.

Panko says nothing more. He neglects his drink and moves not even an eyelash. Only his fingers move to roll a cigarette and to strike a match. He forgets to extinguish it, and burns himself. The flame of the coal oil lamp on the table flickers and smokes, and shadows dance on the walls. Kobzey turns the wick to steady the flame.

The *Khlysty* peasants in that mud-walled dwelling in the remote Ukrainian village sing to the light of twelve wax candles, song after song, until at last a woman rises and begins turning round in a circle. Other women and men step up from their benches, forming pairs, round and round in a circle. Faster and faster they dance, skipping, running crosswise, arms raised, calling on the Holy Ghost. The people of God feel the beating of the wings of the Holy Ghost above their heads. The man and woman at the table are Christ and the Mother of God steering the ark of the righteous towards the Heavenly Kingdom. The peasants cry out, "The Holy Ghost is among us!" and they repeat it over and over until their tongues are numb and their limbs limp from the dance. The man at the table rises, waving his hands, stammering, sputtering, yelling, laughing, crying, speaking in tongues. The peasants huddle on the ground around him, trembling and weeping and crossing themselves.

"Ah," Panko says, "Holy Rollers. They are crazy."

"But that is not all," Kobzey says. Panko is not sure if, even with the liquor he's drunk, he wants to hear much more of this. Foolishness is foolishness, but he's not comfortable the way the priest stares through him. He tells of how the wild dancing continues hour after hour, a confusion of noise and billowing muslin gowns. The floor is wet with the sweat of the dancers. Suddenly they bare themselves to the waist and one by one bow before the man at the table, who whips them with a switch of willow shoots.

Then, as on the day of Resurrection Christ shed his garment of mortality and rose in the spirit, both men and women discard their gowns, dancing in a frenzy. Some fall to the floor in convulsions. The candles are blown out and women unbind their hair and fall upon the men. In sinful encounter they roll on the floor.

"This is how they find God?" Panko asks. "A strange way."

The priest and Panko stare at the lamp, saying

nothing. Panko has to digest what he has just heard. He has to search for some message. Maybe the priest is saying that everyone does the same dance in life's search, only in different ways. Kobzey adjusts the lamp wick to again stop the flame from flickering, and then he talks.

"Before man can find God, he must at first destroy the last of his arrogance and pride, to end the influence of his earthly ego. The way to true submission is through the deepest self-abasement in carnal sin. This is what the *Khlysty* believe."

"How can sin find God?"

"Repentance," Kobzey says. "Maybe they go back to the man at the table and ask to be forgiven. Maybe they carry their sinful burden with them to the next gathering. Maybe it's true that repentance works only if a man is well steeped in his feelings of worthlessness."

"And you believe this?" Panko finishes his drink, then pours another, drinking all of it in two swallows. Then, shaking the drops from the glass, he pours for the priest. Kobzey stares at the liquid in the glass as if gazing into a crystal ball. After a moment he looks up at Panko.

"Is it that in their ecstasy they are drunk in the spirit, and not the flesh?"

"Seems like flesh to me," Panko says.

"Did you have passion for Marusia Budka?" Kobzey asks.

"She was a beautiful woman," Panko says. "But I'm an old man already. At the same time, there is no harm to look. God has beautiful things on this earth. Are they not to be admired?"

"Of course."

Kobzey sips from the glass as if to test the quality of the whiskey, then he too drinks all of it down.

THIRTY-TWO

The police can't hold Vasylko prisoner in Dauphin forever. He doesn't answer questions, as if his apparent uncertainty with the English language has conveniently struck him dumb. His questioner describes the special room in the back of the courthouse. Would Vasylko like to see the gallows with the trap door you fall through when the rope grabs to snap the bones in your neck? A man would dangle like a puppet on a string. Still Vasylko will say nothing. In turn they allow him time and materials to carve things when he's alone in his cell during the day. He suspects that they think he might exhibit some hint, some clue to the murder.

A week is too long to sit in a cell. They do not have the evidence to hold him this long, no facts to lay formal charges. Who do they think they are? Don't they know he has important things to do at home? They can't hang him. They can't keep him locked up. Canada is a free country, isn't it?

Of course, and the police show Vasylko how free it is by letting him go. They are even going to buy him a train ticket to ride back to Topolia tomorrow morning. He'll get off at Fork River. He doesn't have his bicycle in Topolia, and it's a closer walk home from Fork River. So much to do. The potatoes should be dug. He has to get his mail. Saw up firewood for winter. Though it's still a while before snow falls, in truth he really doesn't have that much time. With all his attention to fuss and detail, he doesn't usually get much done, doesn't get finished, doesn't even get started some things because of worry. He's better with the toy world of his wood carvings where he can predict what they will do, where he can count on them, not like real people.

He will go by the swamp. Sitting in his cell all week he's had time to think. His mother is buried out there. They accused her of being a witch and killed her with stones. He knows where the grave is, overgrown with red birch and willow. Years ago he made the cross, forming the cement himself, marking it with the crescent moon and stars, the ancient signs no one remembers anymore. He must remember to pick purple asters for the grave like he does every fall.

He must see to his coins also. More than anything else during his week in jail, he worried that he might somehow give away the secret of his treasure to the police, that they'd somehow smell it out of him. Spit on the Devil that the government would get its hands on his gold. Bad enough he's revealed the one Maria Theresa by mailing it to the woman. The rest will stay buried in the ground, but he will go to the spruce tree now and then. He thinks of the anthill and the woman's buried coral beads. He will dig them up. The bump on his temple throbs as he remembers her naked by the anthill in the forest hiding place, the memory of his carved statue.

He might be released from jail tonight. The policeman was driving to Fork River to catch someone night fishing. Someone has a net in the river. At the same time, the policeman said, it's a good opportunity to look for army deserters. He has a list. If Vasylko will show him the walking trails in the bush by the river they'll go tonight, and Vasylko won't have to spend another night in the cell.

It's midnight, and he doesn't mind the darkness of the bush because he's alone, away from policemen. There's more harm in the daytime facing flesh and blood human devils, then there is walking at night among the spirits. He's comfortable with the light of the crescent moon and stars in the sky over the swamp, the rustle of grass, frogs croaking, the chirp of crickets.

The night is at its darkest when he reaches his yard. He didn't expect a lamp would be burning, didn't expect that someone would be in his shack. Vasylko stands beside the raspberry canes growing by the edge of the bush bordering his yard. He decides to go closer to the window. Sneak in the dark so as not to be noticed, but he must see who's there.

In the lamplight Vasylko's statue of the woman stands tilted in the clutter of sardine cans, egg shells, and soiled papers and box tops on the table. Hryhori Budka bends over the table, an axe and a sharpening stone in his hands. The axe crashes down on the statute, splitting it in two. He chops again and again, wood splintering and sardine cans rattling. He drops the axe and attempts piecing bits of wood together, finally sitting on a box, his hands gripped to his temples.

These two men have been neighbours within a mile of bush from one another. Yet, as if taking different paths, they have kept apart. They have been independent one from the other, keeping out of each other's way, not out of respect, but more so as if they each have a certain loathing for what the other does, and it's not worth it to interfere.

But Vasylko owes him something, even if only to have seen the man's wife in the flesh. Some night in secret he will take the coral beads and leave them for Hryhori Budka to find. As for now, Vasylko will wait by the bush until the widower leaves.

THIRTY-THREE

Early in the morning on a drizzly Sunday, Ivan Stupych lights the first fire before winter in the store's pot-bellied stove. He sweeps chunks of dirt and dust from the mud tracked in yesterday, preparing the floor for an application of oil, a treatment he administers twice a year.

Before he starts he empties the water from the ice-box and puts in a new block of ice. It doesn't last as long in the fall, the ice already old, lined with cracks and grooves, losing its lustre. With his trolley he moves the vinegar barrel from the entry to the back of the store behind the counter, out of the way because he wants to clear the floor in order to mop on the oil.

In his bones he can feel the cold drizzle outside, but slowly the heat from the stove extends itself, soaking into his back like the oil will soak into the floorboards. He stops to roll a cigarette of Ogden's fine cut tobacco. Somehow, in the fall, with a warm fire and the aromas of Ogden's, floor oil, leather harness, bags of flour, and the vinegar barrel, it's not so bad to own a store.

But he shouldn't be so complacent. His reverie is

broken at 7:30 a.m. when Metro Zazelenchuk appears on the front step. Ivan watches as Metro scrapes the bottoms of his boots on the piece of angle iron screwed to the edge of the step. Left foot once, twice, right foot once, twice, but Metro doesn't examine carefully, doesn't wipe what's left hanging on the heels. He opens the door and stands in the entry, brushing excess water from his clothing onto the swept-up pile of dirt at his feet.

"Here," Ivan says, and hands him the broom and a dust pan. "You want to do something, sweep up that pile and throw it outside on the road. Then take your muddy boots off before you come in any farther."

Metro does what he's told for a change. He would never do such a thing for his wife Dounia, but the men are old friends. They are used to each other from many years of visits in the store. If Ivan had a penny for every hour Metro has sat here gabbing over the years it would add up to quite a sum.

"You come from town?" Ivan asks, after Metro completes the sweeping and is drying himself at the stove.

"From town? Of course not. I would be a drowned rat if I walked all the way from town. I'm at the farm. It's harvest time, you know." He proceeds behind the counter, steps up on a Coca-Cola box and perches himself atop the vinegar barrel. He's out of the way of Ivan's mop and oil can. "Pass me your Ogden's," Metro says.

"Help yourself on the counter." The green package sits between them, Ivan mopping and Metro sitting.

The latter has to lean forward and reach, holding one hand against the counter to prevent himself from falling off the barrel. Ivan pays him no attention, screwing the cap off the oil can and pouring a small puddle on the floor. He sweeps back and forth with his mop, working the oil into the wood.

"Crazy bastards let Vasylko out of jail," Metro says.

"Who?"

"Vasylko Gregorovitch."

"I know who was in jail. Who let him out? You mean the police let him out of jail?"

"Who else? Unless he broke out. I saw smoke coming from his chimney when I walked by this morning. He's home. I saw a shirt and underwear on his clothes-line. More washing than drying with this weather." Metro takes off his denim coat. He takes a package from a pocket and drops the coat on the Coca-Cola box. Inside the package he has a bundle of garlic bulbs which he places on the counter. "You sell for me?" he asks.

Ivan glances but keeps mopping. "How could I sell garlic? Everybody grows garlic. Who's going to buy garlic bulbs?"

"For cucumbers. Dounia packs them in a crock."

"Of course. Everybody does. But everybody grows garlic." Ivan pours another puddle of oil on the floor.

Metro butts his cigarette on the side of the barrel. He rubs his hand over his face, feeling the whiskers of a three-day growth. His body has an odour, unwashed and damp, but he doesn't notice.

"Must have been rape."

"What?" Ivan asks. He takes his package of tobacco

and moves a soft drink box away from the vicinity of the stove, sitting down.

"They should never have let him out." Metro's face is puffy with a purplish tinge, not from an excessive over-indulgence, but over the years, with a drink now and then, and heavy foods, the diet has marked him, like it has most of the men. He licks his lips and grits his tobacco-stained teeth, an eye tooth missing. "Rape before he killed her." Metro gazes in the direction of the horse collars hanging on the wall beside the post office cubicle. "Maybe he killed her first."

"Lord save us!" Ivan says. Metro has never stopped talking about the murder to anyone who will listen. People are saying he's a nuisance already. Who's got time during harvest to hear him rant on about what a shame was the murder of Marusia Budka? That for him it was like losing a daughter.

"Who knows?" Metro says. "Maybe somebody English from the air force training base in Dauphin came out to the swamp to hunt ducks. Maybe he ran into Marusia. Such a shame."

"Somebody English. You would know," Ivan says. He shakes his head and picks up his mop.

"You hear what happened Wednesday?"

"No." Ivan mops behind the counter, at the foot of the vinegar barrel under Metro's dangling feet.

"You've heard how those English keep their sons out of the war? Some duke in England? Sent his boy all the way to the Dauphin training base to fly planes. On Wednesday the boy was looping his plane over the schoolhouse at Sifton. One too many loops and he crashed. Even his head came off. That's how he stayed out of the war. Some things are meant to be. Meant to be. Any sausage in that icebox?"

"Of course there's sausage in the icebox."

"Are we going to eat?"

"Are you going to pay?

"Trade you for the garlic."

"Never mind." Ivan takes a ring of sausage from the icebox and slices off pieces on the counter, Metro helping himself, Ivan telling him to watch out if he wants to keep his fingers.

"Something to wash it down?"

Ivan reaches under the counter for a bottle and a glass. He pours a shot for Metro, waits for the glass, then pours for himself. Metro gets off the barrel and goes to the radio, playing with the dial. The sound comes on. Prime Minister Mackenzie King is speaking.

THIRTY-FOUR

Panko wonders if Vasylko should have been released, but the police must know what they are doing. Besides, maybe he's not the murderer. But if he didn't do it, who did? Panko doesn't seem to be convinced one way or the other, and he argues back and forth, trying to convince himself one way this time, the other way the next. Sometimes he is positive Vasylko's innocent, then he imagines him standing by his bicycle watching the women on the railway station platform, his temple throbbing, fingers scratching his knee, and Panko begins to believe that he might be capable of performing the crime.

He wonders also about the poor husband, Hryhori Budka. He had been at Melnyk's threshing, but not for long. After three good days, the weather changed again.

It's wet and cold, raining one day, drizzling the next, and on another there's even skiffs of snow blowing across the meadows. The mood in the district turns gloomy. Stooks have to be loosened and turned to prevent the grain from sprouting, but because the bad weather is so prolonged, people wonder if anything will help to save the crop. If only the sun would shine. Not only would the stooks dry, but with all this moisture, some heat would bring on mushrooms, and there's nothing like mushroom-picking on a warm afternoon to change the sour outlook of the district women. But there is no sun and no warmth. The old women wonder, that with Marusia's death, whether the district is being cursed. Is this the Devil's revenge? Everyone sits and broods, waiting for this long spell of bad weather to break.

Hryhori Budka returns to the swamp path time and again. He hunts for clues. Today it is raining, but he ignores the discomfort. He looks at a mounded depression in the earth; it's one of the three tiny graves dug years ago for somebody's nameless baby before Hryhori came to Canada. Two weathered pieces of wood and a rusty nail are covered over with grass. He picks up the wood. "In the name of the Father, and Son, and Holy Ghost," he says, forming the pieces into their original form of a cross and putting it back, flat on the ground.

The rain falls gently, so gently that Hryhori could even say that it was thinking twice about touching the willow saplings, only a leaf here and there flickering. Whoever had dragged Marusia into the thicket had not been so gentle. Hryhori takes a knife from his pocket and cuts a stout sapling. He would like nothing better than to find the person, pull off his pants, drag him into the thicket, throw him into the willows with his ass showing. Hryhori would whip him.

It's not unpleasant for Hryhori to have these

thoughts. The scent of the muskeg in the rain serves like a medicine in his lungs. His whip is six feet long. *"Whack!"* He strikes one of the posts that used to hold up the church bell. *"Whack! Whack!"* Shreds of willow leaves cling to the wood. He hits the grass, *"Swish! Swish!"* then *"Splat!"* on the mud path. A Cossack warrior whips a fat Turk. *"Splat! Splat!"*

Hryhori stops. He notices that one of his boot laces is undone. He bends to tie it. On the wet ground before his eyes something glitters. He takes it in his fingers. Something round the size of a nickel. Four holes. The glisten of a dark green jewel. A button. Could this be his clue?

IT'S MID-AFTERNOON when Ivan Stupych sees the truck skidding to a stop in the water-filled ruts in front of the gas pump. Panko and Mike Melnyk are at the counter playing cards. Isaac Gruber's in the district selling.

"I wonder did he bring any more chocolate-covered cherries?" Panko says. The Jew huffs and puffs at the doorway, shakes water off himself, kicks mud from his boots, then walks to the men and lifts his heavy sample case to the counter.

"You want chocolates?" Isaac says. "How many dozen boxes?" Panko grins. He knows that the Jew can supply anything, he has even supplied the Holy pictures in their houses. With the war, sugar is in short supply, but he gets hundred pound bags for Panko. He gives the sugar to Panko in return for whiskey to take back to Winnipeg. Everything is in short supply with this war on, and if it wasn't for traders like Isaac Gruber, the city people would have nothing to eat.

But what he brings with him this trip is beyond anything the three card-playing Ukrainians could ever have imagined. After Ivan orders what he wants from the sample case, Isaac Gruber takes out a newspaper clipping. It's the story of the murder reported in the Winnipeg *Free Press*. The men are proud to see this, to see their district making the news as far away as Winnipeg.

"My nephew wrote me a letter," Isaac says. "Filled me in on all the gossip, even about you fellows and the chocolates." Panko and Mike look at Ivan Stupych and laugh, but then Isaac does something where all three can do nothing but gaze at the counter with their mouths hanging open. He tosses a coin on the counter, a heavy coin the size of a silver dollar, but not silver. Instead it is the rich and warm colour of gold. Near the rim a hole has been drilled. Without a doubt it is the coin Marusia wore around her neck that day.

"Where did you get this?" Panko says.

"My wife's brother has a pawn shop in Winnipeg." Isaac tells the men that he bought the coin, a ten ducat gold piece. He wanted it as a keepsake of stories his grandfather told about pogroms in the Old Country, and Jews fleeing with their lives and ducats sewn into their clothing.

"And what should happen after I buy? The very next day a letter comes from my nephew telling about the coin missing from the woman's neck."

Ivan scratches under his ear. His eyes go from the coin to Mike to Panko. "Maybe the police...?" he says.

"Where did your wife's cousin get this?" Panko says.

Before Isaac Gruber can answer, Hryhori is at the door, soaking wet and puffing for breath. "A button! I found a button!"

THIRTY-FIVE

Two days later the police are at Fishing River, at Yuri Belinski's school. They have come to question him. Yuri lets the children out to play.

"Is your name Yuri Belinski?"

"Yes."

"Did you know a Marusia Budka?"

"Yes." The younger policeman writes while the senior officer continues with the questioning. Had he been to Winnipeg lately?

Yes, he had attended a teachers' conference.

Did he visit a pawn shop?

"No!"

Had he ever walked on the swamp path?

"No!"

Had he lost a button from his trousers?

"No!"

Did he kill Marusia Budka?

"No!"

THE POLICE WILL BE BACK, he's sure of it. The words

of Kotsiubynsky appear in his mind: *"Where is Marichka? He feels the need to tell her his whole life, his longing for her, his joyless days, his loneliness among hostile people, his unhappy marriage...."* That evening Yuri drives to Sifton to the priest.

"Please, Father, I must confess!"

Kobzey, sitting at his table reading, lifts his head, staring at the man who enters his house without knocking and falls on his knees before him.

"What is it?" Kobzey asks.

"Marusia Budka. She...."

From Danylo and Nellie's wedding, without a thought for his wife, he had flown away with Marusia, taking her to a hotel room in Dauphin. From the time of his dance with her, until he dragged her to the willows, he could think of nothing else.

He had lusted for Marusia, following her up the hotel staircase, noticing her hands holding up her skirts, and he saw the backs of her legs, giving him the urge to embrace them. For three days they made love.

He bought her coral beads and would have robbed to buy her whatever else she might want, but she said she wanted to go back. Hryhori couldn't manage by himself. And she questioned Yuri about his wife.

"Don't you miss Rose? Buy something for her."

Marusia took the train back to Topolia.

The days passed, and now and then Yuri resorted to Panko's home-brew to lighten his thoughts and relive his moments with Marusia. In the Volga store when Marusia came to him with the chocolates he could not bear to look at her. He saw the golden charm around her neck, and he was jealous. Who has given this to her? Maybe if he could talk to her alone she would tell him there was no other man, and yes, she would come with him, and they could run off once more.

He waited on the path, by the old church space, the place of those babies' graves. An iron bar hung from a post. Grass grew up around it, and three or four morning glories wound around the stems. He began imagining lying with Marusia on a bed of grass. He tramped down a small space hidden off from the path, and then he sipped whiskey from a quart sealer.

He did not know what he would say to her, or what she would say to him. But he knew she had gone to church and that she would return home this way. The sun was beginning to sink when she appeared. He saw her from a distance, the box of chocolates cradled in her arm. Marusia stopped.

"You are here," she said.

"Marusia...."

"Why are you here?" She stepped backwards, away from him.

"Marusia, I saw you in the store...."

"Look," she said, pointing down the path, "in the bulrushes." A boat had been pulled up on shore, partially hidden by the reeds. She ran to it and he followed. A hunter had left empty shotgun shells in the bottom of the boat, and a smattering of duck feathers spotted with blood.

"Take me for a ride," she said. He said nothing, but he pushed the boat off the shore as if it was meant for them to go boating, as if it was a romantic outing in the late afternoon. He began rowing and she started laughing, watching him. "Faster," she said, and began rocking side to side.

"Don't," he said. He noticed the charm on her neck. "Where did you get that, Marusia?" He reached for it but she swept his hand away.

"Don't touch me," she said.

"Who gave it to you?"

"How should I know?"

She was keeping a secret from him.

"What do you mean, 'How should you know'? Of course you know!"

The early evening sun reflected off the gold piece. At once he was reminded of a rival, and he knew it couldn't be Hryhori.

"Who?" he said, then jerked the coin from her neck. She flung herself to the side, one way and then the other, as if purposely trying to tip the boat. The empty shotgun cartridges rolled back and forth at Yuri's feet, unnoticed, jarring something to life on the floor of the boat. A small black object like the silken case of a moth's cocoon slowly unfolded its wings, and then it flew up to cling to Yuri's pantleg. He swatted at it, brushed it off with his hands and kicked it where it landed on Marusia's lap. It spread itself on the palm of her hand, thin black wings like rubber and fur and silk. For a moment both of them sat silently watching as Marusia stroked the wings with the tips of her fingers.

The next moment Marusia glared at Yuri. "My coin," she said, and threw the bat at Yuri's face. He lunged backwards, falling into the water into a tangle of bulrushes. As he sloshed his way to the shore he thought he could hear hostile laughter and far-away voices.

"Are you laughing, Marusia?"

"Of course not, Yuri. I didn't laugh. You must have imagined it."

For a moment he'd forgotten where he was, as if he were being drawn through forest streams in Carpathia, as if they were figures of haunted tales.

When Marusia came to the shore he grabbed her by the elbow, shaking her, and pulling her from the boat.

"You don't have to grab me. You don't own me, Yuri." She stood face to face with him on the path. "And I would like my coin that you tore from my neck."

"No."

She reached up and slapped him.

"No," he said. "No!" Again she slapped. The muscles in his neck twitched, and he clutched her by the shoulders, shaking her until her anger turned to fear.

"Let me go," she said, "please!" and he slapped her. What got into him so suddenly? Was he angry from the drenching in the water? Because she stood up to him? Because he couldn't have her? He became a monster ready to devour Marusia. "You have to love me. I'm telling you to love me," and he held her tighter, but she squirmed and broke away, running. He chased after her, catching her, the two of them wrestling to the ground.

"Get off! Get off!" She kept screaming. He covered her mouth, but she bit him. He drew his hand to his mouth and tasted the blood.

"Bitch!" he said, and slapped her again, then grabbed her throat, pressing hard with his fingers. She reached into his pants and grabbed his testicles, pulling as hard as she could until he let go of her.

On her feet again, she ran at him. "You son-of-a-bitch!" she said, kicking at him, clawing at his face. He ducked, and grabbing the iron from the post, he struck. She fell down and grabbed him by the legs. He hit her again and again....

So, KOBZEY THINKS, STROKING HIS WHISKERS. Here is the one who killed the witch. How miserable he looks. Doesn't he know that he's done everybody a favour?

This is Kobzey's first reaction. He wants to be rid of his passions for this woman, and Yuri's deed has done away with her, even if the priest cannot rid himself of her memory. Then he thinks that this Yuri has erased any chance Kobzey might have had for carnal knowledge of Marusia. This is how it goes with him, a struggle, back and forth. Why is he thinking this way? A sinner has come seeking the grace of God, and the priest must answer to his office.

"You must pay for your sin," Kobzey says. "Go to the police."

"But can you cast out my demons? Pull the bat skins from my hair?"

"I will ask for God's power. Pray with me," the priest says, "for your soul's salvation."

THIRTY-SIX

It would be easy for somebody to tell Rose "I told you so," but who would want to be so mean? Panko hopes at least that she'll be able to hold together. She's a hard worker, and Isaac Gruber has said that she could easily get a job in the city. He'd find her one if she wanted. Panko has always said that matters such as these are never as hopeless as they seem. Who knows, if they hang Yuri, and she doesn't want to go to Winnipeg, there are lots of men around who would make a good husband, better than Yuri.

Panko's daughter Nellie was certain that Rose would go to Winnipeg. What an opportunity, she had told Lena, who told Nick, who told Panko. The Hollywood magazines didn't tell her that marriage would bring a mother-in-law. For ten cents Nellie would trade Danylo for Yuri and go to Winnipeg herself.

Panko felt sorry for Hryhori Budka. "Take him food," he told Paraska. The poor man sits day after day in front of his house whittling a stick. Marusia had been like a mother to him, cooking, carting him from weddings, managing the little money he earned scrubbing bush. Now he is helpless, even letting the cow go dry. It's like he doesn't care to live anymore.

Vasylko Gregorovitch talked about his jail experience with whoever would listen. He showed Nick and Lena the carvings he was making, a model of the police station and the jail cell. He showed little figures of a policeman at his desk, and himself behind bars, all the pieces fitted in a shoe box he stored under his bed. Vasylko had never been away from home before. At the store he'd come and talk about the murder, and about jail. The police had brought him meals from the café, he said. But in all the matters he talked about, he never said a thing about his jar of gold. When Panko asked him about Marusia's coin, he would disappear. Maybe he knew it was dangerous to be different during times of trouble.

Nick worked for the Armstrong Fishing Company. Maybe he was taking too much of a chance with the army, but they hadn't come searching yet. It was odd that the Mounties weren't after him; they could be too busy with the murder. Did the military in Winnipeg even think to bother about someone like Nick out here in the bush? They probably know that one of these days he will show up in Winnipeg. He will have to sit in jail for a month or two, that's all.

Paraska was cooking at the camp, and Lena was gutting fish. Out of school and earning money. She was close to Nick. They said they'd stay up at the north end of the lake until the trial, at first thinking that it might not be till spring anyway. But that's not how things turned out. Panko had to come right in the dead of winter to get them for the preliminary hearing.

The Ukrainians are tiny and mild compared to the lake. In spring the bay laps its water over weeds and stones on the shoreline within sight of Gregorovitch's shack. The land is nearly level with the lake and the meadow floods. What story do the old women tell? Rusalka combs the water from her hair, filling the meadow. The naked goddess is a beauty clad only with her tresses falling to her knees. In spring what man can stand against her beauty? Her song lures him to the water and his death. The fish swim from the lake to shallow water, tossing and gasping, dying in the meadow grass. In fall when the north wind blows, waves slap the meadow. The water promises nothing. Eventually it freezes.

Panko had told Paraska that if she wanted to go fishing it was her business, but to not expect him to get mixed up in it; he was a farmer, not a sailor. As for Nick going, he and Lena Melnyk had been flying together like pigeons all summer, so it was no surprise that they went together to a fish camp. But in the end, who had to go get them? Of course, Panko.

He came to the fish camp by team and sleigh, crossing on the ice. He remembered his poor father saying that the lake was different in the winter, dangerous in a different way. In the summer the water could swallow you up, but in the winter it merely shuts you out, freezing you. A man is small on the ice, snow drifting at his feet like sand around a stick poking up on the desert. When lost out there, he is frightened to the death, his soul shrinking as if it is a dried pea. On the return trip from the fish camp Panko was grateful to see the Topolia homes, and to smell the smoke rising from their chimneys.

At the hearing in Topolia it was as if Yuri was somebody else, showing not a trace of his pride and upright bearing. They dragged him staggering into the hall. He crawled across the floor on his knees, prostrating himself to the judge. Panko had never before seen him like this; it was as if Yuri was drunk and crazy all at once. Maybe he couldn't live with what he had done. He kept yelling about bats, pulling his hair and shouting "Bats! Bats!"

Panko wonders if Yuri has lost his mind, or has someone smuggled him whiskey? The men have been talking about witches. What else could make a man kill a beautiful thing like Marusia? She had power over him, made him forget everything, his job, his family. What torment made him kill her and throw her into the willows? Must not it be recognized that he has fought the Devil, and the battle left his mind full of bats?

"You're bats!" Paraska told Panko. "Struggle? What struggle? Struggle with his pants!" She said Belinski was jealous, that's all. A man wants a woman, wants to do whatever he pleases with her. He can make love to her, slap her, kill her, whatever pleases him. What is the difference between a man or the Devil when either one wants a woman? No difference.

Panko would say a trial is a trial, but he didn't think that. He could see that not much good would come out of it, but for that matter he could see not much good coming from anything else. The people think always there will be a better tomorrow. They don't understand that people come and go, but nature is nature. The Ukrainian came to Manitoba with his strong back. He arrived and saw that for ten dollars he could be a landlord, and the government gave him a paper to prove it. He could make money and buy more and more land. But whose side is time on? The water will wait, the bush will wait, if not a hundred years, then two hundred years. The trees can be chopped, roots pulled, seed planted, and crops harvested. This the people have done. But for what? They are proud to work hard. But the wind howls across the lake just the same, and over the fields, and it whispers through the trees telling the Indians that someday the Ukrainians will be gone.

Years ago when the people came to this country even the women wrestled with poplar trees, because to grow cabbage you need the sun. The tree roots could cling like arms around rocks, but if a horse can't pull the stumps loose, a tractor can. Panko's generation started to clear the land, and Nick and Lena's generation will continue with it. But maybe when Panko is gone and Nick and Lena are very old, will the bush start returning, and Rusalka? Farmers will farm, but the children will scatter.

Some will stick around getting rich, one man on thousands of acres. Some day even he will vanish, and the grass will come back, the fish, and the forests. There will be no more chopped-down trees, and stumps pulled from the soil, but instead leaves, mushrooms, highbush cranberries, and Rusalka.

This trial is over the death of the woman Marusia. Flowers will grow in the swamp nourished with Marusia's blood. The flesh of Marusia remains in the soil. This is the Ukrainian presence.

Panko knows that his could be the last true Ukrainian generation, if it's not already gone to the dogs. The Ukrainians in the lake country are here only a short time. Panko is caught between two times, knowing the foolishness of the old, and the shallowness of the new.

Where have we come, and where will we go? Marusia's murder tells that this life is upside-down. The pattern of Ukrainian life is broken. Who is wise? The priest? Why not Gregorovitch? Soon nobody will live by Kobzey's rules anyway. Here they sit facing the rules of the English judge. There's no mistake. Belinski has murdered. Murder is murder, in Ukraine, or Canada. It's the same.

When the people talk about Marusia Budka, even now that she is dead, they say very little that is nice, nothing about her kindness, her joy, her generosity. All they say is that she was a tramp and deserved what was done to her. Even if they don't admit to it, in their hearts they don't mourn the death of a loose woman. They see it as God's punishment.

Panko feels sorry for her, but then he thinks that she must have done something in the swamp to make Yuri angry, and whether she did or not, she should have left him alone anyway. After all, Yuri has a wife. He lost his head, that's all. As for Marusia, some might say it was the evil power of the Rusalka. No, not Rusalka. Panko would not go that far. He would say that Marusia Budka was real flesh, not a fairy. She died. Yuri killed her. Some people pity him. They believe he lost his mind, a witch made him crazy. But he did kill her. He murdered an innocent woman.

"Baah! Innocent!" That's what some people say. "A whore!" It's always the man who is tempted. Every day he walks a narrow path, and maybe once a week a temptress lures him into the bushes. There he becomes confused. He confuses the act of love with the act of death, especially when it involves a woman like Marusia Budka.

Panko shakes his head. The act of love makes life, the act of death destroys it, both done to a woman, both through a man's passion. Cheap lust, so the district thinks. Some are even pleased that she is dead; a man-chaser, so good riddance. It's as if she can be butchered like a piece of meat. It's not that hard to see why some think this way, because it's how men talk, they laugh about a good-looking woman, comparing her to a piece of meat. How does Panko himself talk when the men are telling jokes in the store? But all the same, Panko considers, isn't it all right to say these things as long as a joke is just a joke? Maybe not.

This murder business gives Panko bad dreams, takes him to his boyhood, to his country village. Across the way from his family's home lived an old man who frightened all the children in the village, not that the man went out of his way to do this, the boys went to him. On a dark fall night they crawled by the edge of his storage shed to reach his wood pile, attempting to topple the logs, stacked in a long row. They did this for whatever reasons young boys have to taunt old men. Panko stayed far behind, outside the fence, for he was the youngest and not as brave as the others. But his fear was no less – the stories of the old man's whip were enough. This unseen whip grew in his imagination to gigantic proportions, and when the boys came running and yelling with fright, jumping over the fence, Panko ran to his parents' house.

It was said that the old man had not always lived alone, that at one time he had a wife and son. Where they might be, none of the boys ever discussed. To them he was a wicked old man who lived by himself.

This attack at the woodpile happened more than fifty years ago, and now Panko's dream brings the memory back. He is venturing into the backyard. The fence and the woodpile are gone, as is the old man. The shed sags and is open at one end. Inside the shed a torn wire netting hangs from the roof, and all at once a bird falls from the hole in the net and flutters to the ground. For a moment it looks up, its brown and yellow feathers in disarray, a bird the size of a dove. It has beautiful yellow feet. As Panko stares down at the bird, it flies away.

On the shed floor are three graves, marked with weathered headstones, as if the years have worn away at the rock. A name is scratched, uneven writing, *Genec,* or something, hard to make out, the name of some ancestor maybe. The centre stone marks a baby's grave, and a gaping hole is worn right through the monument. The three mounds are uneven and sloping upward to the headstones, and the earth is damp and grown over with moss. Panko tries to make out more of the scratchings when another bird darts out from the wire cage. This one is larger, the size of a hawk, but much different. It is coloured blue and streaked with white. Its beak is long and pointed like a needle and it has piercing beady eyes. Its beak snaps repeatedly as if scolding Panko, chasing him from the shed, then the bird flies back into the cage. Presently a female voice calls, from somewhere within the shed, a question, asking for a woman to return to the grave.

Somehow the brown and yellow bird makes him think of his Ukrainian soul. Tears come to Panko's eyes. He sees that the feathers on the bird's wing are out of place. It had shied away from the sharp-bill, the know-it-all bird, the perfect bird that knows when Panko and his people will die. The brown bird will die. This beautiful bird with dancing yellow feet and crippled wings, as best it can will fly away to die.

THIRTY-SEVEN

The lull of the December afternoon draws the card players away from the counter to the warmth of the pot-bellied stove. Panko scoops a handful of peanuts from a burlap sack nestled under the store window. Large flakes of snow float down, forming a rounded cap on the gas pump outside.

Ivan Stupych has stocked the store for Christmas with peanuts, ribbon mint candy, kegs of salted herring, sausages.

Panko throws his peanut shells into the woodbox and glances up to his old friend Stupych standing on a ladder and holding a framed picture of the Virgin Mary.

"Where did you get that?

"Isaac Gruber."

"I'll be damned," Panko says. He wonders if anything exists that the Jew won't sell. "Is it true, Ivan? No oranges this year?"

"Only California." He dusts the shelf and props the picture against the wall. "Just regular oranges." Isaac Gruber had said it wasn't possible for the wholesalers to get Japanese oranges because of the war.

Ivan puts his dust cloth under the counter, wipes his hands on his pants, and pulls up a Coke box, joining Mike and Danylo at the stove. Nick is by the window reading the *Dauphin Herald*.

"Isn't that something about the coin," Ivan Stupych says, scratching his head. "Imagine Vasylko!"

The police had been to the store yesterday. The young constable told Ivan that they had considered calling in Gregorovitch, but at the last minute decided against it. They knew he'd be hard to find, and the case did not depend upon his testimony.

Mike stares at his amber cigarette holder, his blue eyes squinting, sparkling.

"They'd have to tie him to keep him still." He drops ashes into the palm of his hand, from there to the wood box. "He'd make everybody nervous."

"I would like to know where he got that coin," Panko says.

"So would Isaac Gruber," Ivan says, "and he wants to know if Vasylko has any more gold."

Mike pulls the cigarette stub from the amber holder and shreds the remnant of paper and charred tobacco with his fingers. "Vasylko keeps to himself."

"Didn't he have a mother?" Nick asks from the window, directing his question to Panko. "Didn't somebody say she was a witch?"

Panko shells another peanut, saying nothing.

"Maybe somebody," Mike says after a moment. "A long time ago."

"Speak of the Devil." Danylo says. Vasylko appears, holding the door open, and stomping snow from his boots. He steps inside, shutting the door, facing the men at the stove. He stands beside the peanut sack close to Nick, rubbing the fogged-up lenses of his glasses with his fingers. Ivan lifts the board on the mail wicket. "Cheque for you Vasylko. From Sidney I. Robinson. Must be for the Seneca roots."

"They don't pay you in gold?" Danylo asks.

Vasylko backs up even further, almost falling backwards into the peanuts. He notices Nick with the newspaper. He steps wide around the men at the stove, gets his mail, then, keeping his eyes on Danylo, he goes to Nick. "Reading that court case?" he says. "Terrible thing! Terrible thing!" Vasylko reads intently, head bent close to the page. "Terrible thing!"

"How well did you know her?" Danylo asks. "Neighbour and all. Did you ever walk over and help her with the milking?" Vasylko picks up the newspaper. His hands shake as he holds the pages separating himself from Danylo. "Do you make a habit of sending gifts to women?" Danylo asks.

"Come on! Come on, Danylo!" Panko says. "Easy! Easy! Hey, Vasylko. What are you doing for Christmas?" Then he quickly changes his question because he knows that like every year before, Vasylko Gregorovitch will be at home alone in his shack. Not at church. No visitors. Maybe Nick and Lena might take him over a box of Christmas baking. Nick has done that before, but Vasylko will go nowhere. "How is the trapping this winter?" Panko says. "How many muskrats do you have already?"

"Not many." He puts the paper back down on the

counter. "Why do you want to know?"

"No, no. That's all right, Vasylko. It's not my business." Panko shells another peanut. "Hey, you know what, Vasylko? Why don't you come with us to the trial? Don't you think so Mike? He should come with us."

"Why not?" Mike says.

"When?" Vasylko asks.

"Not till after Christmas," Panko says. "January 21st. What do you say, Vasylko?"

"I'll let you know." He reaches into his pocket for his wallet then dumps change into the palm of his hand, counting carefully. "Six cans of sardines," he says to Ivan, "beans, and a pound of tea."

"By the way," Ivan says, "the Jew was asking about you."

"Old man Gruber?"

"About the coin. What did he call it? Maria Theresa? He was wondering if you might have...."

"Sardines," Vasylko says, "six cans, two cans of beans, and the tea. I'm in a hurry."

Either by coincidence, or because the storekeeper was expecting Isaac Gruber, as soon as the Maria Theresa was mentioned, a sleigh drove up outside. The outfit belonged to Isaac Gruber's nephew from Topolia. Isaac borrowed it every winter to come here, the week before Christmas, to write up spring orders – garden seeds, rubber boots, bib overalls, socks, gloves, yard goods for women.

"Is that you, Vasylko?" he says, meeting him outside on the step. "I haven't seen you since I sold the store in Topolia. To where are you running in such a hurry?" Isaac Gruber knows everybody, and he talks to everybody. If it wasn't for the circumstances, Vasylko would have liked to stop and talk with him, but not about the coins, and he knows that the Jew wants to know about the coins. He tugs at the peak of his cap and marches down the steps.

Isaac follows him off the step and walks to the sleigh. "Don't run away yet, Vasylko," he says. "I have something good for you. Free!" He opens a case and pulls out an outdoor thermometer with his business imprint, Isaac Gruber Imports. "Just what you need this time of year." He drops it into Vasylko's grocery bag.

What does the Jew want? Vasylko wonders, and he wonders about his coins. Why did he ever send the Maria Theresa to the woman? Before that happened nobody knew his secret. Now everybody wishes to know. He has to get away from these men so he can think. What if they come to his house? Let them come. Nobody will be at home. He will go to his hiding place in the spruce forest.

By four o'clock it's getting dark. He hears the coyotes, there must be a dozen somewhere across the meadow yapping back to one another. Rabbit runs and deer tracks are everywhere in the snow.

It's dark by the time he reaches the forest, and he can hardly see to gather firewood. Fortunately, dead branches are plentiful on the trees and in no time he has gathered a pile waist high. He breaks off twigs, arranging them carefully into a cone, tearing a corner of paper from his grocery bag and scrunching it into a ball, placing it inside the cone. But he doesn't light his fire until he has broken all the branches and stacked the wood into a neat pile. Only then does he take out a match and strike it, touching the flame to the paper ball, and shredding pieces of twig over the flame.

In a moment the fire catches.

He feels the bite of cold, and fire, the bite of smoke in his eyes, and ice crystals on his hands as he presses down with his palms on the packed snow. He's drawn to pleasure...smell of bark, sizzle of melting snow, warmth.

The dusk has long passed into dark night. Vasylko gazes up to the sky and the movement of the northern lights. His mother's stories come to his memory. *"On such a winter's night spirits swarm and swirl in the splatter of stars belted across the top of the sky. Like in a hurricane a wizard whisks by sitting in a pot. A devil dances in the light of the moon, doffing his cap to a riderless broom."*

Witches and devils inhabit the sky above Vasylko, and in the coals of his fire thousands of little black demons wink at him.

THIRTY-EIGHT

The priest feels it his duty to visit Yuri Belinski at the Brandon asylum, that he can play the role of a Holy Father, like Christ, descending into Hell. The room smells of disinfectant and urine. A woman wearing a green cotton gown wanders about the ward, whimpering, and tugging at her hair. Another stands in a corner wringing her hands and singing a lament. An old man strapped in a wheelchair curses, then hangs his head mumbling.

It would seem that the Devil has congregated his forces here, but Kobzey knows better. There are no special places for demons on earth, no boundaries or confinements other than inside every man, even inside Kobzey, his evils hidden beneath his robes. More and more he thinks about the *Khlysty*. Is it thus that this young man Belinski had fallen to the dictates of his carnal desires, his flesh releasing lust, his sin oozing out as if from a boil cut open? Only God's grace can wash clean the open wound of Yuri's flesh, as the Holy Spirit would descend on couples writhing on the cottage floor of the *Khlysty*.

Is it only trappings the priest can perform with Holy Water? Sprinkle it on devils dancing on the bedposts? But he can bring solace, his trappings can comfort Yuri's soul.

Kobzey stands in the doorway, inert in his black robe, frowning, expecting service. An attendant hurries from across the room.

Yuri sits at a table in a large glassed-in veranda. The priest stands by the latticed windows, absorbing the sun's feeble warmth.

"I have something for you from Panko." Kobzey reaches into the folds of his robe and hands Yuri two packages of Players cigarettes.

"He said you prefer Players."

Panko had made the trip to the priest's house in Sifton, came with the cigarettes and two small jars of home-brew, one for the two old friends to visit over, and one for Yuri.

"He told me to bring you a drink. He said you might need it in this place."

Kobzey produces a drinking glass and a pint jar, pouring for Yuri.

"Panko said you might need some cheer." Yuri sips once, then raises the glass.

"To God," he says, and drinks the rest of it down. "Is there much snow at Topolia?" Yuri leans forward with a cigarette in his mouth, the priest striking a match.

"Much snow."

"Is there news from there?"

"News?" Doesn't he realize that a priest is beyond

the spreading of gossip? Kobzey is here to bring redemption, not rumours. "The bishop will be coming to the parishes this summer."

"Did Panko tell you news?"

"Yes, Panko." Kobzey sits down and pours whiskey for himself, taking the full glass with one swallow. "He has news about his family."

"Nick?"

"Yes, he was fishing, but stayed only until the end of October. And the girl Lena was there too. Panko's wife is cooking at the camp. Panko says that Nick has to report to the army before a policeman comes looking."

"They could arrest him?"

"Apparently he sent a letter telling that he was needed on the farm. To cut cordwood. He's probably safe for now."

Yuri serves himself a drink, then fidgets with his cigarette, puffing, then pulling it away from his lips, inserting it repeatedly from one side of his mouth to the other, puffing each time.

"My wife. Will she visit me?"

"Panko tells me she is baking for her mother."

Yuri butts his cigarette, takes another, and waits for the priest to light it.

"Some Jew is finding her a job in Winnipeg. A friend of Panko. Isaac Gruber. You know him?"

"His nephew has the store in Topolia."

"Do you hear from your family, Yuri?"

"The first year I was in Canada I got a letter from Lviv. Since then, nothing. And now how would they know what's happened to me? Maybe they are not alive."

"Lviv. The young people here don't even know what that is. They care for nothing but English."

Yuri tightens the strings at the waist of his flannel pyjamas, ties them, then blows smoke at the rays of sunlight shining down from the window, the particles rolling and twisting. He shrugs, half grinning, half grimacing. His eyes cloud over and he seems to stare at something unknown and far away. Maybe he sees devils in the smoke. The nurses dress him in striped pyjamas and slippers. They've shaved his moustache.

"What do they feed you?"

"Watery potatoes."

Kobzey returns his gaze out the window. He notices snow on the lattices, snow outside. He notices the grounds bordered with evergreens, and leafless elm trees standing by themselves here and there. He wants to know more about Marusia.

"What were her last words?"

"Who?"

"The woman Marusia."

Yuri's eyes swim in a milky film, focused on the floor. His shoulders slump, his eyes twitch and drip.

Glass shatters above Kobzey's head, and a small bird falls to the floor at Yuri's feet. For a moment it doesn't move, but then it tries to fly, one wing hanging limp, hopping over Yuri's slippers.

"A bat!" he cries. "Get it off!" He clings to his chair, lifting his feet, a strange and silent terror in his eyes.

"No. No. It's all right. Only a sparrow." The priest

bends to pick it up, but it hops out of his reach. He chases the bird into a corner, kicking at it, stomping, and finally it's nothing but a splatter of blood and feathers.

THIRTY-NINE

Christmas morning Hryhori Budka leaves a wandering path of footprints in five inches of new snow. He is walking to the Gruber church. He tries to concentrate on the real name of the church, The Church of the Nativity of the Blessed Virgin Mary. Who could remember that? The people call it Gruber, named after a Jew. The people were calling it Gruber when Hryhori came to this country. The Jew had a store somewhere here. By the river.

Perhaps Hryhori thinks there are services; perhaps he thinks it is Easter. Doesn't he know that the priest would never venture out to the country churches in the dead of winter? How would he get to Gruber? And who would go get him? Who wants to ride with a team and sleigh twenty-five miles to Sifton to get Kobzey? Christmas is better at home with a warm fire in the stove. Every farm in the district will have had its evening celebrations: first star in the sky; twelve meatless dishes. But who knows what Hryhori Budka is doing Christmas Eve? At least when Marusia was alive he wasn't alone.

The winter sun mixes its brightness with the bitter cold, a haze of frozen light hovering over the clearing of the churchyard, motionless and silent, but for Budka, plodding through crystal snow and tinkling a set of three brass bells on a leather strap. Where in his wanderings would he have found bells?

On the church step he stands knee-deep in snow, with one hand pulling at the door, opening it but a few inches, unable to draw it any further. He drops the bells and begins tugging with both hands, but still is not able to squeeze through. The shovels for digging graves are in the bell tower building. He could use one to clear the step. Hryhori might remember about the shovels, he might not. He looks around, and his attention is drawn to a sparrow hopping on the branches of a highbush cranberry tree in the bush bordering the west side of the churchyard. He knows that these cranberries can remain on the tree long after the frosts, and that they get sweeter and juicier as winter comes. He walks over to the bush, unbuttons his fly, and urinates yellow jags into the snow. He counts the berries. There are seven, one or two on a bunch, the rest having been eaten by the birds. He picks one and puts it in his mouth, pressing against his teeth with his tongue. The juice is tart and faintly sweet. The others he picks and stomps into the snow, staining it red beside the yellow crusts.

He hears bells. In the distance a team and sleigh approaches, and then a shout reverberates, "Christ is born! Christ is born!" Soon the sleigh arrives, Lena's father Mike standing at the front of the box, holding on to the reins, turning the horses into the church-yard. The collar of his sheepskin coat is raised up over his ears, surrounding his fur cap. Leather mitts reach halfway to his elbows.

He climbs out of the sleigh box and greets Hryhori. "Christ is born!" he says.

"Bless Him!" Hryhori says.

Mike pulls a bottle from inside his coat. It may be that he is thinking which treasure is more valuable. Is it that which feeds the people and saves them from misery, or that which enables them to forget the world?

"You need to warm up, Hryhori," Mike says, handing over the bottle.

"To God," Hryhori says before swallowing, then wiping his mouth with his sleeve.

"Another," Mike says, and Hryhori hesitates only for a customary moment, then drinks again, this time more deeply. "You know," Mike says, "I need your help."

"Yeh?" Hryhori does not look Mike in the eye. Instead his head is down, his boot scuffing the snow, spreading it around, kicking at his red and yellow stains.

"Fishing," Mike says. "Day before yesterday I went to the shed and looked in the fish box. Anna needed a jackfish to fry for the Holy Supper. I noticed only half a dozen left. How would you like to come with me tomorrow and help set the net?"

"Where is Danylo?"

"He can come too, if he wants. Let's go to the house

and we can talk about it. Later we can have supper. Anna will have food left over from last night."

LITTLE WORK HAS BEEN DONE THIS MORNING at the Melnyk household. Everyone has slept later than usual. In the days leading up to Christmas they have prepared well. They have ample leftovers from the twelve meatless dishes: mushrooms, fish, dumplings, cabbage rolls...and today all that needs to be cooked is a goose. It's roasting in the oven.

Yesterday afternoon, just before sunset, Mike spread hay on the floor of the east room.

"Christ is born," he said to Anna.

"Bless Him," she replied, watching him spread the hay.

A newly washed white linen cloth covers the *skrynia,* its centre-piece a three-tiered *kolach* as magnificent as a church. The *skrynia* spans the width of the room. Not only does it serve as a table, it contains important papers, money, beeswax candles, the household linens, and the bread is kept in it.

On the walls the Holy pictures, decorated with paper flowers and pussy willow sprigs still from last Easter, appear proud and solemn, appropriate for Christmas. On the *skrynia,* just to the right of the *kolach,* sits a bowl of *kutia,* three-quarters full, expected to last the three days of celebration.

If there is one tradition that Lena can cherish, it is *kutia.* On the floor of this room in the early afternoon on Christmas Eves she has sat beside her father.

Candles were lit on the *skrynia*, the light reflecting on the glass of the Holy pictures. He had a grey earthenware pot, a wooden pestle, a two-quart sealer of poppy seed, a cup of water, and sugar. He ground the poppy seed into paste for *kutia*, adding water and sugar. Lena remembers her father every once in a while saying, "Taste it," and handing her a spoon. Her mother had spent evenings sorting through syrup pails full of wheat, choosing only perfect kernels for *kutia*. Wheat, poppy, honey, and sugar, boiled together – the special food for three days of Christmas.

Mike leads Hryhori into the room. Lena and her sister Rose are sitting on the bed-bench reading Nellie's movie magazines. Panko's father, the cripple with both feet amputated, had made this bed at the time of Mike and Anna's wedding. The wood of the backboard is ornately carved in swirls of rose petals, leaves, waves, and spirals, painted red and green. Both girls recline, each on her own huge feather pillow, red cloth showing through the lace trim that edges the white linen pillow cases. "Christ is born!" Hryhori says to them.

"Bless Him!" the girls say, without looking up from their magazines. Mike takes him to the *kutia,* dippers out a portion into a small bowl. The previous evening Mike had followed the tradition of flinging a spoonful into the air. The amount of prosperity that was to come in the new year was determined by how many kernels of wheat stuck to the ceiling. Hryhori motions with his spoon, grinning at Mike and then at the girls. After he eats his *kutia,* he reaches into his shirt pocket. "I have something for the ladies," he says. Strands of red coral beads appear from his shirt. The necklace had shown up one morning on the step outside his house, six weeks after Marusia's death. He had thought it was a miracle: beads, bread, and salt, wrapped in a black cloth, appearing out of nowhere. A miracle, or the work of the Devil. He told nobody. Hryhori holds the beads for Rose and Lena to see. "They were Marusia's," he says. "What for do I need beads?" He lays them down beside the *kolach*. Lena gets off her pillow and comes to look at them. Rose leaves the room.

FORTY

Lena walks to Panko's, if for nothing else, then just to get out of the house. She's been cooped up since Christmas listening to her mother and Nellie gossip. She'd like to scream. For God's sake, Marusia's dead! Can't they leave her alone? She wants to tell them, *"No, it's not 'poor Yuri.'"* He knew what he was doing. Can't they see that? They've even got Rose starting to feel sorry for him.

Lena has to talk to somebody, to Nick. What will he say? She can hear him: *"I'm sorry, Lena. But maybe Yuri couldn't help it. You don't have to feel so bad. Can I get you something, Lena?"*

Maybe Panko will understand.

She sees them standing between the house and a sleigh-load of cordwood. Nick is sawing a log and Panko is watching him.

"Just in time to help us," Panko says. "We need somebody to stack."

"What's to stack?" Nick says. "You've split two logs."

"Never mind! Never mind!" Panko drops his axe

into the snow and sits on his chopping block. "That's a long walk, Lena. Aren't you cold? Or did the exercise warm you? Did you come to see Nick?"

Lena doesn't know what to say. She can't tell them she wants to talk to Panko. Alone. She doesn't want to be rude to Nick. She can't tell them she came to hear Panko play the *sopilka.* All she wants is a little peace of mind, from Panko, or Nick.

"Hey," Panko says, "are you tongue-tied?" He reaches into the bib pocket of his overalls and pulls out his tobacco pouch. "Hmmph! Empty!" He stares at it for a moment, then without moving his head his eyes divert to Nick. Again he says "Hmmph!"

"Why so quiet?" he says to Lena. "Is something wrong?"

"Does the mail come to Volga today?"

"Sure," Nick says, quickly, as if he's been waiting all this time to say something to her. "I saw Stupych on the sleigh coming from Topolia this morning. Are you waiting for something?"

"I have a pen pal."

Nick props his bucksaw against the sawhorse, and picking up a crust of snow, he brushes off the sawdust and licks the snow.

"A girl," Lena says. "I'm waiting for a letter."

"I'll get it!" he says. "I'll get it! I have to go to the store anyway!"

"Bring some tobacco," Panko says. "Tell Stupych to put it on my bill. And sardines or something. Dammit, we need something to eat. What can you do when Paraska is cooking for fishermen? Doesn't she know she has men at home? Nick, get going already.

"Are you hungry, Lena? In the cellar there's chicken. Go down and get a jar. I'll get some bread. Paraska has put it to freeze in the shed before she left. We still have bread, I think."

Lena watches Panko eating, then she concentrates on a strand of yarn unravelling on her sweater sleeve. She tugs at it, breaking off a length of several inches, and begins forming a circle with it on the kitchen table. Then she puts her hands on her knees. Panko waves a chicken bone at her.

"Why don't you eat?"

She shrugs. "I'm not hungry."

"You have something on your mind."

"Oh?" Lena says. "How do you know?"

"You're doing that," and he points the chicken bone down at the table towards her knees.

"What?" Lena examines the palms of her hands, then the floor, as if she has dropped something.

"Your knees. Bouncing. I've seen many times. They bounce when you want to know something."

"When I was little?"

"You're still not so big."

"Do you play the *sopilka* anymore?"

Panko wipes his mouth with the back of his hand. "Just to see you sitting like that makes me sad, knees shaking or not." He reaches over to the cupboard top to pick up his *sopilka*, but he doesn't play it. He just rolls it around in his hands as if waiting for her to ask him to play. Instead, she starts to fidget with the piece of yarn, pulling it along the table-top as if it is a snake.

Yuk, she thinks, crossing her arms, drawing them tightly against her stomach.

"Uncle, what do you think about Marusia?" She calls him "Uncle" because she always did when she was little and right at this moment she wants to be little with no responsibilities, no burden of thoughts of Marusia's death, thinking instead of her splashing in the water at the place where the log bridge crosses over the creek, and picking the morning glory flower. "Did you know her well?"

"Well enough," he says, clenching his *sopilka*. "She wanted to live. She liked to be happy, like everyone else."

"Why does everybody say she was a witch?"

"Paraska doesn't."

"Do you?"

Panko rises from the table and goes to the cupboard, taking a bottle and a glass. For a moment he stands with his fingers on the cork, about to pull it out, but then he sets both bottle and glass on the counter top.

"First I tell you about people. They love to talk. Can't you hear them? *'A witch. Don't you know she's a witch? Mrs. Sawchuk saw a dog running from the barn, and you know, the cow was dry. That Marusia's a witch. You can bet!'* That's how they are. Some story from the Old Country. The witch turns into a dog and sucks the cow dry when no one is looking. People have nothing better to do than talk." He picks up the bottle again, this time popping the cork and pouring home-brew into his glass. He drinks it standing up, in one swallow, eyes watering, then plunks himself down on his chair, the glass and bottle on the table before him.

"Do I think there are witches? What makes a bull roar in the pasture? Maybe I shouldn't be talking about bulls. Anyway, when it comes to women, men are sometimes pulled around by the nose. They are sometimes crazy, and then they have to make excuses."

"But the women also call her a witch."

"That's because they are afraid."

"Of what?"

"They are afraid because she was beautiful. A woman would rather lose her man to a witch than to another woman."

"Do you think she was a witch?"

"No, but I want to think so. Some men and women come together like magnets. One look in the eye and 'boom' that's it. I think that 'boom' is like witches. Maybe there's no old hag in the middle of the bush stirring a boiling pot, but there's magic all the same. Someday it will happen to you. I guess not with Nick, eh? Maybe no, maybe yes? Marusia Budka got this magic from somewhere. Do I think she was a witch? Why not? Why not make it easier for Yuri?"

While Panko was talking she'd forgotten about Yuri, and now she's reminded. He had bashed Marusia's head in with an iron bar.

"Yuri is a murderer!" She pushes the table, causing Panko's bottle to jiggle, and he reaches out to steady it.

"Wait! Wait!" Panko says. "Do you want to spill my

whiskey? Sure he killed her, but should another person die? Would it bring the dead back? Yuri is not well. Wouldn't it be better for Rose if she can blame Marusia? What difference would it make for Marusia? Can't we lie a little?"

"Only fools and children tell the truth?"

Panko puts his hand to his mouth, rubbing his lips and moustache. "Something like that." He pours himself another drink.

That's what he used to say in an argument, *Only fools and children tell the truth.* All the rest, he'd say, be they indifferent, wise, or holy, temper their words to suit their own advantage.

She had expected more from Panko. You can't just explain away a woman's life with a saying. It's as if he thinks the world won't get any better, only worse, so why bother trying to do something about it. She notices his forehead creasing, his eyebrows tight and gathered as if he's shielding something, a pain, something he can't, or won't tell her.

For several moments they remain sitting in silence. His fingers grip his empty glass. There's not another sound until they hear Nick on the step stomping snow off his boots.

FORTY-ONE

Vasylko has made up his mind that he must sell his gold. Ever since he gave Marusia the Maria Theresa, the coins have been nothing but a curse. They are no longer his secret. He must get rid of them. He had dug up the coins, had taken all twenty from the jar and put them in his mother's leather purse. As suspicious as he is, he's not afraid to do business with the Jew, as long as they are alone and nobody else knows.

At mid-morning ten days after Lena's visit with Panko, Vasylko watches for Isaac Gruber's sleigh to come from Melnyk's yard. He knows the cattle buyer stayed the night at Melnyk's. The Jew always went to Mike's farm after the New Year. Mike knows which farmers have calves ready to sell, who might need to buy medicines for cattle, horses, and pigs, and the Melnyk house has room for a guest to spend the night. Not only that, Mike knows what food a Jew can eat and what he can't.

Vasylko scrapes the frost from his window in order to see his new thermometer; it reads ten below zero.

He goes outside to get an armload of firewood. Snow is falling, large lazy flakes, like feathers. A lovely day, he thinks. When there's no wind and the snow drops like a blanket, a puffy quilt all over the meadow, all over his woodpile, and his stove warms his shack, it's more pleasant even than July. He hears sleighbells! Isaac Gruber's team and sleigh are coming. Vasylko drops his wood, and waving his arms he walks with jerky long strides to the road.

Isaac in his buffalo coat appears like a fat fur ball, bundled snugly in the sleigh. "Vasylko," he says. "What brings you on the road?"

Vasylko walks around the sleigh examining it, as if he's deciding if he's seen it before, which of course he has. "Snug as a bug in a rug, eh?" he says. "When I heard those bells I said to myself, that's him all right. That must be Isaac Gruber's team. Then I said he might like a cup of tea." Vasylko climbs halfway into the sleigh, his face just inches from Isaac's. "How about a cup of tea?" he says. "The kettle's on the stove."

"Sure," Isaac says. "Why not? Jump in."

"No! No! You go ahead. Right up to the house." The Jew makes room on the seat, but Vasylko walks around to the front of the horses, leading the way.

"A COZY HOUSE," ISAAC SAYS, "Nice and warm." He stands holding his coat and beaver fur cap looking around for a place to put them. On the table are three empty sardine cans, peanut shells (the only evidence of the Christmas season), the coal-oil lamp, chips of wood from Vasylko's carving, and scraps of paper with curled yellow edges. On the floor are more of these papers, along with bark and woodchips by the stove. On a wooden apple box a cast iron pan contains yesterday's fried potatoes congealed in grease. There's cold oatmeal and water in a pot, calendars dated as far back as 1923 covering the walls, a pile of Winnipeg *Free Press Weeklys* three feet high in the corner, dirty dishes, eggshells, a mail-ordered Dick Tracy ring still in its box beside the eggshells, a rusted pail of wood ashes, a table fork with dried egg yolk on its tines, a ball of string, a box of post-marked stamps cut from envelopes, a gallon can with a rag stuffed in its spout, a tomato can with a dried-up bouquet of last spring's pussy willows. Isaac lays his coat and cap on Vasylko's cot, sharing it with a bicycle wheel with a broken spoke.

Vasylko adds more water to the kettle, and the two men sit at the table waiting for it to boil. Isaac taps the lid on his box of Copenhagen, takes a pinch of snuff, then offers the box to Vasylko, who shakes his head.

"Never touch it." Vasylko stares across the table at Isaac Gruber, saying nothing for a moment or two. It's as if he relishes simply the presence of a guest and is content to wait in silence for the whistle of his kettle.

"Are you going to Yuri Belinski's trial?" Isaac asks. All at once the kettle begins to whistle, and Vasylko jumps up from his chair, then takes his teapot and a jar filled with tea leaves from a wooden box suspended on the wall. He spoons tea into the pot and pours the boiling water.

"Think they'll hang him?" he says. "People go watch that?" He rummages through another box under the table, retrieving a heavy china cup, wiping it with his handkerchief and setting it in front of Isaac Gruber. His own cup is on the table beside the unlit coal oil lamp.

"I remember," Isaac says, "my father saying in the Old Country, 'a hanging is like a holiday,' so many people come."

"They do then? People come to watch?"

"No, no. Not any more, Vasylko. Not here in Canada."

Vasylko stirs the tea in the pot with a spoon, then pours the cups full. Without another word he reaches under his cot and pulls out his mother's leather purse, setting it on the table before the Jew.

"Have a look," Vasylko says. Isaac lifts the purse, shaking it, then dumps the contents carefully on the table. He picks up one coin, then another. Vasylko lights the coal oil lamp for Isaac to see better, then, with the coins spread out on the table, it appears that the light and warmth of the flame are drawn to the gold, absorbed in its rich lustre.

"Hmmmn," Isaac says. "I have not seen such coins. Only the one...." He stops talking, setting the two coins down, walking to the door and spitting out his fresh wad of snuff, then returning to his chair and drinking his hot tea. "Are you selling them?"

"Maybe," Vasylko says.

"You need the money?"

Vasylko scrapes more frost from the window pane,

looks out for a moment, then rubs his nose with his fingers. "What do you offer?" he says. Isaac counts them, stacking them in piles of five, examining each coin before adding it to the pile, until the twentieth gold piece glistens in the palm of his hand. The four stacks of gold sit in a row amid the clutter.

Isaac Gruber stares at the twenty coins. He hesitates. They must have a story that belongs to Gregorovitch alone, and this thought conflicts with his desire to own them. "Are you sure you want to sell them?" he says.

"How much you give me?"

"I would have to figure it out," Isaac says. "These are 10 ducat gold pieces. They would have a face value, and a little bit for collector's value."

"You going to Belinski's trial?"

"No, no. I'll be far away, in Winnipeg."

"Far away...? I think I'll go with Nick Semchuk to that trial, or maybe with Stupych. Stay at the hotel. Buy a suit. Do you think I should buy a suit...? No, I won't do that. Maybe a pair of dress trousers."

FORTY-TWO

Someone has shovelled the snow clean on the walkway to the courthouse. The path is banked waist-high all the way from the street to the front steps, and they are not simply steps, Panko thinks, imagining a walkway rising to the gates of a sacrificial temple. One, two, three, four, five steps lead up to a broad level and the heavy oak doors. This high entry, and the building's red brick walls, make the edifice appear invincible.

Inside, more stairs lead to the courtroom hidden above the waiting room, offices, and library. Panko peeks in the library doorway, seeing the rows and rows of leather-bound books. The English keep records of everything. These books carry the weight of a thousand Bibles, and the judges upstairs have the power of God.

Panko stops halfway up the stairs. He motions with his arm. "This way! This way!" Old man Stupych is staring at a clerk at a desk in the front office. Vasylko taps him on the shoulder. Stupych turns around, then, glancing up at Panko, he hurries to the stairs. "Nick and Lena went up here," Panko says, then puts his finger to his lips just as Vasylko is about to say something. "Be quiet," he says. "The trial is on upstairs."

Before Christmas at the preliminary hearing at the Topolia hall, Panko felt right at home, but he's not so sure of himself in the Dauphin courthouse. When he passed by the woman in the front office he found himself bowing down low to her with hat in hand. She poked the glasses up on her nose, peering at him a moment, then with a sneer resumed typing. That's the English for you, he thought. He looks back and there she is, watching them again. Just above her head the pendulum of a wall clock swings back and forth, *tick, tock, tick, tock, tick, tock, tick, tock.* Panko tries to imagine how this English woman would react if for a change the clock struck thirteen, or better yet that it swore at her, but he knows it won't. Beside it hangs a large oil painting. It is of a captain dressed in a blue waistcoat and shiny black boots. In one hand he holds a three-cornered hat, in the other hand a telescope. The captain looks down on everything, even on the woman, and his strength is reinforced by the painting's massive frame. Wood framework decorates the room's ceiling and walls, all of it scrolled to look like gold ropes, leaves, and rosettes. Up high each segment of the woodcut curls like a devil's tail, one connected to the other, circling the ceiling. The room makes Panko think it was designed to represent an Englishman's vision of heaven's waiting room.

When they reach the top of the stairs the woman calls, "Your boots, gentlemen." She takes off her glasses, wiping the lenses with a handkerchief she pulls from the side pocket of her suit jacket. After three or four seconds of wiping she puts them back, pushes them up on the bridge of her nose, then points.

"The cloakroom, gentlemen, is over there across the hall from the library." Goddamn, Panko thinks, those English. The men and the women deserve each other. Panko and Stupych remove the rubbers from their felt socks and carry them to the cloakroom. Vasylko had taken his canvas overshoes off at the entry so he waits at the top, admiring the shine of his brand-new oxfords.

The courthouse is worse than a church, Panko thinks, the Holy of Holies. Everyone is afraid of judgement, walking around on tip-toe, even if it's only Yuri being judged. Are the rest of us afraid of being caught for something? The oak doors to the court-room are open. The three Ukrainians look inside. A brass chandelier hangs from the centre of a large circle of ceiling bordered with more gilded woodwork. The design is a frieze of Aladdin lamps joined with the same scrolls of golden ropes, leaves, and rosettes. This gold is the only colour in the room. The rest is white wall and dark oak.

Panko wonders if Ukrainians here in Canada will ever be the same as English? Will they meet halfway? Not that he wants this; the English have no soul. They are good for nothing but keeping books. The English believe there is only one way to do things, their own proper and correct way. Take for example a bank book with its debits and credits. Numbers are numbers. You can't wiggle out of it. Panko operates differently. He never counts his money. He keeps it in a paper bag under his Eaton's bed that he got when Paraska bought her hat that she never wears. There's nothing wrong to being modern when it comes to a bed, but there's no sense for him to keep a debit and credit account. You don't pay tax on the profits from selling home-brew. He's no millionaire...ten dollars here, five dollars there. Prime Minister Mackenzie King won't rise or fall on the difference of Panko's five or ten dollars not paid in taxes. They'd put you in jail anyway for reporting income from selling home-made whiskey. It's just that Panko likes to be honest if it can be possible, but sometimes it can't be. And when it can't be possible to do the straight and narrow, the one and only proper and correct English way, you might need to go from the sides, or the back, try this and that, wiggle around and maybe something will come loose. Who knows? For the English it's easy to tell the truth when they make the rules, but poor people are poor people, and they do what they have to do.

Take a calf and tie it to a post. After a while it doesn't move even if the knot is untied. Give it a kick, and when it finally realizes it's loose, it runs like hell. But tie it every day for a month, and before long it will stand without a knot, just as long as a rope is hanging on its neck. Take the Ukrainian out of the bush and put him in the courthouse, he bows his head.

When he dances he leaps to the sky, yet falls to his knees squatting like a beggar. When he does this it looks as if he's meant to serve a master, and for all that it matters to Panko, why shouldn't a man take his cap off for King George? There's nothing wrong with being patriotic, but then again he didn't run to Winnipeg to see the King and Queen in 1939 like some of the English people from Topolia did. The royal family doesn't need Panko. Look at this trial, Yuri Belinski against his Majesty, King George the Sixth. Even if Yuri is innocent, what chance will he have against the King?

Vasylko whispers. "Should we go in?"

"Just a minute," Panko says. "Never mind. Just go. Just go into the room. I have to piss. Go into the room. You don't have to wait for me."

HE STANDS AT THE URINAL THINKING. He thinks of the spring pouring of the water when Metro brought Marusia the shoes. In the house they drank home-brew all night. At dawn Danylo was snoring with his back propped against the wall and the empty jug between his legs. Marusia's simple husband was curled into a ball in the corner. Metro was nowhere to be seen. Maybe he walked back home to Baba Dounia. Panko sat on the bench smoking a cigarette. Marusia came to him with a piece of pickled herring on a fork.

"For you," she said. "You were sitting up asleep when I went to milk." She sat on the floor at his knees, reaching into a wooden chest where she had put the new shoes. "Would you like to put them on my feet?"

Panko had never in his life put a shoe on a woman's foot. If he hadn't had so much to drink he would have felt foolish getting down on his knees with Marusia's shoe in his hand. She sat up on the bench, shoving her bare foot into his stomach. Panko had never before thought of a woman's foot as something beautiful, and Marusia's foot was just a foot, after all. But when he grabbed the ankle and she wiggled her toes into the shoe, his hands shook and all he could think of was climbing up her legs.

"You can take it off now," she said. "It fits, but I will wear them only to church." She stood up, her hand rubbing the hair on Panko's head, and then she danced around him in a twirl, and out the door. What is this, Panko wondered? Catch me if you can? Does she want me to chase her into the bush? He looked around the room. Both Danylo and Hryhori remained as snoring heaps on the floor. Panko went to the door. He saw the hem of Marusia's dress disappear in the trees.

LENA SITS IN THE COURTROOM beside Nick, watching, listening to a policeman testifying. Maybe she should have stayed at the farm. The judge sits wearing black robes. He's at the far wall, high up behind a huge dark oak desk. Above his head hang two pictures, one of King George, and the other the Manitoba coat of arms. It has a buffalo, a cross, and two clusters of maple leaves. Below the judge, behind an oak railing separating the officials from Lena and the rest of the people, Yuri sits in a prisoner's box, the same dark oak. Between Yuri and the judge is another desk with a man writing things down. Lena has no stomach for this, for murders and courtrooms, men, and Marusia Budka. Nick will leave. He has to go back to the army. He's different from the rest of them, only that he wants to stick around until after Yuri's trial, stick around to talk about it for a little while. Will she miss him?

"Two men," the policeman says, "two men from the district took me to the location of the body."

The judge frowns. "Can you identify these two men?"

"Yes," the policeman says. "They are present in the courtroom. Would you stand please, gentlemen. Yes. Mike Melnyk and Panko Semchuk....You may sit down now."

"Continue."

"The body was fully clothed, suspended head down in a clump of willows. She was wearing a white embroidered blouse with a torn sleeve, a dark green skirt, brassiere, underslip, no headgear, no shoes or stockings, and no drawers. A short distance from the body, piled neatly on the ground was a box of chocolates, a pair of women's shoes, a black shawl, and a yellow shawl, and the remnant from the blouse....We discovered an iron bar...."

After the policeman describes the murder scene, the prosecutor brings a document forward, the written confession of Yuri Belinski. The judge asks the policeman to read it to the court:

"I would like to tell from the beginning how she was bothering me until the time I killed her...how she bewitched me in order to have con-

*nections with me the night of Danylo Melnyk's
wedding...how this caused trouble between my
wife and me.*

*I met Marusia on the muskeg path, or was
she a wood nymph who can drain a man's life? I
wanted to take her to Winnipeg. We wrestled,
and the witch showed on her face. "You son-of-a-
bitch!" she said, and yanked my testicles.*

*I struck her with the iron. She fell down and
grabbed me by the legs, trying to pull me down.
She then let go of my legs and I grabbed her by
the hair and pulled her into the bush. I do not
remember how I got home...."*

"DR. MORGAN," THE PROSECUTOR ASKS, "You are a
duly qualified medical practitioner licenced under the
laws of the Province of Manitoba?"

"Yes, sir."

"Did you conduct a post-mortem examination on
Marusia Budka?"

"Yes, sir."

"Could you tell me how long the body had been
there?"

"I estimated from four to five days."

"Would you mind telling the court what you found
in that post-mortem?"

"I found a body, female, in an advanced state of
decomposition, lying out by a clump of willow bushes.
The clothes had been removed from the body when I
got there and there were millions and millions of mag-

gots crawling over it. The scalp, face, and eyes were completely eaten away. I asked Mr. Melnyk if he could locate a wash tub. We had to clean the body. The external examination was extremely difficult."

"And can you give a reason why decomposition should have set in so strongly in such a short time?"

"On account of the extreme heat."

Maggots eating her eyes.... The room begins to spin around Yuri. He gazes to the swirls of golden scrollwork on the high ceiling. In a corner crevice a bat clings to the wood. Yuri grips the seat of his chair. It seems the very life is draining from him as it was in the folktales with Kotsiubynsky's Ivan. *"His eyes were sunken and watery. Life was losing its relish. There was something heavy about him. A worry seemed to be gnawing at him, weakening his body. Something aged and watery was shining in his tired eyes. Marichka asked. 'Have you been ill?'*

"'I've been pining for you, Marichka my love.' He did not ask where they were going. He was happy simply to be with her."

Those sitting in the courtroom, people once familiar to Yuri, his friend Panko, the strange man Vasylko Gregorovitch, all those on the other side of the railing swim before his eyes like devils, shrinking in size and rising from their chairs as if from a swamp. Yuri wallows in the shadows haunting his memory.

"The forest was growing thicker. The putrid odour of smouldering stumps wafted to them from a thicket where dead fir trees were decaying and poisonous mushrooms sprouted. The boulders were cold to the touch under their

*covering of slippery moss, and the bare roots of firs
entwined the paths, which were covered by a layer of dry
needles."*

The bat in the crevice unfolds and flies to the chandelier, its wings draping over crystal globs, bat wings
like dark forest moss hanging on dead tree limbs.

From their chairs as if from a foggy sea Panko and
Nick rise to perch on the chandelier, playful squirrels
on tree branches, sounding music with their instru-
ments, luring the alabaster maiden singing as she rises
out of the mists.

> *See my friend, the sky,*
> *See, the cranes on high;*
> *Wing to wing they fly together,*
> *Fading as they fly.*

The bat flutters to her, covering her white breasts
with its black silken wings. She beckons to the carver
Vasylko Gregorovitch, and they chase together into
lavender clouds. Light envelopes them, peach and
mauve shining through the billows. Vasylko and the
woman float steaming in the glow, rolling in the bed
of coloured clouds, her fingers playing on his back,
lifting his shirt-tail from his sides, stroking his belly.
Temple throbbing, glasses slanting, Vasylko squeals
with laughter, rolling over and over, kicking off his
shoes.

"A witch!" Yuri yells. "I thought I was rid of her. Are
you Marusia?"

"Order! Order!" The judge pounds on his gavel.

Only Yuri sees Panko and Nick with *sopilka* and *tsymbali,* perched on the chandelier like the little black demons. Faster and faster they play, and in the clouds the Devil's two cherubim roll quivering to the sound.

"Yes, Marusia! Yes!" Yuri covers his face with his hands. "I killed you, and now you come back."

The judge stares down from his desk. "Court is adjourned for the day. Remove the prisoner."

FORTY-THREE

I t's somehow fitting that the trial would soon be followed by six weeks of Lent, as if everyone in the district has to purge himself of evil, restrain from the appetites of lust and rich food. Even Panko has restrained himself, believing that he's been in mourning both for Christ, and for Marusia and Yuri. On Good Friday after church he wanders on the path by Willow Swamp. He remembers that Good Friday in the Old Country had better weather. Of course last year in Manitoba it had not been so bad with Easter coming later than most years. On top of that, the spring thaw had arrived much earlier than usual, making many people believe that the celebration of the Resurrection was more glorious than ever before.

But it isn't to be this year. So far it's been grey sky every day, no sun, no warmth, but this doesn't deter Panko. He welcomes the dreary weather. The gloom of Good Friday and the sky suit his mood. He wants to be out on the frozen swamp all by himself. He does not even wish for the coming of spring; maybe he's too old to wish. The coming of Easter used to well up inside Panko like the springing bud of a pussy willow. It used to be that the signs of renewal enthralled him, that he also could rise up anew time and again, like Friday transforms to Sunday, winter to spring, death to life. Ever since he can remember, the promise of tomorrow excited him. It's what keeps people going. But yes, maybe now he's getting too old to wish. His walk to the swamp doesn't excite him. It calms him, if anything.

Any melting that has taken place hasn't removed the snow, but has only covered it with a crust of ice. He carries a bottle of his whiskey to console his gloom. With each sip he can produce tears in his eyes, appropriate for the sorrows and sufferings of Christ Himself.

Panko has taken two *pysanky* that Paraska had so carefully decorated. Normally he should be waiting for Easter Sunday to celebrate with the eggs, but somehow he has been driven to take them from Paraska's basket and to come out here to the frozen swamp. No one can say he hasn't helped Paraska with the eggs. He made her a brush she wanted for painting. He used a pig bristle. Took a piece of the metal strip from a Massey-Harris calendar and pinched it on the bristle. Paraska drew a curved line of hot wax, in curls like a devil's tail – one connected to the other – around the egg, running to eternity. Paraska's *pysanky* are almost as beautiful as Anna Melnyk's.

He stands at the spot of the old posts that used to hold the church bell, the place of the three babies' graves, the clearing where the people used to gather many years ago. Marusia's place. He stumbles. The pathway is icy and he's had a little too much of the whiskey. He recognizes that he's not able to stomach as much of his home-brew as he used to, that he can't keep as clear a head. Drink used to liven him up; now it dulls him.

He has come out here to offer the *pysanky*. "Christ has risen!" he says to no one in particular. There is no one to say it to, only himself. "Praise Him!" he answers. The people will use these greetings all day Sunday, but not on Friday. On Friday Christ has not yet risen. But Panko says it anyway. He takes another drink. Carefully he bends over and with his fist makes two shallow holes in the snow. More tears come to his eyes as he sets each egg in its hole.

Nick will be leaving on Monday. That is good, he thinks. Get out from here. A young man would be a fool trying to live as he, Panko, has lived, as Metro and Baba Dounia have lived. That can't be anymore. Even Kobzey doesn't make sense anymore for Panko, let alone for the young people. The young can't escape from the English even if they wanted to, and they don't want to. They will go into the English world and be boiled out like a pea in a pot of borshch.

Nick and Lena wish to be English. Because she has been born a little bit later, and because the Melnyks had a radio long before Panko, Lena wants to be English more than Nick. He has enough *tsymbali* in his blood to play a merry tune when he needs to.

Nothing much changes in this life. In the Old Country, Panko's father went cap in hand many times to his Polish landlord, and kissed his ring. One must bow even before a monkey if it is in power. When Lena gets older, will she bow?

ON MONDAY AFTERNOON Nick and Lena are standing on the concrete bridge in Topolia, he reminiscing in his slow manner about the outcome of the trial weeks ago, and she gazing out at the frozen river, not hearing. She doesn't want to think about anything. But even if she doesn't want to, she can't forget the trial. She wonders if the English judge thought all Ukrainians were weak in the head. Why else would the court allow Yuri Belinski to get off? The jury decided in twenty minutes, that's all! That's all it took for them to agree with the judge's advice. What if she had been the judge? Or what if Baba Dounia? Wouldn't that be something? A woman might have seen the matter through Marusia's eyes.

"Baba Dounia made lunch for us; we'd better go."

"Why not?" Nick says, "I could eat."

Dounia said for them to leave enough time before Nick has to go on the train. Tata Paraska and Panko are here, coming to town to see him off. Paraska says she had to come to town anyway to sort through garden seeds with Dounia. This year's Easter Monday is sad for Panko. He would have wanted to be out on the roads with the young men collecting *pysanky* from the girls and pouring water into their cupped hands. But no one was going out. Only he and Danylo went last year. This year, nobody.

Dounia made a big lunch. "Eat! Eat!" she says, as if they have been starving all through the Lenten weeks. She dishes out canned chicken, boiled eggs, cottage cheese that Anna sent from the farm with Lena, and cabbage rolls. She slices sausage on to a plate. Metro produces a bottle for the men and they talk about the winter that will soon be passing, about the biggest event of this particular winter, the trial.

"Sure," Metro says, "the doctors decide everything." Yuri was kept at Brandon for weeks before the trial and the doctors watched him. Kept charts on his behavior. Yuri had complained of dizzy spells, and his memory was poor. The medical evidence saved him from hanging. "Hardening of the arteries in the brain," Metro says. "That's what the doctor claimed. And what did the judge advise? Guilty, but insane." Panko and Nick nod their heads.

"Baah," Dounia says. "Is that all you talk about?" Paraska digs a piece of jellied chicken from the sealer and puts it on a piece of bread.

"Hardening of the arteries," Paraska says, scowling. "Maybe, but not in the brain."

"Never mind, never mind," Baba Dounia says. "That's enough already. Eat, and forget about arteries!" Like all old Ukrainian women, Dounia spends much of her life encouraging everyone to eat. "It's a long ride on the train without eating," she says to Nick, touching nothing for her own nourishment, but making sure everyone else is properly served. She mutters about how spring is coming, to leave the dead alone, and let things be born. Think about gardens.

Soon the ice will break and the meadows will fill with water. The fish will come up from the lake. Dounia turns to Lena, nods her head, and leaves for her bedroom. In a few minutes she returns wearing an old sheepskin vest. "Come, Wasylena. I'm going to give water for the cow."

Snow covers the backyard. A path leads to the well, and another to the shed that houses the cow. Lena and Dounia argue at the well, each determined to carry the water, and they compromise carrying one bucket apiece. The cow drinks, nuzzling one pail, then the other, while Dounia, in her slow but determined fashion, forks hay from a stack in the corner of the barn into the manger.

"Metro milks the cow sometimes. All my life I did it, but now, how do you say? We're retired? Metro has nothing else to do." Dounia leans on the fork just as Metro would when he is about to roll himself a cigarette. For a moment her face loses its softness. "You still upset about Marusia Budka, Wasylena?"

"Didn't it bother you, Baba?"

"Bother? *Oi, oi, oi,* bother. All my life is bother. What can you do?" The cow splatters wet manure in a steaming pile at their feet. Dounia forks it away onto a larger pile by the door. They move away from the cow. Dounia's eyes are somewhere else, far off, in the past.

"Sometimes we have to smell things. One time my mother boiled cranberries in an iron pot...."

Lena's mother makes jelly from highbush cranberries. "They stink like dirty socks."

"No, no. Not so bad. Not the cranberries. I was nine years old. Mother told me to take them from the fire, take the pot down from the hook. I tried, it was heavy and spilled on my foot. 'Eeeee!' I cried, and my mother ran to the barn. Right away she was back with a pail full of that wet cow dung. She made me step in it. Made me keep my foot in the pail for three days. That's what stinks. But I lived after that. And not one scar on my foot. I went to weddings. I danced...."

"You came to Manitoba."

"Yes, Metro and I. 1903. I left my family behind. It was hard. I remember the day I walked to the store at Gruber.... On my way back from that store, as I got closer to the homestead, I thought I had heard a cry, like a ghost wailing. Was it my daughter Anna? Had she left the *buda?* Or was it wolves? *Oi, oi.*"

Lena sits beside Dounia on a trunk that came from the Old Country, listening to her baba's story. She's heard it before, but Dounia likes to tell it. Lena listens as if she is hearing the story for the first time:

HOW FAR YET TO GO THROUGH THE BUSH? How far to the girls? The young Dounia heard it again, "*Momka? Momka?*" She adjusted the sacks on her shoulders; one flour, one sugar. She groped for the bottle of medicine and the gift of candy from the Jew, both safe in the pocket sewn in her dress.

Dounia told her daughter before leaving in the morning, "I go to Gruber. The cow is sick." She remembered the time when Metro bought the cow, what the Jew said. "Dr. Bell's medicine," he said. "Good for sick cow."

But Metro said, "Why should I buy medicine? The cow she's not sick."

She had to get the Dr. Bell's medicine, and why not get some more flour and sugar? And salt. She was out of salt. Metro had said he might write a letter, that she might walk to Gruber on a nice day to get it. Maybe the letter had come to the store already. She wanted to write and tell him there was another baby coming in November, and maybe it would be a boy.

The path had been easy to see in daylight where Metro had chopped the notches in the trees, and where he broke branches. When she had left she knew that Anna was as good as anybody with the baby, as good as any mother, as long as it was daytime. But night was a different thing with the wolves howling.

Dounia hadn't thought she'd be gone long, less than a day. She'd be back before dark. But to play safe she had told Anna, "Don't leave the *buda*. Look after the baby." She hadn't counted on having to wait at the river.

Pray to God she stays at the *buda*. Metro had said to watch out for the wolves. Surely Anna wouldn't leave the *buda*. Surely she would listen to her mother.

Metro had come home with money after the haying. Now he's gone back harvesting for the English-man at Sifton. He said he must earn more to buy the plough, and the horses. Why hadn't he bought the Dr. Bell's?

When they came last fall from Ukraine, thanks be to God they had money enough for the cow. Thanks to God Dounia had brought seeds in pouches on her belt: onion, beets, garlic, poppy, even buckwheat, and soon the cabbage would be ready. This coming winter they would have cabbage. Last fall the two of them had worked fast and hard to build the *buda*, and she had been heavy with the baby. Metro said to be careful with the axe, she could hurt herself, but she had been happy to work. She had lost many babies in Ukraine since Anna was born, but all the same, God had watched over them. How could they have managed on the big ship crossing the ocean if she had had babies to care for? In Canada she could work hard and have babies all the same; she was strong to swing the axe to cut the bush.

Metro had said, "Take only straight rails for the wall, Dounia. Lay the sods so they don't slide down, Dounia. Cut some hay from the meadow for making the plaster, Dounia." She shredded the hay. Stomped it with bare feet in water and clay in the floor hole. She and Metro plastered the sloping walls, inside and outside. Their home was the best, not like Semchuk's *buda,* leaking from rain, and dirt always falling.

"More plaster," Metro said, "I weave a chimney with the willows. Plaster inside and out for the chimney. Ya," he said, "our *buda* will not be full of smoke like an Indian tent." Metro said their shelter looked like an Indian tent he saw at Gruber, with the smoke hole at the peak. But they would have a chimney. They would not have to live like an Indian.

"What is an Indian?" Dounia said. "You mean those dark ones? Gypsies?"

"No, Dounia, don't be afraid. The Indians have a

boat to take us across the river if we need."

She was afraid all the same, but at least Dounia had a better place to live than Semchuks. They had only a hole in the ground to make the fire, and an iron plate. Dounia had a big *pich* just like in the Old Country. If only they had had enough flour last winter to bake bread in the *pich*. But the stove had kept them warm; Metro had made it big enough for all of them to sleep on top.

If last winter they wanted bread, at least they hadn't starved. She had seen that the bush was full of mushrooms. One day of picking and mushrooms were hanging to dry in a sack above the stove. Berries of all kinds she found. Metro had snared rabbits, knocked the stupid grouse on the head with a stick, netted fish in the lake, and of course they had the cow.

After they had built the shelter, and another for the cow, they cleared bush to make a garden space. In the spring she planted the seeds...but not all of them. What if nothing grew? But the seeds did grow, and now they had beets and onions for borshch. She was so happy with the garden. So happy that last Sunday she fed two beets to the cow. What would Metro say? Would he laugh at her?

At the store the Gruber Jew said to her, "So you are Metro Zazelenchuk's Dounia? Aren't you late coming? Do you know it's long past noon? Almost supper time?"

"There was no...Indian at the boat. I had to wait."

The Jew laughed, and then asked her, "What do you need?"

"Is there mail from Metro?"

He looked in the cubby holes. "Nothing," he said.
"There is nothing?"

"No. I get the mail two times a week. I go to
Dauphin tomorrow. Maybe something is there."

"The cow is sick," she said. "I need that medicine.
What is it? Dr. Bell's? And salt. I need salt. Maybe give
me small bag of flour, and sugar. Just small bags.
When Metro comes from Sifton he will bring home
things for winter."

As she left, the Gruber Jew said to her, "Take this
candy for your children – a gift from me, and now you
better hurry to get home before dark."

AT THIS POINT IN HER STORY Dounia adds something
that Lena has not heard before. The old woman
appears suddenly older. She holds the palms of her
hands to her cheeks and her eyes flit from side to side.

"I have to tell you something," Dounia says, her
voice a mere whisper, as if it's a confession in her life's
last breath. "I came to the swamp. There were no
babies' graves yet, only the church bell in the clearing.
I saw at dusk, hell's fire on the water. Heard a woman
laughing, a woman as white as the moon. It made me
think of a dream I had of Vasylko's mother on the
meadow, dancing with Metro at midnight. Vasylko's
mother was a good-looking woman. A young widow."

"What happened to her?"

"You don't want to know. Everyone was suspicious
of her, the way she kept to herself in the bush, charming who knows what. My baby had died at birth the

day before Metro returned in the fall after harvest. I had lost babies in the Old Country, but this was the first boy. Two more mothers lost babies that fall."

"But Vasylko's mother couldn't have...."

"She died a witch's death. The men buried her in the trees far enough away from the babies." She says no more about Vasylko's mother, and Lena doesn't ask.

AFTER DOUNIA HAD SEEN THE *Rusalka* she walked fast away from the swamp into the thick bush. How long could she keep the pace? Dounia was not a big woman, and the sacks were becoming heavy on her shoulders. It would soon be dark, and Anna would be afraid. Dounia had left milk with sugar warming on the *pich,* and there was buckwheat *kasha* for Anna. She had told Anna to feed the milk with a spoon if the baby was hungry. If still she was crying let her suck the cloth pouch with poppy seed. Dip it in the milk.

It was getting too dark to see the notches. In the morning the sun had broken through the trees. But now the sun was gone and shadows appeared to move deep in the trees. How far away were the wolves? Her neck was hurting from the sacks. Everything would be fine if Anna stayed in the *buda.* Would she try to light the lamp? All at once she heard not far away but high in the trees, *tok, tok tok tok.* A woodpecker somewhere. Loud tapping, *tok, tok tok, tok.* She stepped quieter, listening. The sound distracted her from the worries; she marvelled how the tapping carried in the air. She liked birds, and to hear the woodpecker assured her that she still had some daylight; the birds had not yet gone to sleep. But as she walked further, the pathway became harder and harder to follow. Soon she heard another bird, but this time she was afraid. An owl, the night bird, *oooo, oooo.* High up somewhere. She saw it on a branch, the owl and the moon up high. All at once, *swoosh!* The bushes exploded beside her in a fluttering of branches and feathers. Dounia's heart jumped from her mouth almost. *Oi, oi.* Only a grouse. God was telling her. Think of Anna. She heard a cry, "Momka? Momka?" Anna's cry. The sound was closer. Had the child wandered from the dwelling, or was it only that Dounia was that much closer?

"Momka?" She could no longer see the broken branches, but God was telling the way. Dounia heard the cries. She had to go to the cries.

"Stay! Stay!" Dounia yelled. "Stay at the *buda.* I am here. Your mother is here." She ran and then tripped on a root, falling with the sacks. "Stay! Stay!"

On her knees she lifted the flour and sugar to her shoulders, checked her pocket for the Dr. Bell's medicine, the packet of salt, the rock candy from the Jew. "I come right away," she said. She heard a bell. The cow. The moon was overhead. It lit the way into the clearing. The *buda.* Anna was in the doorway, bouncing the baby in her arms, trying to make it take her poppy seed soother. "Momka!" Anna cried.

"MY MOTHER," LENA SAYS.

"Yes, your mother." Dounia shifts her body on the

old steamer trunk, and reaches inside her vest. "She isn't so bad, you know. But I have something for you." She pulls out a folded cloth, spreads it on her lap, a square of green cashmere with red and yellow flowers.

"A babushka." Lena tries to smile, tries to appear grateful.

Dounia's face hardens. "The English say 'babushka' and now you young ones say it. Babushka is for an old woman. I am a babushka." She brushes the back of her hand across the material, her eyes downcast. "I wore this at my wedding. We call it '*khustyna*,' not 'babushka.' *Khustyna* is a nice headscarf for a nice girl. My grandmother gave it to me, and I give it to you."

Lena takes the scarf, holding it up. "*Khustyna,* not babushka." She rubs it against her cheek. "Thank you, Baba," and then she folds it on her lap.

LENA STANDS ON THE LITTLE BRIDGE over the creek where she and Marusia had splashed in the water. It's frozen over now. The sky appears heavy over the scrubbing, the landscape a dark crust of snow, the tangled roots of upturned stumps somewhat softened by the snow.

Rose has a job in Winnipeg. Will she visit Yuri in the Brandon asylum? Rose says the asylum is worse than a jail, but at least they didn't hang him. Sometimes Lena thinks he should have been hanged, but she shouldn't think that. How is it that people can blame Marusia?

Lena touches her grandmother's headscarf draped

on her shoulders, the *khustyna* for a beautiful young woman. All her life Lena had heard only the word "babushka," reminding her of a fat old woman like a heap on a bench, not a young girl running on a hillside with ribbons in her hair. *Khustyna* is Marusia; *khustyna* is a bluebird's feather. This Easter Monday afternoon Lena wears her *khustyna*, but she would never wear it in town. She'll have to put it away.

Her mother has prepared food to take on a picnic at the cemetery tomorrow, her beautiful *pysanky* to be peeled and eaten over graves, the shells to remain on the snow. What does Panko say about *pysanky?* "The woman paints, the man eats." He has an answer for everything. He says that some things never change even if you think they do. He says what sense is there to change if it gives you no time to sit on a bench after supper and play the *sopilka?* What good to change if you lose what you are?

But Lena believes that her life has to get better, without *pysanky*.

From the bridge she can see the smokeless chimney of her country school. She likes her school in town much better. She'll go there for another year, and after she gets her Grade Eleven she'll move to Winnipeg. She gazes up into the sky above the school house, imagining the tangled hair of Dounia's witches mingled in the clouds. At least she won't have to live with that when she leaves.

ACKNOWLEDGEMENTS

I thank the Saskatchewan Writers Guild, without whose programs I would not have acquired the craft to write a book. At the risk of missing some people, I also wish to thank Sharon MacFarlane, Margareta Fleuter, Glenda MacFarlane, Jane Urquhart, Janice Kulyk Keefer, Myrna Kostash, W.D. Valgardson, Geoffrey Ursell, Nellie Beyak, Helen Warwaruk, Fred Rozmarinovitch, Mike Smilski, Steve Beyak, Leah Northrop, and my mother.

The Ukrainian Wedding is a work of fiction. I have taken liberties with place names and locations in the Interlake in order to suit the narrative.

Any similarities to actual persons or places are purely coincidental.

— *Larry Warwaruk*

GLOSSARY

Baba: grandmother
Babushka: old woman; headscarf worn by an old woman
Borshch: beet soup
Buda: primitive A-frame shelter
Dido: grandfather
Harbuz mami tvoyii: a pumpkin to your mother
Holubchyka: a twirling dance
Hospody pomylui: Lord have mercy
Hutzul: mountain people
Kapeliukh: a hat
Kasha: porridge
Khustyna: headscarf which in tradition a girl may bind to her suitor's arm
Kolach: decorated bread – has different styles and names for different occasions – Christmas, Easter, weddings
Kolemeyka: a lively dance of Western Ukraine

Kosa: braid of unmarried young girls
Pan: equivalent of "sir," or landlord
Pich: large clay stove and oven
Praznyk: celebration for name-day of a church
Pysanky: decorated Easter egg
Rusalka: water spirit, nymph, or princess
Seech: Cossack island fortress on the Dnieper
Shliak trafyv: may you be struck by lightning
Shyshka: pine-cone-shaped fertility loaves given out at weddings
Skrynia: cabinet serving as table and place of storage for bread and precious items
Sopilka: wooden flute
Tata: aunt
Tsymbali: many-stringed instrument played with two small wooden hammers

ABOUT THE AUTHOR

LARRY WARWARUK is the author of one other novel *(Rope of Time, 1991)*, a number of short stories published in *Grain, NeWest Review,* and elsewhere, and broadcast on CBC radio, and a non-fiction work, *Red Finns of the Coteau,* published in 1984. He is also active in community theatre – he helped found the Snakebite Players in Beechy, Saskatchewan, and has received several Best Director awards in Saskatchewan Community Theatre festivals.

Born in Regina, Larry Warwaruk grew up in southern Saskatchewan, took his education degrees in Regina and the University of Oregon, and was a teacher and principal in central Saskatchewan for many years. He currently works as a crop insurance adjuster and lives with his family in Outlook, Saskatchewan.